DEFECTIVE FOR HIRE

A BUMBLING BRIT ABROAD MYSTERY, BOOK ONE

D. R. LOWREY

Late Bloomer Books

Editing assistance by Rachel Stout and Brooks Becker.

Proofreading by The Pro Book Editor

Beta reads by Peter Anthony and Mark Boren

ISBN: 9781734108255

1. Main category—Fiction

2. Other category—Humorous/General

Second Edition

Dedicated to my mother, Mary Ann Lowrey, who thinks that by writing this book I've accomplished something.

PROLOGUE

"Those are some flashy shoes you're wearing, but I'd admire them more if they weren't on my desk." Having voiced his disapproval, the man leaned forward and spat on them.

"What are you doing?" shouted the shoeman, wiping away the spittle with a handkerchief. "Each of these shoes cost twice as much as your desk."

"Really?" said his tormenter with an acidic huff. "They must have come with a bowling alley attached."

"Bowling?" said the indignant shoeman. "I'll have you know these very shoes were worn by Taps Henderson in the 1931 production of *Speakeasy or Forever Hold Your Piece*. They are the last surviving footwear from Mr. Henderson's collection. Had they not been forced to exhume his body, even these would have been lost forever."

The man on the other side of the desk appeared unimpressed. That is, if mouthing "Whoop-de-doo" was any indication. "Let me get this straight," he said. "You're proud of wearing a dead man's shoes?"

"Well, he may be dead now. In fact, he is dead now, but not then. That's why they were forced to exhume the body.

Turns out, he was just sleeping one off after crashing a Hollywood gin party. He wouldn't actually drink himself to death for another five years. But someone had the presence of mind to realize that shoes of this caliber don't belong on the feet of one who sleeps through burials in shallow graves. Thankfully for the shoe aficionados of the world, these dual-toned wingtips were liberated. And here they are," he said, admiring their spit-polished sheen.

"Enough about your damned dead man's shoes. Did you get the papers?"

The shoeman produced a stuffed manila envelope. He tossed it on the desk where it landed with a splat, as manila envelopes do when tossed. "I'm no expert, but I still don't understand why you need these documents. Seems to me we're better off leaving them be."

"You're right. You're no expert. It's a matter of housekeeping. I'm making sure that when the old lady goes, all is in proper order. No entanglements. Clean and tidy. That's how I do business. Now, about the old lady ...." He stopped and gurgled something unspellable before backing his chair away from the hound sniffing his crotch. "Would you get this beast away from me? Why did you bring this mongrel mutt? I thought you detested furry animals."

"A matter of housekeeping," said the shoeman. He pulled back the ugly dog, which had taken to snarling. "I'm relocating this hideous brute to prevent any complications. Believe me, the faster I get rid of him, the better. I'm done shoveling his shit."

"Well, keep him on your side of the desk and away from me," said the dog-intolerant man while brandishing a pointy letter opener. "Now, as I was saying, the old lady... What was I saying?"

"I don't know, but if you can't remember, it must not have

been important. The important thing is that we've found our mule. Have you made all the arrangements?"

"*You* don't need to ask *me* about arrangements." The man was clearly perturbed at losing the inquisitor's role. He took the folder and dropped it in a desk drawer. "I'll provide the package and give our mule his orders when we meet here day-after-tomorrow."

"Day after? Wasn't tomorrow to be zero hour?"

"Have you seen the weather forecast, by any chance?"

"You mean we're going to wait for the hurricane to pass?"

"Bingo, Sherlock." With no sniffing dog to get wedged in his groin, the man leaned forward over the desk and spoke in a low voice. "Once the delivery is made, you go into action. Then, within a few weeks, a wedding, a funeral, and a payoff, in that order. You get what you want. I get what I want, and the bride.... Well, the bride gets a honeymoon she'll never have a chance to forget."

After sharing a chuckle, the shoeman asked, "How much are you paying our mule?"

"Nothing."

"Nothing?"

"The bride is paying.

"The bride is paying for her own—"

"It was her idea."

"And the mule—"

"Knows nothing. He's just doin' a job."

"You are slick."

"Not slick. Evil. Pure and unadulterated," he said proudly. The man rose as though buoyed by his own badness. Suddenly, anger filled his face. "Hey! What's that?"

"What's what?" asked the shoeman.

"That, by the plant," he said, pointing toward the plant. "That yellow puddle."

"Oh, that. Think nothing of it," said the shoeman, waving a hand as if shooing away a fly. "Since you don't have carpeting, a pair of paper towels will do. You'll have it clean in no time."

Steam rose from the dog-hater's collar. That was before he let loose with an even louder yowl. "What is he doing?" A stubby index finger extended itself past the shoeman's ear.

The shoeman's eyes followed the digit's trajectory down to the dog. "Why, I'd say he's taking a dump. That's what dogs do in the face of pure and unadulterated evil. It's good that I've given up shoveling his shit, and it's good that you don't have carpet." The shoeman rose and flipped on a driving cap. "Our business is done here. Good day, sir."

1

DEATH, WHAT A TEASE

Annie, returning from work, noticed her pale lump of a husband sunken deeply into his La-Z-Boy. Not so unusual, but this evening, something was different. She noticed a lack of vibrancy, a paucity of animation—an absence of *joie de vivre*. She'd noticed, to put it succinctly, that he was dead. She'd also noticed the front door handle needed polishing, a scuff on the wall needed cleaning, and a baseboard needed painting. All of this before she had kicked off her toe-pinching shoes, and none of it made her happy.

She hung her purse on the rack by the door and perused three pieces of mail, tossing each into a nearby wastepaper basket. She turned toward her husband, the cadaver. As a former cop with twenty years of experience in the Houston PD, she knew a stiff when she saw one. She was seeing one now.

"Nigel, Nigel, Nigel," said Annie. His name, let's assume, was Nigel. "Wasn't I saying just this morning to lay off the Cap'n Crunch?"

Annie moved closer to inspect the body. Aside from an off-putting deathly pallor, he looked good—better rested than she'd seen in years. He had a grin on his face. This did not put a grin on her face. What would a dying husband, without his wife by his side, be grinning about? Nothing respectable, she was certain.

Looking down at her late beloved, Annie swiveled her head from side to side, repeating a motion she'd used earlier that day after discovering a half-package of moldy cheese. What a waste.

The cause of death was not apparent. There was no sign of struggle and no indication that death was anything but a pleasure. That is, until her eyes landed on the hands. They were positioned atop the chest, one over the other—a perfect funeral pose had they lightly clutched a lily. But there was no lily, and the clutch was not light. Rather, the hands were white-knuckling a crinkly sheet of yellow notebook paper.

Leaning forward, Annie grabbed the yellow sheet and pulled. The cadaver's hands held tight, gripping the paper in —what else?—a death grip. The dark secret to Nigel's unexpected demise might be revealed if Annie could just wrestle the note from his damned corpse. What might this document be? A suicide note? Shocking news from a loved one? An ancient contract penned in blood? Whatever it was, it wasn't availing itself without a fight. The dead preferred their secrets buried with them.

Annie, asserting her dominance one last time, finally prevailed. She straightened the crumpled sheet. It was Nigel's to-do list—the one she had cultivated for him, item by item, over the past several weeks. She scanned the roster of home improvements, first one side and then the other. Not a cross-out or a check mark to be found. From the deepest folds of her epiglottis, Annie emitted a chiffy blast not unlike that of the green iguana when finding its tail attached to the toothy end of an ocelot.

Shaking the paper over his lifeless face, she huffed,

"Nigel, Nigel, Nigel." Nigel had never appreciated his own name, and certainly not when said by his wife three times in succession. "What have you been doing with yourself all this time? Are you completely useless?"

A fly, alert to the dynamics between domineering wife and dead husband, circled down to land on the quieter of the two. The corner of Nigel's smiling mouth provided a prime landing location to plant the flag and declare first dibs. Annie thought about shooshing away the pest, but what really was the point?

Brrringg! Brrringg!

Nigel, being dead, afforded Annie the opportunity to answer the phone.

Brrringg! Brrringg!

Nigel, much to his surprise, felt his blood start to sizzle. He had been under the impression that corpse blood, if not entirely coagulated, was at least cold. Yet he quite distinctly felt the stuff going warm and fizzy.

Brrringg! Brrringg!

Bloody hell. Yes, Nigel had agreed to handle the domestic duties, but couldn't Annie, under the circumstances, man up just this once? Had death come with no privileges?

Brrringg! Brrringg!

Hells bells! thought Nigel, hurtling himself from death to wakefulness at an injurious pace. Half conscious, he ejected himself from the La-Z-Boy, sending his stockinged feet and a crumpled piece of yellow notebook paper onto the linoleum floor. Attempting to catch his breath, Nigel instead caught something small and fluttery in the back of his throat.

Brrringg! Brrringg!

Nigel scanned the room for the source of his unpleasant resurrection. It was the landline phone Annie had recently installed for her business calls.

"Ack, ack." He coughed into the phone, attempting to clear his throat.

"Are you okay?" Annie asked from the other end of the line.

"Yearrrgh, ack! I'm fine. Ack! Just something in my throat. Yeaccch! You'd think I'd swallowed a fly. What's up?"

"So, the phone is working?"

"Yes. Yes, it is. Blasted thing could wake the dead."

"Good. I've got a mailer ad out today, and I wanted to make sure the phone was still working."

"Indeed. Tricky devils, those phones. Hard to differentiate between the ones not being used and the ones that are broken. How to know except to test? Consider ours tested."

"Are you working on the to-do list?" said Annie, moving on.

"Absolutely," said Nigel. "What else would I be doing? Sleeping?"

"You seem a bit sharp today."

"Sharp, dear?"

"Sarcastic—"

"Sorry. I'm a little out of sorts. For one joyous moment, I thought I'd died. Purgatory, maybe. Not to worry. I felt you by my side the whole way. It was your call that pulled me back from the gates of heaven—or hell. I'm not sure which. Sarcastic? Don't think so, dear. Just happy to be among the living and to hear your lovely voice."

"It's good you're back," she said, accompanied by a sound which may have been eyes rolling skyward. "I called to let you know that rain gutters should go on the list. I noticed this morning that we have none in the front, and some are missing in the back. They definitely need to go on the list."

Annie was always so matter-of-fact when weaving new things into Nigel's list. And why not? Weaving, like knitting, is a bloody relaxing activity, even when the end product is a crown of thorns for your spouse.

"Okay," said Nigel. "That would be item forty-seven, if memory serves. Or maybe it's fifty-three."

"It should go on top."

"On top? I was going to pounce on that leaky toilet today, and then there were those nail pops you find so gruesome. Any reason why rain gutters are the new crisis *du jour*?"

"Yes. There's a hurricane heading our way."

"A hurricane? Do rain gutters protect against hurricanes? If I were a rain gutter—I'm not, of course, but just thinking out loud. If I were a rain gutter, I believe I would rather go up after a hurricane, wouldn't you? If you were a rain gutter, I mean. You know," said Nigel, interrupting himself with a whooshing sound, "all that wind."

"We're a hundred miles inland. We don't worry about the wind, but we do need to worry about flooding rain. Rain gutters—top of the list. Also," added Annie, "while you're out buying the rain gutters, pick up something for dinner and some bottled water."

"I certainly will, dear," said Nigel.

Two engineering degrees and thirty-some years in industry had never taught Nigel how to counter a directive from the wife. She spewed orders like a drill sergeant at bayonet practice. Nigel once thought she'd acquired this proficiency in the Marine Corps. Then he met her mother.

"Have dinner ready when I get home," said Annie.

"Aye, aye." Nigel ended the phone call with a salute. *Nice conversation*, he thought. What was he to add to the list? Rain gutters, was it?

It wasn't always like this. A few months ago, he'd held a respectable job working for an oil company back in Houston. What precisely he did at that job was, to his wife, an enigma. Nigel, tucked away in his tiny cubicle, often felt the same way. Nevertheless, for nineteen years, he dutifully executed his responsibilities until that one day when—out of the blue—he was summoned to a bare meeting room occupied by his boss, a three-year company vet; his boss's boss, a six-month company vet; and an HR person he'd not seen before. This makeshift collective informed Nigel that he'd been a fine worker, a corporate asset, and a pleasure to be around. Be that as it may, the company's prospects looked grim as long as he kept showing up. A stay-at-home incentive program was enacted in the form of no more paychecks.

Even though Nigel had been expecting something like this for at least sixteen years, he was, nonetheless, shocked. At the ripe old age of fifty-six, he'd been put out to pasture. Thinking of it that way made him feel better, but the thought of telling Annie made him feel worse.

Annie worked as a detective for the Houston Police Department, having worked her way up from patrol officer. Nigel knew that her colleagues held her in high regard, though sometimes put off by her enthusiasm for "law and order." This mirrored her experience as an MP in the Marine Corps, where she'd been informally crowned "Miss Gung Ho." Nevertheless, underneath her spiky exterior, through a thick layer of tungsten steel and below a rock-hard mantle, lay a rich, gooey caramel center. It was this sweet core that Nigel planned to drill into while explaining to his adorable pitbull how their main feeding dish had gone bye-bye.

Upon receiving the news, Annie was pleasingly placid— almost disconcertingly so. Nigel congratulated himself on a finely nuanced delivery. It hadn't been easy because, truth be told, he was still giddy at not going to work in the morning. But giddiness was not an emotion he dared exhibit at this stage. Instead, he kept it solemn—not dark, not despairing, but solemn, with hints of not-so-badism. To end on a high note, he threw his hands in the air and let loose a breezy, "But what can we do?"

Much to his surprise, Annie told him exactly what they could do. It seems she'd been harboring a secret plan. She was tired of life on the force and tired of the big city. She wanted to start her own private detective business in a small town like the one she was from. In one of those not-so-bizarre coincidences, she revealed that her younger brother owned a small fixer-upper in her hometown that was available for a pittance.

Nigel, you understand, had lived in Houston for the past thirty years, and he had been raised in the suburbs of London. He knew nothing about life in small-town Texas. What awaited him there was yet to be defined, but an hour before, he was a man without a plan. Now he had one. A new existence was gaining momentum faster than you could say "snowball."

Their new life would be simple. Annie would grow her business while Nigel made a home. After three decades in the corporate rat race, he looked forward to puttering around the house, fixing this doodad, polishing that doohickey, growing bell peppers, and baking sugar cookies. Move over, Martha Stewart. As they dismantled their old life while preparing for the new, his mind drifted to thoughts of new hobbies. Perhaps he would smoke a pipe.

And then, within a week of moving into their small-town slice of heaven, a monster sprouted between them. Nigel knew it was bad—monsters often are—but at the time, he had no idea. Annie was making a list, you see. It was a vast list of home repairs and improvements, which by the terms of their agreement, he was obligated to do. Each new item was like a nail in the coffin of his dreams for a leisurely semi-retirement. Even after that coffin lid was shuttered by a thousand nails, additional items continued to fall like spadefuls of dirt.

You might ask why Nigel didn't sit his lovely wife down for a heart to heart. Wouldn't have worked. Annie was not the type of gal to say, "Relax, dear. Don't worry. All in good time." Nope. Nigel could hear her say, "If you need a straw, soldier, I can lend you one." That's marine-speak for "Suck it up." That's the kind of gal Annie was. To put it in perspective, Nigel may have worn pants, but Annie wore *the* pants— pants constructed of soft, pliable threads stripped from Nigel's backbone.

But enough of the daydreaming. Nigel picked up the crumpled piece of paper. He glared at its yellow blackness, breaking into a cold sweat. The to-do list glared back in silent, mocking contempt. He recalled—maybe a month back, though it felt like years—when victory over the to-do list seemed conceivable. Not anymore. The list grew longer and stronger by the day, while Nigel's soul—along with his dreams—shriveled like a raisin stranded on a tombstone during a hot summer day.

He had long known the key to his own happiness was to make Annie happy. After all, what planet thrives while orbiting an angry sun? Not Planet Nigel. He would do anything for Annie. Anything. Anything at all. Anything but that to-do list!

"Oh, deliver me from this pestilence!" shouted Nigel, falling to his knees while thrusting the paper in a trembling fist toward an indifferent heaven.

Brrring! Brrring!

2

A MISSING DOG TO THE RESCUE

The new day arrived with thin strips of shimmery sunshine squeezing through the shutters. Sunshine at such an hour—whether shimmery, in strips, or through shutters—could find a warm, moist place to stick itself as far as Mrs. Sandoval was concerned. She burrowed beneath the sheets and bade the rising sun goodnight. Later, when the sun bore its rays at less offensive angles, she would grumble herself out of bed.

Mrs. Sandoval's first morning encounter was normally with Duffy, a regrettable-looking mutt who stationed himself outside her room at the appropriate hour. On this day, Duffy was conspicuous by his absence.

The second to greet Mrs. Sandoval in the morning was usually Gastrick, the butler. He stationed himself downstairs and awaited the sound of footsteps and ghastly utterances, which would signal Mrs. Sandoval's survival through another night. Gastrick, as always, was conspicuous in his presence.

"You slept well, I trust?" Gastrick asked his employer as she stepped hard onto the ground floor. The grand staircase always confounded Mrs. Sandoval—more steps going up than coming down.

"Mmmmmmm Mmmm," she moaned, interpreted by Gastrick as "So-so." "Where is Duffy this morning?"

"Where's who?"

"Duffy. You know, the dog."

"Oh, that. Don't know."

"What should we do, Gastrick?"

"Pop a bottle of champagne?" Gastrick did not approve of dogs in his workplace.

"Why would we do that?" said Mrs. Sandoval.

Wry humor was not her forte, especially in the hours between sunup and tequila. A subsequent search of the house and grounds confirmed a dogless estate. Contrary to Gastrick's supposition that dogs were wild creatures not suited for life in a home, Mrs. Sandoval resolved to find her animal. But where to begin? Gastrick mentioned animal shelters and dog pounds. His lurid descriptions of those institutions left Mrs. Sandoval with a sense that no dog, having been in such a place, would be reclaimable as a pet. If Duffy had been there, she wouldn't want to know about it. "What are we to do, Gastrick?" she moaned.

"If I may say so, you are entirely too stressed about this. Please have a seat. I've brought you the mail and a replenishing tonic. I suggest you rest and leave the matter to me."

"To you, Gastrick? What do you propose to do?"

"To find dear Puffy."

"Duffy."

"Of course."

Mrs. Sandoval, a handsome, middle-aged widow, stretched herself out on the red velvet divan. In terms of fashion, Mrs. Sandoval was an experimenter. Today, it showed in the form of a crinkly, crinoline-fueled strapless gown that, had it been worn to a function, would have made every critic's best- *or* worst-dressed list. Nothing of that sort would happen today, not while Duffy roamed untethered in a dangerous world. Mrs. Sandoval slammed back the "replenishing tonic," which tasted comfortingly like fine tequila. Upon clearing her head with an after-snort snort, she thumbed through the assorted junk mail until happening upon an ad for a detective agency. She had never in her life seen an ad for a detective agency. Rather suddenly, she found herself believing in divination.

Worth a try, she thought.

Brrringg! Brrringg!

Nigel got off his knees, expecting to hear his wife on the line. "Yes? Another addition to the to-do list? Emergency root cellar? An urgent gazebo, perhaps? A drawbridge?"

"Excuse me?" answered back a distinctly non-Annie voice, one that sounded like Betty Boop after a night spent on the floor of a cantina. "This is Mrs. Sandoval. To whom am I speaking?"

Nigel, realizing the errors of his ways, saw a stack of his wife's business cards placed strategically by the phone. *That woman thinks of everything.* "Sniffer's Detective Agency and Security Service," he read. "At your service."

"I have a case for you, I think," said Mrs. Sandoval.

Nigel had just become a temporary receptionist, but Annie had provided no instructions. He'd have to wing it.

"You think you have a case? You mean, you're not sure?" he said. "I'm not sure we could take a case if you're not sure you have one."

"I'm not sure you'd be the right agency."

"I assure you, *madam*, we are the right agency. But are you the right client?"

"I don't know. Do you handle dogs?"

"We're not a kennel, if that's what you mean."

"That is *not* what I mean. Do you handle cases involving dogs?"

"Are you implying what I think you're implying?" asked Nigel, warming to the task of playing the detective's receptionist.

"I don't know what you think I'm implying, but most assuredly, I'm not. I would never. You seem to me to be sort of … What's the word I'm looking for?"

"An imbecile?"

"I was going to say presumptuous, but you know best."

"Do I?"

"You're an Englishman, aren't you?"

"I might be. What does that have to do with it?"

"Nothing, I suppose. An Englishman can be an imbecile, though in this country, we'd probably say moron. Now that you've declared yourself an imbecile Englishman, I'm not sure I want you on the case. I was coming around to that conclusion anyway. You just saved us both some time."

"Just to clarify," Nigel broke in, "I wasn't declaring *myself* an imbecile. I was just trying to help you place a word. I took a guess as to what you were getting at, you see. And," said Nigel, perhaps making too fine a point of things, "in my experience, there is no distinction between imbecile and moron based on country."

"I see. I'm inclined to agree that either would do. Imbecile, moron, whatever. At least you seem expert on something."

Nigel, not ready to lose a client over trifling verbiage, opted for a brass-tacks approach. "Maybe we should talk about your case."

"I'd like nothing better," said a surprised Mrs. Sandoval.

"You say it involves dogs?"

"A dog. Singular."

"Okay, one unattached dog. So, what's this dog done?"

"I don't know," said Mrs. Sandoval.

"Well, this is a puzzler," said Nigel. "You have a dog that needs investigating, but you don't know what it's done. A conundrum."

"He's missing."

"And he's missing to boot. Bear with me, ma'am, while I write this down."

Nigel picked up a non-functioning pen and began to make a series of indentations on a nearby legal pad. "So, this missing dog, do you know where he is?"

"No."

"No? Sounds difficult, but that's what we're here for. Tell me, what would you consider a satisfying result in this case?"

"Getting my dog back."

"Alive?"

"Of course, alive."

"Just needed to make sure it wasn't one of those dead or alive thingies. So, all you really want is for us to find and return your dog—alive. I've made special note of that," he said, carving an "A" into the helpless pad with the hapless pen. "This type of case falls under the broad heading of what we loosely term 'missing-persons cases.' "

Nigel found himself being pulled into the investigation in the manner of a moth being pulled into a campfire. If he'd owned a deerstalker cap, he would, by this point, have donned it. "I have a few questions. They might sound a bit personal. I ask that you not get upset, okay?"

"Sure."

"Is it possible the dog just ran away?"

"Why would he do that?"

"I don't really know, ma'am, but it happens. Dog wanders off. He meets up with a traveling circus or a train-hopping hobo, and the next thing, he's in Cornwall, or Iowa. I just want to know if it might have been voluntary. Had there been a spat?"

"Nothing of the sort. I don't think he would have wandered off. He likes to get fed."

"I see. I don't want to upset you, but I must ask, could the dog have fallen victim to an accident? If not an accident, foul play?"

Nigel, inkless pen at the ready, waited for a reply. Rustling sounds—not of the cow variety, but more like moving fabric —spilled from the receiver. This was followed by a couple of grunts and then a sound like a squeegee being run across a balloon. Nigel imagined the scene at the other end. A lonely woman kneeling by an empty dog bed—one hand softly touching the surface where her pooch should have been, and the other clutching a tissue and wiping away tears while the phone lies unattended on the floor. Nigel afforded her time to regain her composure.

"Hello?" she said after the extended break.

"Yes?"

"I'm sorry. I was rearranging my, um, brassiere. Sometimes they get away, you know. Jump the fence, so to speak. The lambs are back in their pens now, for sure. Taped 'em up. Now, what were you going on about?"

"I was asking if you felt the dog had left voluntarily, or if you suspect foul play?"

Rustling noises again. Maybe now she was reaching for a tissue, though Nigel could not put aside the image of a pair of lambs tumbling from overburdened hammocks.

"I'm sorry again. I was just attaching my garter clips—"

"Excuse me, garter clips?" Nigel looked around for a calendar to affirm the century.

"Yes, garter clips. The things that keep your nylons up. Come now. You're a man of the world. I'm sure you've seen garter clips."

"Yes. I'm sure I have. I'm a man of the world. Please proceed."

"I would not have called if I thought Duffy had left on his own. Believe me, if he had wanted to leave, I'd have thrown down a hell of a going-away party. No, I think he's been snatched."

"By who?" said Nigel.

Silence.

"Aren't *you* supposed to answer that question?" she said.

A pause ensued.

Right, thought Nigel. "For now, let's just say foul play is possible, and that everyone is suspect. That way, we don't bias the investigation," said Nigel, impressed by the sound of his own investigatorliness. Using the inkless pen, Nigel repeatedly impressed the word "Duffy" onto the legal pad. It was the single most important fact in the case, and he had cataloged it to the extent that a blind person could see it.

"Will you take the case? I'd like it resolved before that storm hits tomorrow night."

"I'll have to confer with my partner. I'll let you know by tomorrow morning. It depends on our caseload."

"Oh!" said the lady, as if surprised.

"I'm sorry, but that's the state of things."

"No, no, it's all right. It's just that"—grunts and groans ensued—"they've gotten loose again. Some days, they have minds of their own."

3

SHOWERHEADS AND GUTTERS

Annie's ancestors were Texas pioneers: tough, independent, and hygienic when possible. From an early age, Annie received semi-reliable, third-hand accounts of cowboy life on the great western cattle drives. She recalled vivid descriptions of her cowboy forebears plagued by billowing clouds of dust, pummeled by sheets of wind-blown sand, and irritated by saddle rash—the unhappy result of a continuous diet of stewed beans coupled with the ever-present grind of sweat-lubed grit between denim and skin. It was no wonder that after weeks on the trail, a young buck tucked into his bedroll had but one thought on his mind: to secure a room in some wild west cow town where he could stand in a porcelain tub unleashing a torrent of clean water upon himself from an oaken bucket hoisted overhead. His deepest desires having been satiated, he could then enjoy a glass of cool lemonade on the veranda. Granddad related this story with tears welling up in his eyes.

In contrast to her cowboy predecessors, Annie regarded the shower—with its adjustable water temperatures, selection of flow patterns, assortments of anatomy-specific shower gels, shampoos, conditioners, and scrubbing utensils—as a chore. Not today, though. Once home, she marched straight to the bathroom, stripped off her sweat-soaked clothes, and turned on the shower. Stepping into the stall, she unleashed a "Yeehaw!" her ancestors would have been proud of.

In her eagerness, she did not notice the shiny new showerhead, nor did she see how the pulsing projectiles of water punished the tiles on the opposing shower wall. Stepping into this crossfire, Annie grabbed the showerhead to save herself from the liquid pummeling. She gave the head a twist, causing the entire assembly to rocket forward and wallop her on the forehead. She screeched and wobbled as the showerhead crashed near her feet.

Nigel, stepping through the front door with a bag of groceries, heard the commotion and rushed to the bathroom.

"Don't tell me you tried to take a shower," he said to his wife, standing naked and wet in the shower stall.

"What else would I be doing?"

"I would've advised against it."

"I take showers every day. I took one yesterday."

"*Yesterday*, we didn't have a new showerhead. You wanted a new one, remember? Number twelve on the list. I *installed*," he said with air quotes, "a new, massaging, adjustable, multi-flow model." Nigel rotated his hand as if to demonstrate its function.

"When I tried to adjust it," said Annie, mocking his rotating hand gesture, "the *newly installed*," she said with air quotes, "showerhead flew off and hit me on the head. What kind of showerhead does that?"

"The kind that's not fully attached. I needed to buy some Teflon tape before I screwed it on for good. I'd have hung a sign, but I didn't expect you to come home at four-thirty and take a shower. How often does that happen? Once, I'm guessing. Are you injured?"

"I can feel a bump."

"It looks like you're sprouting a horn," said Nigel. "You'll have a bruise tomorrow. Here," he said, pulling her closer and kissing the bump, "that should fix your head. If you can wait two minutes, I'll fix the shower's head."

"And you can fix dinner. You have something for dinner?"

"Absolutely. Pizza!"

"You do remember we had pizza last night, right?"

"Ah, but this is different. That was the cheap frozen stuff. Tonight, we have the Tuscan medley special from Marco's Italiano and—I kid you not—wine. Not just any wine, but a box of America's finest red, straight from Walmart's bargain basket. That's where they keep their best stuff, you know."

Annie shook her head and felt her bump. It was hard to be too mad at the guy. He was trying, after all. And he was smart enough to buy wine.

After de-weaponizing the showerhead and convincing Annie it was safe to shower, Nigel turned to re-heating the pizza and pondering his plight. This latest incident provided yet one more reason why the to-do list was a bad idea. Turning one's home into a construction site just wasn't safe. Accidents are bound to happen. Bound to. Of course, he would never mention this to his wife. She had a way of turning such discussions against him, making him seem like a shirker. *So not completely true*, thought Nigel.

Having showered without further injury, Annie entered the kitchen in bathrobe, frizzy hair and glasses. To Nigel, she seemed just as enticing this way as any other. The table awaited with warm pizza and wine glasses. Annie nodded her approval, especially at the box of wine sitting as a centerpiece.

"I love a girl with a bruise on her forehead," said Nigel, pulling her close and kissing her bump once again. Annie was a strikingly beautiful woman, though you wouldn't know it just by looking at her. Her beauty was, shall we say, not lovingly presented for all the world to see. That didn't matter. He was lucky to have her, and he knew it. She also knew it.

"You're turned on by girls with bruises?" asked Annie, furrowing her brow, which hurt a bit.

"Let me rephrase. The girl I love has a bruise on her forehead. I'm sorry about that, but I was only trying to please. Really, I was." He kissed her fully on the mouth and pulled away, smacking his lips. "Nice shower gel," he said, stroking his chin. "A hardy flavor. Would mate well with roast beef. Pina Colada?"

"Lavender."

"Close," said Nigel, still embracing her. "You must have had an active day to come home at four-thirty for a shower. Any noteworthy sleuthing?"

"I spent my day traipsing through a cow pasture. How about you?"

"Me? The usual. Showerheads and whatnot. I'm more interested in your cow pasture."

"Looking at fences for signs of theft, delinquency, bad ranching, whatever."

"So, you've branched into fence inspecting?"

"Rustling. The Gilbert Ranch, north of here, has been missing some cows, so they've hired me to find out what's going on."

"Cows? Really? I don't recall you mentioning any cow work in Houston. You have training for this? They teach you how to track cows at the Police Academy? How to take a hoofprint? How to file an MCR?"

"An MCR?"

"Missing Cow Report," said Nigel, administering a critical eye. "Are you sure you're qualified for this type of work."

"A cow theft is pretty much like a car theft, except they seldom use the cow as a means of escape."

"Ah, grand theft cow." The conversation had taken a fortuitous turn. "What about dogs?" asked Nigel.

"Grand theft dog?"

"I mean, if someone wanted you to find a missing dog, would you be interested?"

"No way. Stolen property is one thing. Missing pets, I'll leave to dogcatchers."

"I see. Is this going to keep you busy, all this cowlifting?"

"Busy enough. After this, I have a couple of deadbeats to locate."

"You know," said Nigel, thinking out loud, "if you're getting busy, I mean, if you could use a little extra help with your investigations, I could—"

"Hahahahaha! No," said Annie. Then she added, "Hahahaha! Thanks, but no thanks." That was followed by, "Hahahahaha!"

"Glad I could bring some cheer," said Nigel. Maybe if she had actually heard him out, she—

"Hahaha! That is—What is it you say?—rich. You helping with investigations? That's rich. Hahaha!"

Nigel was pleased that her business was succeeding, though he never doubted it would. His wife was a marvel. He was quite sure the private eye industry in New Antigua, Texas had never seen anything like her. "So business is roaring, is it?" asked Nigel between sips of wine.

"Holding my own," said Annie. She quickly added, "This is really good pizza." She said it, but her blank stare did not communicate pizza rapture.

"You look as if you need more wine," said Nigel, pouring it for her.

Annie snapped to. "Why do you say that?"

"Staring into an empty glass with a faraway look is like asking for more. Isn't this wine spectacular? I give it seven and a half stars."

"On a scale of what?"

"One to thirty-four—thirty-four being best in class. On second thought, make that one to thirty-three. It's kicking in, so I'm feeling generous." Nigel held his glass up to the light. "A lean wine and delicate, but not too lean and not too delicate. There is a hint of flab and a touch of brutality. I like that. It does have edges—quite a lot of them, though not terribly sharp. These softened edges give this wine its semi-well-defined shape. And that shape is...a dodecahedron. Not a raw dodec, but one that's been worked over a bit, like with a sixty-grit sandpaper." Nigel took a sip, and after some slushing and sucking noises, he continued, "The flavor hints at hickory with a pinch of leather. Kangaroo leather, perhaps. Is this an Australian wine? I detect emu and a dollop of plum, with tangerine peeking from around the corner. The aftertaste is Robitussin. The wine is dry, but not so dry that the bottle's empty. That's my humble opinion. What say you?"

"Honestly, I've been careful not to let it touch my tongue, and I've held my breath to avoid the smell. However, the aftertaste implicates alcohol, and that's a positive."

"We should be writing for Wine Enthusiast. We know our stuff," said Nigel, taking Annie's hand and kissing it just above the third knuckle.

"Speaking of stuff, what else did you get at the store?"

"That store! The storm's first casualty. After being at that place, I don't see this hurricane as anything but a welcome change of pace. I'm sure there are already bodies in amongst the rubble."

"You got bottled water?"

"I got it, though I'm not sure I trust it. It was the last they had."

"What brand?"

"Brand? It has a white label that says, 'Water, for to drinking.' I think it's an import. At the price I paid, it had better be. What kind of catastrophe are we expecting here anyway? I mean weather-wise."

"We're in the path of Hurricane Pelham, a category two, maybe a cat three by the time it makes landfall tomorrow evening."

Nigel loved the way she said cat three. An image of Annie as a sexy TV weathergirl flashed in his mind. "And the winds? Powerful?" Nigel knew the answer, but he wanted more weathergirl.

"No, but flooding is possible." An image of Annie holding her wineglass in one hand while gracefully gesticulating with the other in front of a map of colorful blobs, arrows, and lines invaded Nigel's brain space. He wondered if Annie had ever imagined him as a hunky newscaster.

"Did you get the gutters?" asked Annie, vaporizing the newsroom fantasies. Gutter talk was not sexy.

"I bought some gutters," said Nigel proudly.

"How many downspouts did you get?"

"Downspouts?"

"Don't tell me you bought gutters but no downspouts."

"Okay. I won't."

"You can buy them tomorrow," said Annie, retrieving a firearm from her purse. "If you put up the gutters this evening, it shouldn't take long to install the downspouts tomorrow."

"You're forcing me at gunpoint?"

"No, but maybe a pistol-whipping. That is," she said, smelling the barrel of her gun, "if you're a good boy and get those gutters up."

As he laid out the materials and set up the ladder, Nigel reckoned he had two hours of usable daylight. Outwardly, he was a man doing a man's work. Inwardly, he perceived an uneasiness, a vague tension, and a bloated hollowness. This he attributed to the inner frustrations of a man who, after sharing multiple glasses of wine with his wife, was putting up gutters. Then he burped, and he was fine. He still regretted wasting a buzz on home improvements, but on the bright side, the job provided tangible evidence of forward motion against that albatross of a to-do list. An albatross getting heavier and smellier by the day. As Nigel climbed the ladder in the stifling humidity, he sensed something oozing from his pores. It wasn't sweat. It was his life force. He needed an escape. Tomorrow, he would give himself one.

4

MRS. SANDOVAL, SEA CAPTAIN

Nigel turned off FM1024 onto a shady two-lane blacktop known as Country Club Drive. A mile later, the road split into a one-way lane, circling in front of the only destination on Country Club Drive, the Sandoval estate. Nigel drove past an empty parking lot and right up to the house.

He slowed as he approached. The imposing antebellum-inspired structure had clearly been designed as a grand gathering place for a certain class of people. They must have been out fox hunting because the place looked deserted. The stillness induced a foreboding. Nigel's gut—the most prescient of his organs—urged him to circle around the loop and head back to the highway.

But the car crept onward. The sound of tires slow-rolling on coarse asphalt was suddenly overtaken by the sound of haunting laughter. *Hahahaha. No.* Nigel quickly pinpointed the source as a ghostly, foot-tall image of Annie sitting on his dashboard. The laughter, a replay from last night's conversation, had taken on an almost taunting quality. *Hahahaha. Rich.* The interloping phantom of the dashboard vanished when Nigel jerked the steering wheel to avoid drifting into a ditch.

What did it mean? If Nigel had gotten the gist of it, Annie's laughter had been her way of voicing skepticism regarding his value as an investigating partner. So here he was—not her partner—on a dog case, which she had no interest in. *So what's the problem, phantom wife?* Nigel didn't see one. Certainly not if she never found out about it. Of course, this assumed little phantom Annie wasn't a two-way messenger.

Nigel parked the car just to the side of the house. His palms wet themselves while his mouth filled with cotton. What on earth had possessed him to come here? A gentleman's agreement to accept the case? A resolution to squeeze more juice from his life than he could fixing toilets and hanging gutters? Had he bitten off more than he could chew? He had no answers, but he knew it was too hot to stay in the car.

As Nigel stepped out, he noticed a middle-aged man, outfitted in stylish dinner attire, approaching with purpose. The man's dress, his deliberate pace, and his steely countenance pegged him as a hard-charging executive type. Nigel had encountered his kind far too often in his previous career. These men of the self-imposed ruling class wielded their brand of aggressive, back-slapping friendliness as a tool to impress upon the serfs how lucky they were to be under the thumbs of such amiable owners. Nigel would not cower to such manipulation this time. He took two hops forward, grabbed the man's hand, and squeezed and pumped like nobody's business. The man blanched, taken aback. Nigel, having telegraphed his refusal to submit to a servant's role, stood tall.

"Mr. Blandwater-Cummings of the Sniffers Detective Agency?" asked the man, leaning backward.

"That I am. Pleased to meet you," said Nigel, pulling him

forward while emphasizing his dominance with a reach to the shoulder.

"We've been expecting you," said the man, retreating as best he could. "I'm Gastrick, the butler. Please follow me."

Inside, the house was tastefully appointed, leaning toward the ornate. Gastrick directed Nigel through the foyer and into an alcove that served as a sitting room. A middle-aged woman, dressed like a fifties teenybopper primed for the hop, sat on a Louis XIV loveseat. Gastrick completed the formal introductions in a manner suggesting he might soon be asleep.

"Please have a seat," said Mrs. Sandoval. "Do you have a card? Gastrick recalls names. I do not. Helps if I have something solid."

Nigel, in a rare moment of clarity, had anticipated the need for a business card. Before his appointment, he had stopped off at the New Antigua Print N' Post. The dead-eyed clerk there didn't look as if he'd know a business card from a biscuit, but Nigel wrote down what he wanted and got his order back in minutes. New Antigua lacked plenty of amenities, but efficient printing, apparently, was not one of them.

"Sure thing," said Nigel, reaching into his pocket for a freshly minted card. "There's more where that came from."

"Very good," said Mrs. Sandoval, holding up the card. "Nigel Blandwater-Cummings, defective for hire."

"Ha ha." Nigel chuckled. "That's detective for hire."

"It says, 'Defective for Hire.' "

"No, no. That's detective. I don't think anyone would care to hire a defective. It's detective."

"Looks like defective to me."

"May I?" said Nigel, reaching out for Mrs. Sandoval's card. Judging by his horrified eyes, one might suspect the card had been dusted with anthrax. As if to underscore the point, animalistic growls escaped from behind tight lips stretched over clenched teeth. Nigel pulled a pen from his pocket and marked on the card. He handed it back to Mrs. Sandoval, commenting, "Detective for Hire."

Mrs. Sandoval looked at the modified card, which had a "t" superimposed in blue ink over the "f" in defective. Of course, such a cosmetic trick would have worked better converting a "t" into an "f," but Nigel played the cards he was dealt.

"I'll try to remember," said Mrs. Sandoval. "Do you mind if I just call you Mr. Blandwater? Blandwater-Cummings seems rather drawn out. I get a little short-winded sometimes."

"Actually, I prefer Nigel. People seldom pass out when saying it." Nigel felt somewhat relieved. Despite Mrs. Sandoval's odd getup, the surroundings evoked a refinement not expected in New Antigua. Rich people were the same the world over.

"Perfect. I'll call you Nigel, then. Would you care for something to drink?"

Mrs. Sandoval exhibited quite the rational temperament compared to her telephone persona. "Water would be fine," said Nigel.

"Gastrick, could you bring a bottle of water and two tequilas? Thank you." Turning to Nigel, she continued, "About our little Duffy. I'm just heartbroken that he's lost— out there with no one to care for him. It must be absolutely terrifying. He's not used to fending for himself, you know."

"I didn't know, but you're right. It must be terrifying."

"It's like this, Mr. Nigel. He's a wonderful pet, but he's not the kind of dog likely to be adopted into a family environment. You see, he's not exactly a friendly-looking dog."

"Does he bite?" said Nigel, pushing past the aesthetics.

"Well, he hasn't bit anyone except for veterinarians. Oh, and their assistants. But really, I don't think that should count against him. I mean, it's understandable biting a veterinarian, given all the cruel things they do. The last one stuck a thermometer—a very cold thermometer, I imagine—where you shouldn't really stick things in a dog. Of course, he bit. Wouldn't you?"

"Wouldn't I?" asked Nigel, recalling a similar experience which he'd submitted to without so much as a growl. That experience would be kept to himself. He didn't want to make Duffy sound like a brute.

"Wouldn't you bite a veterinarian that stuck a cold thermometer up your pooper?"

"Well, that's a tough one. For one thing, I don't think I have the flexibility."

"You might want to try plyometrics."

"Plyometrics?"

"Exercises to increase your flexibility."

"I'll consider it before my next appointment with the vet," said Nigel. The interview, having drifted where no interview should drift, needed a refocus. "Now, about poor Duffy, when did you discover he was missing?"

Before Mrs. Sandoval could answer, Gastrick arrived with the drinks on a tray. After transferring a cloth napkin, juice glass, and bottle of water to the small table siding Nigel's chair, he lowered the tray with the two tequila shots for Mrs. Sandoval. She took them both, one in each hand. She downed one in a single motion, then downed the other. She concluded this impressive feat with a gruff, exaggerated *aaaach* while waggling her head back and forth, presumably to free up any droplets clinging to the tonsils.

"I don't always drink in the morning, you understand. But when I have morning callers, I like to be hospitable and offer them a drink," said Mrs. Sandoval.

"I quite understand," said Nigel, holding up his glass of

water. "I see how it works. It's like eleven o'clock tea back home, but earlier."

"Really? What do you drink for eleven o'clock tea?"

"Tea," said Nigel.

Mrs. Sandoval scrunched her face, as if trying to imagine it. "Well now," she said. "We can talk freely. At least I can. Are you sure you wouldn't like a drink, Mr. Nigel?" She leaned forward while framing her face between the two shot glasses as she rotated them with her fingers. A minute earlier, Nigel supposed he was talking to a doyenne, a matriarch, a regal, fifties-style, plantation-house *grande dame*. And now? A sea captain on shore leave.

"I had better not. I'm on the job," said Nigel, hoping to get the interview back on track.

"I hope you won't take this the wrong way, Mr. Nigel, but you seem like the nervous type. You're new around here, aren't you?"

"Is six weeks new?"

"What brings an Englishman all the way to New Antigua?" Mrs. Sandoval's original sitting posture had been like something out of a 1950's charm school instructional manual. Now she was starting to resemble a mudslide.

"Well, I did stop in Houston for about thirty years," said Nigel. "But I got here as fast as I could. Actually, my wife is from here."

"Really? What's her name? Maybe I know her."

"Her original name was Annalee Novak."

"Novak, Novak," she whispered, casting her eyes up and away as if a school yearbook were perched in a corner of the room. "I think I may remember her from elementary school. Does she have braces? Does she wear her hair in a Buster Brown cut? Does she draw ponies? I'm sure I remember her."

"Doesn't ring a bell for me," said Nigel. If Nigel had heard a bell, he'd have assumed it was in Mrs. Sandoval's belfry.

"But we've only been married for twelve years." Course correcting, Nigel asked, "Now, perhaps we could talk about your missing pooch, eh?"

"Whereabouts are you living, Mr. Nigel?"

"We're out east, near No Way. Perhaps we can—"

"No Way, very nice."

"So, you're familiar with the area?" replied Nigel, trying to observe a certain civility.

"No, not at all. I do know that Cam Logan has a place out there."

"Does he? I'll have to stop by and say hello."

"I'm sure *she* would appreciate it."

"Right. Now about this dog, exactly when and where did you discover him missing?"

"That's a hard question."

"Why is that?"

"A missing dog doesn't have an exact when and where, does he? I mean, it's kind of like, you don't see him here, and then you don't see him there. And then, after a while of not seeing him here and not seeing him there, you think to yourself, 'I haven't seen him anywhere.' After you think that to yourself a few times, you call an investigator. Isn't that how it works?"

"I see," said Nigel, coming to grips with the kind of keen intellect he was grappling with. "And you've looked in all the places he usually frequents?"

"Yes."

"Have you looked in the places he doesn't frequent?"

"Imbecile!" exclaimed Mrs. Sandoval, as if divining an eight-letter word meaning idiot.

"What? I beg your pardon?"

"Imbecile or moron. I remember we were talking about that yesterday. I wanted Gastrick to weigh in. He's quite clever," said Mrs. Sandoval. "Gastrick!" she shouted.

"You called?" asked the butler.

"Imbecile or moron?"

"Might you be kind enough to enlighten me as to the context of the question?"

Mrs. Sandoval jerked her head toward Nigel.

"Mmmmm." He hummed for a half-second. "Imbecile. Anything else?"

"No, Gastrick. You may go," said a satisfied Mrs. Sandoval. "There. Settled."

Gastrick was a first-rate butler. He maintained a haughty disinterest, no matter the task.

"Okay. Let's just review here," said Nigel. "Based on what you've told me, I know Duffy's not in his most frequently visited places. That narrows the search considerably. Wonderful. Do you, by any chance, have a picture of your beloved pooch?"

"I thought you might want one. Here you are."

Nigel held the picture at various distances from his face, closing one eye and then the other while shifting his head to various angles. "I'm having a little trouble drawing a proper bead on this one. Mrs. Sandoval, this is a living animal we're talking about, right?"

"Very much so."

"And the animal in question—Duffy—is, in fact, a dog?"

"Absolutely."

"Is it possible it might be only part dog?"

"What do you mean?"

"I don't mean to be negative in any way, you understand. I'm sure you love your pet, with its sparkling soul, warm personality, and all that. But looking at this picture, I'm just not sure."

"Not sure of what?" asked Mrs. Sandoval, whose head kept creeping to one side while an eyebrow kept creeping upward.

"Do you have another picture by any chance?"

"Yes. Here's one. Not as recent."

"Aha, that looks a bit more dog-like. Do you know the breed?"

"Don't know. What would you say?"

"To me, it looks like a cross between a schnauzer, a chihuahua, and maybe a 'possum or muskrat."

"Mr. Nigel," said Mrs. Sandoval, shaking her head like a wet lizard, "I assure you he's one hundred percent, pure dog. Won a blue-ribbon at a dog show."

"I didn't mean to imply that he's not a stunning animal. Indeed, he is. Just looking at his picture, I'm stunned. You said he took home a prize at a dog show?"

"The Tonkawa County Fair, 2015. First place for Ugliest Dog—All Breeds."

"You must be very proud—should have entered him in state. This is all very good information, absolutely stellar, but I'll need a lot more boring information like personal habits, visitors, possible motives, enemies—the usual stuff for a dognapping case. You understand, don't you, Mrs. Sandoval?"

"Of course." She raised her hand as if hailing a taxi. "Gastrick, please bring me two scoops of butter pecan, and crush some Tums on top." Turning to Nigel, she asked, "Would you care for some ice cream, Mr. Nigel? It's delicious."

"No, thank you. I'm good with water."

"I don't know what it is about tequila. Sometimes it leaves a burning sensation in my throat. Ice cream is the best remedy. Do I drink tequila to get ice cream or the other way 'round?" She snorted.

"Now, before we get to the more mundane questions," said Nigel, "I wanted to ask about something you mentioned in our phone call. You seemed to believe that Duffy's disappearance was connected to some nefarious activity. Is that correct?"

"If nefarious means someone took him, then yes."

"Any idea who would do such a thing?"

"No."

"Well then, why do you suppose someone would take him?"

"I don't see another explanation. I mean, he was here, and then he wasn't. Beloved pets don't just get up and walk away, do they, Mr. Nigel? I mean, they're not silverware."

Nigel was on the verge of agreeing when he spotted, out of the corner of his eye, an approaching wheelchair. The black-clad pilot of this mechanized contraption appeared to be a skeleton—a skeleton the skin had refused to let go of.

5

ABUELITA APPRECIATES A GENTLEMAN

Mrs. Sandoval, tipped off by the expanding whites of Nigel's eyes, spun around to view the source of his terror.

"Abuelita? What are you doing out?" she said.

The only reply was the whir of a tiny engine as the wheelchair phantom approached. Upon closer inspection, Nigel determined that the driver was not as initially supposed—a skeleton—but a pre-skeleton.

"Abuelita, this is Mr. Nigel," said Mrs. Sandoval. "He's a detective who has come to help us find Duffy. Mr. Nigel, this is Abuelita."

The scrawny pilot, head down, continued to barrel forward. Nigel stood to welcome her into the proceedings.

"So nice to meet you," said Nigel as the wheelchair approached.

Mrs. Sandoval scrunched her face. She knew something Nigel didn't. What Abuelita lacked in depth perception, she made up for with a keen racing spirit. Wherever she went, she went at top speed: 2.5 miles per. The permanent residents of Sandoval House had all mastered the bullfighter's *molinete*, a spin move designed to shift one's vulnerable body parts away from a charging opponent. Mrs. Sandoval observed Nigel executing something more of a *parar*, standing one's ground. Her shins ached in empathetic anticipation.

"Ummmph!" Nigel throated.

Abuelita, having detected a collision with two semi-solid objects, reversed the chair, giving Nigel room to rub his bruised shins.

"So nice to meet you," said Nigel through smiling, gritted teeth.

Afforded a closer look, Nigel saw not a helpless invalid, but a formidable, glowering presence encased in a bag of wrinkles. Her vulture's eye—for only one eye appeared functional, the other an untethered free agent—fixed upon Nigel like the point of a barbed harpoon. The eye scanned head to toe, invoking a shiver under its hovering focus.

Sensing the outsized personality in his presence, Nigel opted for a show of deference. He bent at the waist and offered his hand for a delicate shake. The eye latched onto it, inducing a momentary frostbite before moving its cold laser to the forehead. She then unbuckled her seatbelt and—to Nigel's horror—initiated the preliminaries to standing up.

"Please, don't get up on my account," Nigel implored.

Abuelita paid no heed. With just minutes until liftoff, she busied herself, methodically shifting her weight to various limbs as part of a pre-mission stress test. A mountain climber would not have checked her equipment more thoroughly.

"Please, no need to stand," Nigel implored, but she was determined. Nigel consoled himself, thinking this must be normal. He glanced at Mrs. Sandoval for reassurance. She had one hand clenched near her neck and one over her mouth, which appeared to be shrieking at inaudible frequencies.

"God help her!" she seemed to be saying.

There was nothing Nigel could do but shout encouragement and hope for the best. While Abuelita struggled, one side up and then the other, Nigel shuddered to think what stresses were occurring below that shriveled hide. Those papery bones could not have been held together by much more than habit. If even one gave way, the whole structure might collapse into dust, and Nigel would be blamed as the destroyer of a precious, living heirloom. He made the sign of the cross. He wasn't Catholic, but God might be.

"No hurry, ma'am. Take your time. Rest if you need to," coached Nigel. Unless she'd been born deaf, her hearing wasn't what it used to be. Eventually, she obtained a position allowing her to slide free of the chair. Nigel and Mrs. Sandoval each cradled an elbow to help her rise upright. Once it was clear she wouldn't topple, they each backed away.

"What the hell?" said Abuelita. "Where'd everybody go?" Her de-chairing process had oriented her opposite the other members of the room.

"Abuelita, yoo-hoo. Here we are," toodled Mrs. Sandoval.

A standing Abuelita was intimidating in her own way, sort of like an ancient five-foot Jenga tower.

"So nice to meet you," said Nigel, taking her tiny withered hand in his. After such a life-and-death struggle, a handclasp hardly seemed adequate. He lowered himself into an awkward curtsy, leaned forward, and gently placed his lips to the back of her claw. He swooned for a moment as a pungent mix of vapors—mothballs, ammonia, and roses—snaked their way into his nostrils. He had little time to wallow in the smellscape before being snapped to attention by what felt like a collision to the side of his head by a large flying insect.

"Abuelita! Don't strike the guest. You know you shouldn't do that," said Mrs. Sandoval.

"Hand-slobberer!" barked Abuelita. "Where's my pistol?"

"Now, Abuelita," said Mrs. Sandoval, retaining a voice of

calm and reason, "you don't carry a pistol anymore. Mr. Nigel was just saying hello. That's how they do it in England."

"Really? If I had my pistol, I'd show him how we do it in Texas."

"I'm sorry, Mr. Nigel. She gets a little wound up," said a contrite Mrs. Sandoval. "Gastrick!" she hollered. "Two more tequila shots. Now, Abuelita," counseled Mrs. Sandoval, "be nice to Mr. Nigel. He's here to help us find our dear Duffy."

"He wouldn't be here if I still had my pistol," she said, glaring at Nigel with her good eye.

"You don't mean that," said Mrs. Sandoval.

Nigel was pretty certain she did. Abuelita seemed a woman of her word.

"I do mean that. If you hadn't taken my pistol away, I'd a shot the hideous mongrel."

Nigel was starting to feel unwelcome.

Abuelita continued, "That no-good mutt. I'd a put him out of his misery long ago. Then this hand-slobberer wouldn't be here putting the moves on me."

"Now, you know you love Duffy," said Mrs. Sandoval.

"That dog chewed my slippers!"

"Abuelita, I'm sure he meant no harm," said Nigel, seizing the opportunity to play peacemaker. "It's in their nature. Dogs will often chew things they find lying about."

"Lying about? They was on my feet at the time. I needed three stitches and a tetanus shot. Lying about! When you find that dog, I hope he finds your pants 'lying about' your tender parts. You don't seem like much of a detective to me," she said, sizing him up with her working eye. "You packin' iron?"

Nigel was alarmed by this statement until he realized she meant a firearm. "No. I've never felt the need."

"I always said if you're halfway attractive, or if you got anything someone would want, then you better carry a piece.

You"—she painted Nigel with a squinty eye—"you don't need one."

Gastrick arrived with a silver tray bearing a porcelain dish of ice cream and two more shots of tequila. He transferred the ice cream dish, along with a cloth napkin and small silver spoon, to the coffee table in front of Mrs. Sandoval. He then lowered the tray with the two shots between Mrs. Sandoval and Abuelita. They each took one, simultaneously relieving the glasses of their contents with a sweeping 180-degree throw back. They returned the glasses to the tray, which Gastrick—comprehending the brevity of the operation—was holding at the ready. The two tequila-slammers then produced a kind of post-tequila anthem, opening with an extended note of inward rushing air through pursed lips followed by the sound of two cats expelling hairballs. There followed a fallow period of a self-conscious Nigel being gazed at by three inquisitive eyes.

"Well then, shall we talk about the missing dog?" asked Nigel.

"Why aren't you drinking?" blurted out Abuelita. "Why isn't he drinking?" she demanded.

"He doesn't drink on the job," answered Mrs. Sandoval, licking her ice cream straight from the bowl.

"A man shouldn't sit there while ladies drink. A man like that can't be trusted. He's biding his time, waiting for an opening. If I had my pistol, I'd give him one."

"Go easy on Mr. Nigel. He's a dog detective and a proper English gentleman. Why, look at him. He's not interested in sex. Look at those shoes. I bet sex isn't even in his...umm... that thing-of-a-bob. It's not in...that thing you have. The English have a word for it. Sex is not in your... Oh, what do you call it?"

"Call *it*?" said Nigel, looking up from his shoes.

"Bailiwick! Sex is not in your bailiwick, is it? You're not

even interested in sex," she said. A shiny red fingernail played about the corner of her mouth. "*Are* you, Mr. Nigel?"

A stifling silence occupied the room. The kind of silence made by extinct mastodons thundering across a marble floor. The unbearable noiselessness was broken by the gentle rustling of crinkly petticoats as Mrs. Sandoval shifted from one butt cheek to the other. A bat, had there been one in the room, would have heard tiny high-pitched squeals made by pores squeezing out droplets of sweat on Nigel's upper lip.

"Are *you*, Mr. Nigel? Interested in sex?" repeated Mrs. Sandoval. One eyebrow arched upward like a cliff diver positioning for the descent. "You're not a Lothario, are you?"

A Lothario? The old vocabulary wasn't what it used to be. As Nigel opened his mouth to speak, he caught a glimpse of Abuelita's tiny vulture eye drilling a borehole into his forehead. He steadied himself by addressing the other eye, which fell lazily toward an empty space on the floor.

"I don't think I am," said Nigel. "My wife worries about me, but she bought some pills that are supposed to fix it. All in all, I'd say I'm relatively normal…and harmless. Normal and harmless, that's me."

"That's what they want you to think," growled Abuelita.

"Really, I would prefer to talk about the dog," said Nigel.

"Dale Griesen took the dog. Bet a cobbler on it," said Abuelita.

"Really? Why do you think it's this Dale Griesen person?"

"He's a scoundrel—always has been—him and his whole gang."

"A gang? He has a gang? Dale Griesen and his dog thieves?"

"Wouldn't put it past them. They're a bad lot. They stole the town bell," said Abuelita.

"The town bell? Brazen fiends," said Nigel.

If Mrs. Sandoval had a belfry of ringing bells, Abuelita had one full of bats.

"Worse than that," said Abuelita, her voice intensifying. "They stole just the clapper. On Halloween, for Christ's sake."

"Last Halloween?" asked Nigel.

"Not last Halloween. Nora, when was it that Dale Griesen stole the clapper?"

Mrs. Sandoval, who had slid out of her chair and onto the floor, spoke with her tongue crammed into one of the shot glasses, "Nideenfiffhefyb."

"Fifty-five," said Abuelita, translating.

"That's quite a while back. So, you think the old gang is still up to no good?" asked Nigel, envisioning a band of marauders in wheelchairs and walkers.

"If it's not Dale, then it's some other Griesen. They're a bad lot, the whole bunch of them."

"And this Dale Griesen? Where's his hideout?" said Nigel.

"Sleeping Willow Cemetery. Been there twenty years. You might say he's gone underground." Mrs. Sandoval laughed. "Pay no attention to Abuelita. Yesterday, she saw a ghost. Maybe it was Dale."

Abuelita grunted a snore. Mrs. Sandoval was licking the ice cream dish. Looking at the wreckage, Nigel decided he'd received all the useful information he was likely to get on this visit. He didn't have much to go on, but there wasn't much to stay for, either. He announced his departure and rose to leave.

"What about your fee?" asked Mrs. Sandoval.

Nigel had neglected to consider this detail. A fair market price for recovering an ugly dog was not the type of thing he went around knowing. "I'll have to check with the home office," said Nigel, pulling out his phone. "We have an app," he said, grasping for credibility. "Let me see. Duffy's a large dog." Nigel twiddled his thumbs on the phone. "Is the dog fast?"

"Pretty fast."

"What breed of dog?"

"Mixed breed."

"Right. Got it," said Nigel, working the thumbs. Regret washed over him for not quizzing Annie over the financials of her cow work when he had the chance. "The app's doing its stuff." His initial wild-ass guess came to a thousand bucks. Being his first job, a discount was in order. "Here we go. That will be...two-hundred, and..." Nigel paused to monitor Mrs. Sandoval's reaction.

She was bouncing a spoon off her tongue.

"Fifty...four dollars."

"Two-hunnerd and fifdy-four? Dollars?" said Mrs. Sandoval.

Nigel found it unsettling how she said dollars as if doubting the currency. Nigel sensed the need for a correction. "Wait," he said, looking into his phone. "There's a special this week. One-hundred and ninety-nine dollars and ninety-nine cents. How's that?"

"Two-hundred? Dollars?" she repeated a

gain with a finishing flourish, as if she suspected the quote was in shekels.

"Too...high?" squeaked Nigel.

She laughed.

Like a far-sighted snake handler, Nigel realized he had grabbed the wrong end of the deal.

"How do you stay in bidness?"

"We pride ourselves on being the low-cost provider." Nigel would have preferred a different business model, but he'd locked himself in.

"And expenses, I assume?"

"Aha," said Nigel, sensing a new stream of income. "Expenses. Of course. There will be expenses."

"Those expenses will be...what?"

"There would be, uh, travel expenses while on the case. Standard mileage rates, of course, and, uh, lunch—"

"Lunch? What kind of lunch?"

"Nothing extravagant, mind you. You said your dog was pretty fast—fast food, mostly."

"No alcohol?"

"Not while I'm working. Unless, of course, it's needed for the investigation."

"How would that happen?"

"If, for instance, I was tailing the suspect, and, say, he dropped into a bar. I might need to go in to observe, see. Naturally, I would need to blend in with my surroundings, so a beer would be part of my disguise, a form of camouflage."

"Surely not in this case."

"One can never tell," said Nigel, hedging his bets. "No need to worry about that now. You can just pay half the fee today and half when I return your dog back. If I don't find him, I refund your money."

"Okey-dokey then. Gastrick, could you show Mr. Nigel the way out and pay him his hunnerd dollars?"

"Very well. I'll dig into the penny jar."

As Gastrick was showing Nigel out the front door, Mrs. Sandoval stumbled forward.

"Oh, Mr. Nigel. I just got a message on the thing," she said, holding up her phone. "The game tonight—canceled. No game."

"The game?"

She must have noted the baffled look on Nigel's face. "You know, football. Our Copperheads." She held up her right hand as if giving a victory salute, but with her two fingers drooping forward.

Nigel hesitatingly returned the salute.

"They had a game, but now they don't. I thought you ought to know."

"Ah, so since there is no game, I should not attend. Is that it?"

Mrs. Sandoval converted her salute to a thumbs up.

Gastrick walked Nigel to his car, pulled out his wallet, and doled out five twenty-dollar bills. Behind him, Nigel noticed a sunflower yellow Lamborghini—or was it a Ferrari? It was definitely yellow. He knew his colors better than his super-cars. As he reached out to collect his hundred, he suffered a vision of the butler behind the wheel of the sports car swinging out to pass his Ford Fusion. The butler had one hand on the wheel while the other lit a cigar with a twenty. He slowed just long enough to deliver a contemptuous sneer before rocketing forward in a spray of gravel and derision.

"One-hundred dollars, sir."

"Thank you, Gastrick."

Nigel normally looked a man in the eye when receiving money, but not in this case. He feared the smirk. Nigel was secretly relieved that the butler did not tip.

6

FORTY-SIX, PART ONE

Nigel left the Sandoval estate with little more than a picture in his pocket and a demoralizing collection of qualms. He had hoped to receive a treasure trove of telling details and tantalizing clues, but his one big takeaway after meeting the Sandoval ladies was that Duffy was likely better off wherever he was. But Nigel was hired to find the dog, not protect him.

Nigel drove north toward town, passing the Sleeping Willow Cemetery—the eternal hideout of his only suspect, old man Griesen. He opted not to stop, even though buried remains might have more information than the tequila-soaked Sandoval women. Instead, Nigel's first stop was the New Antigua Animal Shelter, located in a one-time bank building.

In contrast to the dour exterior, the interior was disarmingly cheerful. The walls were splashed with over-sized, hand-painted primitives of dogs and cats interspersed with the odd rabbit or turtle. The local mural artist seemed to delight in providing her subjects with eyes the size of dinner plates. Nigel found it unnerving and wondered about its psychological impact on the lost and frightened animal inmates.

The service desk was manned by a single staff member hunkered behind the counter, perhaps amusing a kitten with some string.

"Hello, miss, I wonder if you might help me. I'm looking for—"

The young lady craned her neck around. Nigel staggered backward. She pulled up to the counter and swiveled around to face him. Nigel staggered a second time before straightening up into a wobbly version of himself. Having recaptured a sense of mission, he addressed the lady once again.

"I'm, uh, looking...for...dog." He wheezed. Any sense of pride Nigel felt for completing his sentence was undone by the onset of a feverish tremor. The sudden affliction was not borne of a parasite, but the predictable consequence of a surprise encounter with a shimmering goddess.

Nigel was suffering a bout of venustraphobia, a kind of thunderstruckedness in the presence of beautiful women. It didn't happen often—Nigel had high standards—but when it did, it left him gaping like a codfish on a slab of ice.

And there he stood, codfish-like, mere feet from an unsurpassed beauty. "Unsurpassed beauty" was his own terminology—a well-established part of his lexicon—having been used forty-five previous times to describe forty-five previous girls, each presumably more beautiful than all those before. Nigel's nomenclature might be up for debate, but not his taste. He knew his stuff. To call this girl attractive would be like calling the Taj Mahal a nice little shed. Metaphors aside, the girl was a looker.

"Well, we are the place to find dogs," she said, moving up her chair and raising her arms to desktop level.

Her arm—or rather what was wrapped around it—sent Nigel teetering once again. This latest bout of wobbles resulted from a surprise appearance of a large, shiny black snake.

"I'm sorry. I didn't mean to scare you," she said. "This is Blackie, our indigo snake. Would you like to touch him?"

Nigel shook his head. Snakes, in the appropriate context, didn't bother Nigel. He was, in fact, almost a fan. Should he happen upon the odd serpent, he was prone to give it a good look-over. In his youth, he studied snakes, lizards, insects, and arachnids in books and in the wilds of his native Surrey. At the age of ten, for a period of two weeks, he maintained a respectable herpetarium, complete with a living grass snake. The little serpent, imaginatively named Grassy, occupied the finest dwellings a snake could hope for—the equivalent of four-star lodging with meals and cleaning services thrown in. Grassy earned these extravagant digs by doing absolutely nothing. A sweet deal, one would have thought. But Grassy, demonstrating a mind-blowing lack of situational awareness, failed at doing nothing, and at the most inopportune time. The damn thing moved while Nigel's mum was changing the bedsheets. There was, predictably, a scream, some yelling, and an expulsion. The emotional scarring was minimal since Nigel held little affection for a creature that seldom moved. Still, an interest in such things survived.

No, the snake itself was merely a momentary jolt. The snake's handler, on the other hand—Unsurpassed Beauty Number Forty-Six—was a tormentor from hell. Women of unsurpassed beauty, all forty-six of them, did this to Nigel. You couldn't fault the woman any more than you could fault a campfire for incinerating a moth that flies into it. They were just doing what they do, which is to say, having no use for Nigel whatsoever. He knew it, they knew it, they knew he knew it, and he knew they knew it. That kind of vicious circle leads to internal friction, and eventually, self-combustion. The snake was no more than a marshmallow on the fire.

"You were asking about finding a dog? You've come to the right place, but probably not the best time. You're free to look around, but we're prepping the shelter for the hurricane, so no more adoptions today," said Forty-Six, unwinding the serpent from her arm.

Feeling as if he had a burlap bag in his mouth, Nigel replied, "Not looking for a new dog. I have a lost dog." He pulled out the picture. "I wondered if this dog might have shown up here."

"Jeeze Louise!" she said, peering at the picture. "You say that's a dog?"

"I've been told."

"Is it a menace?"

"No, just a pet."

"Pet, huh? I love dogs. I love, love, love dogs, but this"— she tapped the picture—"would scare the bejeezus out of me. This guy would more likely end up with the animal control. It's just a couple blocks away, east on Main, at the county courthouse. You can't miss it."

"I see. Thank you." Nigel turned and took a deep breath. As he walked away, he watched his feet hit the floor, considering each step a success. His tendency under such circumstances was to crash into things. If things weren't available, his own feet would do. Exiting into the suffocating embrace of ninety-six-degree air, he felt relatively okay. Least ways, the encounter hadn't devolved into a humiliating mishap as had occurred in the presence of unsurpassed beauties Two, Three, Four, Seven, Thirteen, Sixteen, Twenty, Twenty-Four, Twenty-Nine, Thirty, Thirty-Six, Forty-One, Forty-Two, and Forty-Four.

Nigel climbed into his car and started it up. He closed his eyes as he straightened out his tense body, raising his butt off the car seat. He took in a massive breath, filling his lungs right up to the jowls. He held it momentarily, then let loose a torrent of used-up air through a fluttering mouth, like a horse might do after swallowing a hot-air balloon. While his lips flubadubbed, Nigel shook the tension from his arms. There was a knock on the window. Nigel went limp in his seat and opened his eyes.

"Sir, you left your picture. I thought you might want it back," said Forty-Six.

Nigel felt himself shape-shifting into a worm beneath the radiance of her smile.

He rolled down the window before his arm disappeared. "Thank you. I was just doing relaxation exercises."

"You might try plyometrics. You seem tense."

7

LOCAL AUTHORITIES

The towering Tonkawa County Courthouse was easily the most regal building in town. They don't make 'em like that anymore. This architectural jewel, a monumental work crafted from massive blocks of red sandstone, loomed above the New Antigua town square to impress upon the occasional visitor this community's enduring will to exist. Today, that visitor was Nigel, and the courthouse—having been declared unsafe—was closed indefinitely. Animal control had been relocated to a tiny office within an adjacent one-story structure, which was known as the Annex.

Nigel made his way to a dim office at the back of the building, where a uniformed county official introduced herself as Leslie Dole. Leslie appeared to be one of those take-charge gals who reeked of competency and efficiency. In that respect, she reminded Nigel of his own wife—kind of intimidating.

After fumbling through small talk about the impending hurricane, Nigel handed Leslie the photo of Duffy. She had not seen the animal, regardless of whether it was—or was not—actually a dog. "Mind if I ask who the owners are?"

"The Sandovals."

"Surely not that rich family that bought the golf course."

"Could be," said Nigel, imagining the house as a country club. "They live south about ten miles."

"That'd be them. They bought the golf course down there. Closed it up and turned it into their own private ranch. A lot of the local golfers were pretty upset. I guess if you've got that kind of money, you can do what you want." She took another look at the photo and shook her head. "Goodness. Not what I would envision walking around a country club. Does the dog have a collar with tags on it?"

"Not sure about that."

"Has the dog been microchipped?"

"Don't know that either, I'm afraid."

"Is it a male or female?"

"I'm going to say male."

"But it could be a female?"

"Fifty-fifty," said Nigel. This girl really knew her business.

"What's your relation to this dog, if you don't mind my asking."

"Aren't we getting personal?" said Nigel, feigning an indignation that felt uncomfortably real. "You might say I'm sort of a dog detective in this case."

"You're a dog detective? That's what you do?"

"Well, not a proper one. I heard they had a missing dog and thought I could help."

"They're paying you?"

Nigel was suddenly aware that he was talking to a potential business rival, and a formidable one at that. This lady knew all the right questions. He'd keep his cards close to the vest.

"A little bit," said Nigel. "I mean, if I bring in the dog, I'll get paid a little bit. The butler will pay me."

"The butler?"

"He does the paying. It's how rich people work, you know. The butler manages the money."

"I guess I didn't know that," she said. "If you'll leave your name and phone number, I'll give you a call if I come across the dog. Of course, if the dog is microchipped, I'm obligated to call the registrants, but I can let you know all the same. I'd hate to see you lose your money."

"Did someone mention money?" boomed a friendly voice.

"Ah, Sheriff," said Leslie, giving a one-finger salute. "This is Mr. Blandwater-Cummings. Mr. Blandwater-Cummings, this is Sheriff White. And that standing behind Sheriff White is his loyal minion, Deputy Willard Winjack."

The sheriff was a robust man, tall and wide from every angle. He had a big, proper sheriff's hat and a big, proper sheriff's sidearm. He engaged Nigel with a big, meaty handshake, using a cushiony pressure that said, *"Be friendly and behave."*

Popping out from underneath the sheriff's armpit was the aforementioned deputy, a wiry, jumpy type with a rubbery face. Not like tire rubber, but more like the raw stuff that's been pumped from a tree, rolled into bails, and allowed to sit on a loading platform in the tropical sun for eight hours. Droopy, sticky—that kind of stuff. Unlike the sheriff, whose uniform fit nicely except across the belly, the deputy's needed some serious growing into. The deputy's handshake said, *"I don't like handshakes."*

"You might want to show the sheriff your photo," Leslie said to Nigel. "He's around the county a lot, so he sees things."

After a rehash of the previous conversation—"Yes, it's a dog," the Sandovals, golf course, and so forth—the sheriff asked, "You new around here?"

"Relatively," replied Nigel. "I live out in No Way. Moved in a few weeks ago from Houston."

"I see. If you're near that creek, you might want to find another place to stay tonight. What brings you to New Antigua?"

After a condensed version of their immigrant tale, the sheriff asked, "What's your wife do?"

Nigel perceived a need for caution. It was his understanding that local police viewed private eyes the way prisoners view weevils in their biscuits: pesky opportunists taking advantage of unfortunate circumstances. "She works with livestock. Not sure what exactly. That's her business. Yesterday, she was checking out the cows on some ranch up north."

"Would that be the Gilbert ranch?"

"Sounds right."

The deputy, bobbing and skittering like a prairie dog, interrupted with additional snickering.

"What are you giggling about?" asked the sheriff.

"He sounds like that funny guy, Benny Hill," said the deputy.

"I guess he does at that," said the sheriff. "You know Benny Hill?"

"I know *of* Benny Hill," Nigel replied, thinking that he sounded like Benny Hill as much as Sheriff White sounded like Jerry Lewis.

"It was nice to have met you, Mr., ah…Nigel. We need to be getting along with our work. This hurricane is keeping us busy. We're letting people know the game is off for tonight." The sheriff and his minion departed.

"I had better get along as well," said Nigel.

Leslie Dole gave him a tug on his shirtsleeve as he turned to depart.

"You know, they call the deputy 'Barney,' " she said, sounding amused.

Good to know, thought Nigel. *Strange nickname for someone named Willard.*

8

BIG SMALL-TOWN LAWYER

Annie was furious at her pounding heart. She wanted it to just stop for a while. Annie had once stared point-blank into the barrel of a loaded shotgun and convinced the triggerman that a third murder was bad for his future. On that occasion, her heart had kept to itself and let her do it. But introduce a scurrying cockroach, and the damned organ was about to burst out of its cage.

She was not one to give up though. Pulling back the box of trophies, she swung down hard with a tightly-rolled July edition of *Police* magazine. *Whap! Whap!*

The door of her tiny office swung open. "What ho! An old-fashioned pummeling!" shouted Nigel. "Good form, ol' girl. Get the shoulder into it. More shoulder."

Whap! Whap! Whap!

"Where's the gun? I'll finish him!" yelled Nigel.

Whap! Whap! "No need. He's a goner," said an exhausted Annie.

"How do we dispose of the body?"

"I'll leave that to you. You brought him in. You take him out."

"Me?" asked Nigel. "What do you mean, I brought him in?"

"He was in that box of trophies you brought."

"Ah, the trophies. Aren't you going to use them to spruce up the office? Trophies lose their impact sitting in a box on the floor."

"I'll use the plaque. The rest of them, out." She never discussed the trophies because most of them were given as gags. That Top Marksman trophy, for instance, was received after posting the lowest grade in the division. Of course, the guys all knew she'd taken the exam following a forty-two-hour stakeout and a quart of coffee, but that was part of the joke. Nigel was great for ego-boosting, but Annie never thought of herself as a supercop. There were only two citations that meant anything to her: a medal of valor award that was safely locked away, and the Investigator of the Year plaque for 2014.

Nigel looked pained. "You had such a great career. You might as well show it off. It's good PR. Lets people know you're hot stuff."

"Not relevant here. They'd just gather dust. I'd appreciate it if you took them back home."

"As you wish, milady, but they'll not escape the dust, I fear."

"You came to watch me whack a roach?"

"No, ma'am. I was in the vicinity, having visited the local downspout dispensary. Thought I would drop by."

"You got the downspouts?"

"Negative. Cub Scouts beat me to it."

"Cub Scouts?"

"There's been an outbreak of downspout derby activity among the local tribes. Those scouts pillaged every downspout for miles around. This is a dry county regarding downspouts—"

There was a knock at the door, followed by the appearance of a large, round head.

"Am I interrupting?" said the head.

"Not at all. Just talking with my partner. Come in," said Annie.

"The name is Gerald Fitzgerald O'Reilly, attorney at law, but it seems I'd do a better business sticking folks with needles."

"Similar work," said Nigel.

"What makes you think," interrupted Annie, "there's a market for needle-sticking?"

"I just had a fourth person walk into my office expecting to find an acupuncturist. The next time it happens, I'm going to sit them down and go after it. We'll see how it goes."

"Yes, I see it now," said Nigel. "Once they've discovered your lack of credentials as an acupuncturist, you offer up your legal services to sue for malpractice. You stick it to them on either end. You'll make a mint. Are you Irish by any chance, Mr. O'Reilly?"

"Greek," he replied. After a pause, he continued, "Teasing, of course. Yes, the name is Irish. Full-blooded Irish on my father's side, and double that on my mum's. And how about you? You're not from here, by the sound of it."

"UK—Surrey, to be precise."

"Please have a seat, Mr. Gerald Fitzgerald," interjected Annie. "Please excuse the messy office. We're still moving in. I've been in business less than a month, you see."

"Thank you," he said, man-spreading himself across the flimsy chair. He was among the larger sizes for an attorney, especially his belly, which looked to have been stuffed with a sofa cushion. "I've been here for three months, and I'm probably less moved in than you are. I'm your neighbor, by the way, a couple doors down. I'm setting up shop as a family attorney."

"Excellent. Someone to borrow paper clips from," said Annie.

"Or a phlebotomy kit," said Nigel, receiving a savage side-eye from Annie.

"What brings you to New Antigua?" asked Annie.

"Well, I practiced in Dallas for many years. It was a comfortable life—a solid practice, a home in the suburbs, a wife and two kids. Well, once the children moved out and my wife departed, bless her soul..."

"Your wife left?" asked Nigel.

Annie shot him a stern gaze.

"She departed," said O'Reilly.

"Oh, departed," whispered Nigel.

"On my own for the first time in many years, I gave in to some serious reflection—where I'd been, where I was, and where I should be going. It's my belief that we should all take stock from time to time. Nothing beats a deep, critical self-examination—"

"Indeed," interjected Nigel. "I've talked to my wife about the benefits of self-examination. It's a money-saver. I'm a staunch practitioner, but the prostate—that's a tricky one. I leave that to the professionals."

Annie was laughing on the inside while simultaneously receiving a reminder of why Nigel could not be hanging around her office. His jokiness would not mix well with clients in need of a detective.

"Ahem. Yes," continued O'Reilly, rolling his eyes to the ceiling as if looking for a pigeon that had soiled on him. "My self-examination indicated that my current path was not fulfilling my destiny. I needed to begin a new chapter. The content of that new chapter was not immediately clear to me, but one thing was certain: I wanted to help people, real people—people in need. Do you know what I mean?"

"I think I do," said Nigel. "You wanted to help people. Got it."

"At first, I considered the ministry. I asked to be shown a sign from the Lord. The Lord put me on a different path. With my skill set, I was called to provide affordable legal services in a small-town setting. I had in my office a large map of the state of Texas. From my desk drawer, I extracted my professional-grade tungsten dart set, a gift from one of the partners. I used one of those high-quality darts to determine a location for my future professional activities."

"And the dart, as luck would have it, landed on New Antigua?" asked Annie.

"Eventually. Thereabouts," said O'Reilly. "Three years later, here I am. No longer a soul-deadened big-city lawyer practicing tedious, specialized law, but a re-invigorated, case-diversified small-town attorney dispensing much-needed legal assistance to real people."

"We know what you mean," said Nigel. "We just came from Houston. Full of automatons, robots, and cyborgs these days. We now provide investigative services for real people."

"Please excuse my partner's sense of humor. It's what we call, in the detective trade, a blunt instrument," said Annie.

"I understand. It's that dry English wit. So very, very dry," he said, stroking his beard and expelling a moist, cynical chuckle.

The attorney continued, "I won't take up your time. I just dropped in to introduce myself. In my game, we occasionally need the services of a *good* detective," he said, addressing Annie. "Perhaps someday, I can send you some business. I'll leave you my card. Likewise, I know your business sometimes generates the need for an attorney. Please keep me in mind for you or your client's legal needs. Divorces, estates, small businesses—I run a diverse practice.

"We will certainly keep you in mind, Mr. O'Reilly," said Annie as the big man lumbered out of the office.

"See there," she said to Nigel. "In a small town, you don't even have to leave your office to meet nice people."

"Nice?" said Nigel. "He stocks his aquarium with lampreys."

"Why would you say that? You don't think he's trustworthy?"

"Trustworthy? I'd trust him as far as I could throw him. I think he's a well-practiced liar."

"Oh, yeah? I've had a bit of experience identifying liars. Look who I married," said Annie, patting his shoulder.

"Ha ha. Seriously, you think he was being honest?"

"Tell me why you think he wasn't."

"Well, I will admit he was good," said Nigel. "Too good. His story sounded rehearsed, practiced. How many times would you tell that story? If you were telling how you came here, it wouldn't sound that way."

"He *is* a lawyer. He's trained to be an orator."

"Okay, try this. When he sat down, he splayed himself out like an octopus. By the time he finished, he was drawn up like a clam. Also, when he got to the dramatic parts of his story, his lips rolled inward. I had this guy, Rollo, working for me. According to Rollo, his projects were always on time and doing great. I learned to watch his lips. If they rolled inward, Rollo's project wasn't so great.

"Also," continued Nigel, "whenever I interrupted this guy, his hand when straight to his beard. He wasn't picking off fleas, I don't think. It was a sign of anxiety that I was about to uncover something. Furthermore, this guy kept looking up to his right. Why? Nothing to see there. Shall I go on?"

"You're pretty good at this," said Annie. She had to admit it sounded plausible. Then again, Nigel sometimes pulled things right out of his ass. If allowed to go on long enough, the joke—if there was one—would reveal itself. Annie didn't always have the patience. "Or maybe you're bullshittin' me, and I'm too hopeless to detect it."

"I'll tell you what else I know about this guy. I think he's been attacked by aunts?'

"Ants?"

"Not ants, aunts. Notice how his face bulged out—bulgy eyes, bulgy nose, lips; ears? A clear sign of aunt attacks in his formative years. I imagine he had a family of large, powerful, possibly childless aunts who put the squeeze on him every chance they got."

"Anything else?"

"Yes, I predict in ten years, he's in jail, or alternatively, a Santa Claus at a discount mall."

"Okay, enough," said Annie, laughing. She usually played the straight man while Nigel riffed, but the Santa Claus line got her. "I've had courses in this stuff, but I don't keep my BS detector out all the time. That would be exhausting."

"If you're not using your detector for a lawyer, then when?"

"Now that you've forced me to get it out, how's that to-do list coming along?"

"Coming along great," said Nigel, looking to his right, stroking his chin, and contracting himself into a ball. "Could not be better."

"I thought so," said Annie. "You forgot to do the lip thing."

"I made that part up. Anyway, I must leave to do you-know-what."

"Good for you. I'm heading out as well. A pasture is waiting."

"In that case, turn on your bullshit detector," said Nigel, heading out the door.

Annie wondered if Nigel might have perceived something she had missed. Her husband, lovable lout that he was, could be surprisingly perceptive. He possessed an absent-minded professor's intellect that converted the simple into the complex, and the complex into the simple. For him, no job was too easy to screw up, nor was any problem too intractable to solve. You never knew quite what to expect.

A pang of guilt played upon her soul as she watched him drive away. She detected a certain raggedness in his spirit of late, and she knew why: adjustment anxiety. He was a square peg whose edges needed filing to fit into his new round hole. Fortunately for Nigel, a plan was in motion to make it happen. Annie's plan.

She had read up on the subject of early retirement, and frankly, had been appalled. Based on an avalanche of anecdotal evidence, early retirement appeared to be a form of lazy man's suicide. Life expectancy plunged when one decided to take it easy. Living a little, as it turns out, kills. Nigel was a wonderful man, but left to his own devices, he enjoyed the deadly pleasures of doing nothing—a skater, as they called it back in her marine days. After considering the pluses and minuses of a premature widowhood, Annie decided to take steps.

The to-do list was central in her campaign to keep her husband upright. He may have embraced it like a cactus, but in Annie's view, it was working. A period of adjustment and self-doubt was inevitable, not unlike her sixth week of marine boot camp. But as boot camp had demonstrated, an understanding, hard-driving, butt-kicking drill sergeant was the answer. The fact that Annie had never been a drill sergeant couldn't stop her from dreaming. Playing the kind and loving drill sergeant to her husband could be painful, sure, but service and sacrifice were what she did best.

9

AN ESCAPE FROM THE HOLE

The morning's activities were all well and fine, but after a scant four hours, Nigel's doggie dragnet had hit the doldrums. He had exhausted his search strategies without spotting so much as a paw print. Worse, an ensuing cold-eyed appraisal of his situation exposed a shocking reality. Nigel's dog-sleuthing venture had failed to blunt his creeping angst in any way whatsoever. Matching wits with a dumb animal was supposed to have engaged the gray matter to an extent that nothing was left for to-do list fretting. But Nigel had underestimated himself. He could, in fact, obsess mightily about two things at the same time. He was on the verge of a breakdown.

On the bright side, a hurricane was coming. But to reach that blissful distraction, Nigel would have to weather the calm before the storm. The sky over City Park was now blue but for a few thickening clouds. A steady breeze animated the trees, and the sun's rays glittered upon the water. It *looked* lovely, but unseen were the heat and humidity. Like many Texas days, the beauty was best appreciated from behind the window of an air-conditioned space, but Nigel had placed himself outside. Reclining on a bench with his back braced against a picnic table, he admired the ducks paddling about in serene little groups on the sun-dappled waters. They seemed to have found their place in this world. *They had not one to-do list among them.*

Nigel removed the yellow sheet of paper from his pocket, unfolded it, and winced at the sheer volume of ink on the page. He took a deep breath and redirected his thoughts to the peaceful, glistening pond. Before long, he found himself wondering if there might be a body somewhere in it. If so, there might also be a to-do list. Nigel wouldn't be at all surprised.

He wanted to rip his list into a thousand tiny pieces and feed them to the ducks. But his wife was a detective—and a damned good one. She was also determined—utterly, insanely, bulldoggedly, illogically determined when it came to this to-do list.

Her persistence was no surprise. Annie was equal parts mule, bull terrier, and rabid wolverine. It was one of the reasons Nigel loved her, but the way she pushed that to-do list down his throat, at every opportunity, was frightening. If he didn't know better, he'd swear she was bent on driving him to an early grave. And for what? Home improvements?

Their old place in Houston, a house of notable anonymity in an average neighborhood, had been permitted to age gracefully. Cracks and stains were plentiful if one cared to look. But no one did. Nigel recalled the saga of a two-inch hole in an interior wall of the master bedroom. It had been placed there one moonless morning in the wee hours when Annie, after a long night of police work, entangled her feet in a pair of men's boxer briefs someone had left on the floor. Somehow, she ended up putting the heel of her boot through the drywall some four inches above the baseboard. Two years later, Nigel, by his own initiative, repaired the ugly depression. So proud was he that he summoned Annie around to inspect the results. She'd have been favorably impressed had she been able to remember a hole ever having been there.

But now, if she spotted so much as a pinhole, she wanted it fixed. What was this obsession? More to the point, what to do about it? Nigel began to shake as if contracting heat stroke. Perhaps he was, but more importantly, he had an idea. It went like this:

Annie had lived in the presence of that Houston hole for seven hundred straight days, but at some point during that span, it had—for her—ceased to exist. It was as if the hole had fallen into a hole. This was a conceptual breakthrough, the hole-in-the-hole phenomenon. Based on this principle, Nigel's solution was—drum roll—to do nothing. Given enough time, the house's blemishes would cease to be visible. The concept had already been proven. Execution on a mass scale could begin immediately. In fact, it was already underway.

Of course, he couldn't do nothing all at once. That would draw suspicion. Certain bugaboos would be corrected via honest work. Many others could be slyly ignored, precipitating, at an appropriate time, their quiet removal from the list. This plan—so cunning, yet so simple—was, by Nigel's way of thinking, a kind of genius. Had he the flexibility, he would have kissed his own forehead.

Nigel rose from the bench and bid the ducks adieu. While he'd struck out on the dog search, he reckoned he'd just saved himself two years' labor on the house. Not a bad afternoon's work. Unfortunately, Nigel was in no position to rest just yet. The outer bands of the storm would arrive within a matter of hours, and despite his failure to secure downspouts, the rain gutters still beckoned. He had previously installed them, but mostly in a decorative mode using only every third hanger clip. They would not withstand a heavy breeze.

Climbing the ladder, Nigel braced himself against some hefty wind gusts. Thick cloud banks formed in advance of the storm while intermittent downdrafts provided temporary heat relief.

The height offered him a sweeping westward view in this semirural community. He could look straight down the road, through an assortment of homes, almost to town. A small moving speck caught his eye. It appeared to be moving in his direction. Nigel decided to have a look. *If one is to be a dog detective,* he thought, *one must look for dogs.*

He scrambled down the ladder, walked down the street, and kneeled about fifty feet from the mongrel, causing the scraggly animal to stop and sniff the air. Hard to believe, but this animal had to be his runaway. A state the size of Texas could not hold two dogs that ugly.

"Duffyyyy, oh, Duffyyy, here boy, come on, Duffyyy." The dog's ears popped up, and he sauntered toward Nigel. The gnarled snout, the asymmetric face, and the scruffy muskrat coat all indicated that Nigel had found his dog. He looked friendly, but Nigel was apprehensive. "Come here, Duffy." The dog's tail wagged, and he came straight over.

After a minute of being petted, the dog lay down and offered up his belly for a rub. This was obviously not the fearsome monster implied by his picture. A few minutes of belly rub was the only persuasion needed to get him to the house.

Finally, something had gone right. Nigel figured he had just enough time to return Duffy to the Sandovals before finishing the gutter installation. If he could do all that, *and* tonight's hurricane blew the house off its foundation, all his problems would be solved.

Then his phone rang. It was Annie.

"I'm at the police station," she said.

"Cool. Good facility?"

"I've been arrested."

"Arrested? For what?"

"Rustling."

"Rustling? I thought you were meant to catch the rustlers. Did I misunderstand?"

"Of course I wasn't rustling. They spotted me near one of Gilbert's fences. There was a break in the barbed wire, and I was putting a temporary fix to it. This deputy walks up out of nowhere, pulls a gun on me, handcuffs me, and takes me to the station."

"A deputy? Little guy, bounces around, has a rubbery face? That guy?"

"I don't know. He looked like a pelican."

"Exactly. A rubber-faced pelican. That's him."

"I guess. How do you know him?"

"It's a small town. I get around. I know people. I make friends."

"You got a ticket?"

"Absolutely not," said Nigel, thinking it a strange time to make such an accusation. "I'm a law-abiding citizen. But enough about me. Didn't you explain that you were trying to *catch* the rustlers?"

"Sure, but he wasn't going to be convinced. Neither would I if I were him. I mean, I'm standing there in a field, middle of nowhere, with a toolbox that happens to have wire cutters, and there's a gaping hole in the fence, on a ranch that's reported missing cattle. This guy doesn't know me from Adam. Why wouldn't he arrest me?"

"Why was he in the middle of nowhere?"

"That's the crazy part. He said he got a tip. From who? How? I don't understand how he'd get a tip."

Nigel didn't either, exactly, but it wasn't something he wanted to delve into, either. "It's a small town. Word gets around."

"But who knows I'm out there other than the Gilberts…and—"

Nigel perceived the conversation taking a nasty turn and heading straight for him. "Drones," he said.

"What?"

"Drones. They're everywhere these days. They can see for miles. Somebody saw you with a drone. That's what I think."

"I haven't seen any drones."

"I have. They're all over. Even if you don't see them, they see you."

"Right, whatever. Now is not the time to discuss. You need to come to the police station and pick me up."

"So, you're free? No big house? No necktie party? I thought they didn't cotton to rustlers in these here parts."

"I had them call Mr. Gilbert. He explained everything. I'm no longer in custody. You need to pick me up."

"What happened to your truck? Confiscated?"

After a pause, Annie issued a slow and deliberate response. "When you've been arrested and handcuffed, they don't let you drive your own vehicle. You need to pick me up at the station, then take me to my truck so we can each drive home."

"Right." Nigel could tell by the way she slowly enunciated each word that her patience was wearing thin. He needed to change the subject. "You know the game has been canceled?"

"Yes, Nigel. That's all anyone was talking about in the Tonkawa County Slam. Now, come pick me up."

Pick her up he did, but he was hardly greeted as a liberator. Perhaps by the time she arrived home, she'd recognize the humor in the situation. He hoped so because the early going had been frosty.

In Nigel's mind, doing time in a small-town pokey for cattle-rustling was just the type of life experience likely to improve with every telling. A half-dozen such harmless transgressions equaled a life well lived in his book. Annie, on the other hand, didn't seem to appreciate the gift she had been given. One might suppose that twenty years in the Houston PD had de-glamorized jail time.

Nigel pulled into the driveway, followed by Annie a minute later. As Nigel exited his car, Annie stomped past him to the side of the house and stared upward at the rain gutter. Not at just any part of the rain gutter, but at the neatly cut hole where a downspout should have been had the Cub Scouts not gone on a rampage.

"Like my handiwork?" asked Nigel.

"So, the water just drops in a torrent right onto the flower bed?"

"Well, it could be worse," said Nigel.

"How?"

"Drought."

Annie shot him a look suggesting he should spend the night standing where the downspout was supposed to be. As if to drive home the point, large drops began to swirl down from the sky. Annie stomped into the house, slamming the door behind her as a gust of wind blew leaves and a beach ball across the yard. Large drops pummeled the side of Nigel's head as he weighed the relative dangers of facing the tempest outside versus the one inside.

Outside, he at least felt the crazy excitement of an approaching storm. His inner eight-year-old urged him to run down the street, holler, and climb tall objects, but as often happens to eight-year-olds, he heard a scream from inside the house, indicating that it was time to come in.

"What is that?" shouted Annie, pointing to a spot along the baseboard in the living room. It wasn't the baseboard itself that held her attention, but a shadowy pyramid shape on the wall accompanied by a small yellowish pool on the linoleum floor.

"I'll clean it up," said Nigel. "Don't get excited."

"Where did it come from?"

"Just an accident. I'll get some paper towels."

"Just an accident?" Annie's brow began to scrunch. Her lips pursed, her eyes widened, and her mouth dropped open. "You?"

"What?"

"You did this?"

"Goodness no. Of course not! No! I wouldn't do this. How could you think?" said Nigel. "It was Duffy."

"Who is Duffy?"

"A dog."

"A dog? Where did we get a dog? We don't need a dog."

"Just for tonight. Just until the hurricane blows over. He was lost, so I took him in. We can't leave him outside. There's a hurricane."

"Where is he? I want to see him."

Of course she did. And judging by Duffy's reaction upon being let out of the utility room, he wanted to see Annie even more. He could not have been more welcoming. Annie, by contrast, had endured a difficult day, what with the cockroach and the arrest. The difference in enthusiasm levels told all. By the time Nigel had pulled Duffy away and helped Annie off the floor, she wanted nothing more to do with him.

Annie took a shower while Nigel prepared catfish parmesan, a proven crowd-pleaser. He hoped it would ease the tension. Outside, the rain came down in sheets that sometimes turned sideways. The trees stretched one way and then another, releasing tiny bits of themselves into the windy current.

"Dinner is served," announced Nigel.

"Good. I am so hungry." Her remark was punctuated by a metallic clatter from outside. "What was that?"

"Must have been the wind," said Nigel.

"You better check it out."

"Let's go ahead and eat. If it happens again, I'll go have a look."

"It came from outside."

"No doubt. Could you pass the vegetables?"

"It sounded like something hitting the house. Something metal."

"Possibly. The fish is really good. Try a piece."

"If it struck the roof, it could cause a leak."

"Could you pass the pepper, please?"

The steady roar from outside rose to a howl as a long gust of wind screamed through the trees, accompanied by three distinct metallic clashes.

"Okay then, I'll just go have a look," said Nigel, shoveling a last piece of fish into his mouth.

In a storm with sixty-mile-an-hour gusts, all sorts of things may get blown around. Be that as it may, Nigel suspected a particular type of hazard: rain gutters. A look out the bedroom window confirmed his suspicions. A properly attached rain gutter should have been scarcely visible. His new rain gutter was not just visible, but animated, fluttering in the wind like a ten-foot windsock—a predictable outcome when proper installation is interrupted by a lost dog, a wife in jail, and a hurricane. The solution was to release the flailing gutter from its anchor point.

As Nigel put on his shoes, a hardy gust sent the rain gutter flailing upward before clattering against the bedroom window. Then, the new gutter, having suffered enough, went gentle into that good night, receding into the blackness as Nigel watched with gaping mouth. Under the illumination of multiple lightning strikes, the tortured stick-like form bounced, rolled, and twisted its way toward a new destiny.

"Did you find out what that noise was?" Annie yelled from the kitchen.

"Yes. Something in the wind. It's fixed now."

The lights flickered, then went out.

The blustery, rainy, electricity-free night passed almost without incident. Water on a bathroom floor indicated a leak of some kind, adding to the to-do list, but the house remained standing. Electricity was restored by mid-morning, and in the afternoon, the rainfall became spotty. Nigel took advantage of a dry spell to step outside for a damage assessment.

Aside from a few missing rain gutters, the little house appeared sound. The damned thing would outlive them all. The house belonged to Annie's brother, the brother who was never discussed in Nigel's presence. When he'd asked Annie how long they could live in the place, she just said five to ten. The ramshackle bungalow wasn't inherently awful, just evil. Evil for somehow persuading Annie that it could be turned into a pristine habitat.

Nigel walked down the street inspecting the storm's after-effects. Aside from the litter of windblown debris, Nigel saw no lasting damage to cars or structures. He walked a few hundred feet to a bridge spanning a creek that was now swollen with rushing brown water. The small bridge acted as a strainer for the hurricane-generated debris deposited within the creek's watershed. Entangled among the collection of branches and rubbish were the bent and twisted remains of Nigel's gutter. Nigel envied that gutter, unmoored from its life of purposeful servitude, crumpled beyond any notion of reclamation.

As he turned to walk back, a passing pickup truck crawled to a stop. The young man in the driver's seat rolled down his window.

"You folks okay? Need any help?" he asked.

"No thanks," replied Nigel. "We came out all right. And yourself?"

"I'm okay. I was living in a mobile home up near the river. It's gone now. Washed away."

"Goodness!" said Nigel, experiencing a vision of himself waving goodbye to his own house, to-do list included, as it bobbed its way down a raging river. But this was no time to rhapsodize. "Do *you* need any help? You have a place to stay?"

"I'm good. I've got family in the area to stay with. I had time to save the important stuff. I got my guns. I got my heads—"

"Heads?"

"My deer heads. You know, hunting. Not such a big deal, really. I didn't own the place. I reckon insurance should cover the loss."

10

A PICKUP SUNK DOWN

By Sunday morning, the floodwaters had receded somewhat, and the sun shone brightly once again. The hurricane had cooled things down for a while, but now the intense sun lifted the scattered waters into the air to form a ghastly soup. Stepping into it from the comfort of an air-conditioned house was like walking into an armpit. Intolerable, it was, but not atypical. The weather of early September in this part of Texas did not distinguish itself from that of early August, which, in turn, did nothing to differentiate itself from that of early July, which could not be discerned from the inside a slow-roasting turkey. Alas, a turkey has just a few hours to endure its inferno.

"I'm going to take this dog in," Nigel yelled to Annie as he stepped from the comfortable confines of his air-conditioned house into the armpit.

"Take him where?"

"The animal shelter in town."

As Nigel scooted out the door, a great ape seemed to lift off his back. Within the hour, he would simultaneously solve his first case *and* close the book on his career as a gumshoe.

Despite proving the adage that it's better to be lucky than good, Nigel couldn't expect future subjects to waddle up to his doorstep and show him their underbellies. It happened once. It wasn't likely to become a tradition.

But the big relief would be the end of the deception. Annie, had she discovered Nigel masquerading as a detective for her agency, would have been unkind, possibly barbarous. His stomach did a rumba just thinking about it. And find out, she would have. Nigel's advice for anyone heading into marriage thinking they would deceive their spouse: Don't marry an investigator. He felt enormous relief as he loaded Duffy into the car.

The effects of wind and rain were everywhere to be seen in the form of broken branches, swollen creeks, and wind-blown clutter. He passed a couple of abandoned cars left in place by owners, who were frustrated by their lack of amphibian capabilities. Having lived in Houston, with its history of catastrophic floods, he understood the relationship between water and cars. Water wins. Drivers unaware of that relationship often lost their cars, and sometimes themselves.

Nigel turned onto Country Club Drive and into a gusty, drizzling rain. A few hundred yards in, the road submerged into a mass of moving brown water. He put the car in park and got out to take a closer look. Standing at the water's edge, he could see the maximum depth across the roadway was only a few inches. He'd not previously noticed the creek, nor the culvert bridge now acting as a ford. Of course, two days before, there would have been little to notice. He would have rolled unperturbed across the two-lane blacktop, across an unmarked and unobtrusive ditch.

Back in the Fusion, Nigel eased the car across. Midway into the stream, he spotted something odd to his left—something smooth, metallic, and immovable. Nigel crept the car forward past the stream, stopped, and placed the car in park.

Grabbing an umbrella, he got out to investigate. Beneath the plink of raindrops, the brown flowing stream barely made a sound except for the gentle gurgling of water bouncing across various obstructions. Most of the obstructions were natural—logs, rocks, and branches—but one, sitting center-stream several feet from the road, was not. Broad eddy currents swirled about a smooth, white, rectangular shape sitting just below the surface. Nigel put his clenched hands to the top of his head as he realized he was staring at a fully submerged pickup truck.

He paced in one direction and then the other. Horrific images flashed in his head. The most distressing involved a lost struggle to exit a rapidly-filling cab. Stepping up to the water's edge, he gazed at the scene. He saw no bubbles, no steam, and no plumes of mud-roiled water. The truck must have been swept off the bridge when the water was a couple feet higher. The accident, Nigel concluded, happened many hours ago, maybe a day or more. He calmed himself by imagining the occupant in his home discussing the incident with his insurance agent.

Nigel returned to his car and called 911. While waiting for an officer, he leashed up Duffy, and the two of them walked up the lane. After a few minutes, a large, dark SUV barreled down the road from the direction of the house. Spraying water high in either direction, the SUV did not slow down at the bridge. Ten minutes later, a cop arrived.

After a handful of questions, the female officer handed Nigel a report form on a clipboard, which he completed sitting in the back of the squad car before handing it back.

"Okay, Mr. Blandwater-Cummings," she said, looking over the document. "So, you live in No Way, huh? You know Cam Logan has a place out there?"

"So I've heard."

"You'll be around for the next few days?"

"I plan to be."

"Okay." She handed over a business card. "Here's my contact information. If anything else should come to mind, give me a call."

Nigel returned to his car and proceeded to the Sandoval mansion. He parked his car next to the yellow sports car and was met by Gastrick, the butler, on the front steps.

"Mr. Blandwater-Cummings," said the butler.

Impressive, thought Nigel, *that he could remember the name.*

"To what do we owe the pleasure of this visit?"

"I came to return Duffy."

"Really?" he said with the enthusiasm of one who had lost a bet. "Mrs. Sandoval will be pleased."

Duffy was eager to exit the car, but upon seeing Gastrick, he cowered. As Nigel handed over the leash, Duffy pulled back, emitting a low rumble.

"Have you been stealing his bones?" asked Nigel.

"He doesn't like me, and I'm afraid there isn't much to be done about it. Part of the job, really. Mrs. Sandoval has me take his temperature once a week. The dog has come to regard me, quite literally, as a pain in the ass. If you'll follow me, we can walk him back to his pen."

"Is Mrs. Sandoval in today?"

"She is, but you will not see her. She sees no one during the Cowboy game. I'll tell her you are here at an appropriate time."

"You mean after the game?"

"During a commercial break. Most favorably a commercial break following a Cowboy score in a game they are winning by a wide margin. Should circumstances be otherwise, it can be unpleasant."

"Will Abuelita be watching the game?"

"Without a doubt. She's not missed a game for decades. It was during the final year of the Wade Phillips era that we had to confiscate her pistols. Big-screen TVs were expensive back then. Now we just see that she has an adequate supply of nuts."

"They keep her occupied?"

"Occupied? Yes, and far less damaging than hot lead. I shall return once I've notified Mrs. Sandoval that Duffy is safe among us."

Nigel looked around the grounds at the back of the house while awaiting Gastrick's return. To the left and slightly behind the house was a garage large enough for a half-dozen cars. Straight back was an Olympic-sized pool with tennis courts beyond. Everything appeared maintained and functional, though it begged the question: For whom?

The drizzle started up again, so Nigel retreated to the covered porch. The dog's "pen" to the right was a fully enclosed cage covering an area as large in area as Nigel's current house. At the far end of this enclosure, abutting the house, was the "doghouse" built in the style of a mini-mansion about the size of Nigel's bedroom. Any agrarian hermit worth his salt could have maintained a reasonable existence in such a setup. Of course, the cage, enclosed at the height of about four and a half feet, would have favored a hermit of diminutive stature. A hobbit hermit, perhaps.

Nigel's musing on the agrarian life of hobbits in dog enclosures was interrupted by a loud pop, a crash, and the muffled sounds of a confrontation. The verbal melee lasted a few seconds before fading to silence. The pop was almost certainly not a gun, but the sound of something being broken.

Gastrick soon returned to accompany Nigel back to his car.

"I couldn't help but overhear a commotion in the house. Any problems?" Nigel asked.

"Nothing to worry about. Abuelita just threw a dish of peanuts at the television."

"My goodness."

"These things happen. Even great quarterbacks throw interceptions from time to time."

Nigel was hesitant to discuss the incident at the bridge for a bunch of different reasons. No doubt the police would soon appear with a more complete account. Still, he felt an obligation to bring it up. "That reminds me, did everyone come through the storm okay?"

"All present and accounted for. Why do you ask?"

"On my way up, I spotted a pickup truck in the creek, submerged. I called the police about it. They're on the scene now. You didn't know anything?"

"No, I haven't been out since the storm. My car is very low to the ground, so I can't drive across that bridge during any kind of flooding. No one here drives a white pickup truck, so I'm not sure who it could have been."

"Does anyone here drive a big, gray SUV?"

"Don't tell me there are two trucks in the creek."

"No, it's just that I saw an SUV come up the road from the house. I thought it might belong to someone here."

The butler stared out toward the road. "Sometimes people come down this road by mistake. They usually just do a U-turn when they see it's a dead end. Maybe it was one of those dead-enders."

"Perhaps," said Nigel, "a dead-ender."

"Before you go, I was instructed to pay. How much do we owe?"

"Another hundred plus expenses." Nigel showed him his phone for the expense totals he'd calculated before leaving the house. The numbers were fabricated approximations, but they could have been true.

"Here you go. Keep the change," he said, pulling seven twenties out of his wallet.

"Thanks," said Nigel. All his working life, Nigel had been

paid a pre-arranged salary for work of a highly indeterminate value. He contrasted that with this job. Do a certain thing, get paid a certain amount. Simple. Of course, the pay was about a thousandth of his corporate rate, but still, it felt like honest money.

11

THE TRAGEDY AND THE COOKERY

Nigel returned down Country Club Drive to find the area now littered with emergency vehicles. On the scene were two marked police cars, a fire department ambulance, a tow truck, and another car of unknown providence. The submerged pickup truck had been pulled partially out of the water, and the passenger's side door had been opened. Nigel parked nearby and walked toward the original squad car. The officer was busy calling in her report. Nigel positioned himself out of her line of vision, but close enough to listen in.

"We've got an accidental drowning. The EMT guessed he'd been in the water at least twelve hours. We'll need the ME's report to establish a proper time of death."

Nigel's stomach dropped to his knees. Being first on the scene, he felt he had more at stake than just a passing connection.

"Male, white or Hispanic, average height, average build," she continued. "I have the driver's license. The name is an Oscar Preston Griesen. The birthdate is April 20, 1997."

The name Griesen sounded familiar. He thought back to his conversations in the Sandoval house. Wasn't Griesen the name of that prankster clan that Abuelita had raged about? Given her animation on the subject, one might suppose there were some ill feelings, if not an all-out feud between the Griesen and Sandoval families. That would make this an altogether strange location for a Griesen to meet a lonely end.

The officer continued, listing other personal information obtained from documents in the wallet. Finishing that, she began to list the items found in the truck. "We've got an unopened package from Wylie's Drug containing some supplements. There was a backpack full of photography equipment. There was a bouquet of ten roses; they look hand-picked, not from a store. There's a large toolbox in the bed of the truck. Once the truck's out of the water, I'll rummage through to see if there's anything interesting. That's about all I have for now. I'll see you back at the station once we're cleared."

Nigel approached the officer as she stepped out of the car.

"So, what's the story?" asked Nigel, feigning ignorance.

"Fatality. Oscar Griesen is the name. Mean anything to you?"

"No, not really. Any idea why he was here?"

"We made a call to the owners of the house up the road. They knew of no reason for anyone to be on the road at that time and couldn't identify the vehicle or the driver."

"Did they know anything about the truck before you mentioned it?" asked Nigel.

"No, they seemed surprised," said the officer, looking over the scene as if searching for answers.

"Who did you talk to, if I may ask?"

"Someone named Stefanie."

Nigel had not heard of a Stefanie. It occurred to him that he didn't know Mrs. Sandoval's first name. She didn't seem like a Stefanie.

"I talked to the butler up there just ten minutes ago," said

Nigel. "He didn't know anything either. He said a lot of people come down this road by mistake. Maybe he was one of those."

"Maybe so. I'm about to call it quits here. That truck's not moving until this water goes down some more. I'll be back here later with a tow truck. Maybe I still have time to see the end of the game."

"Don't you need to notify the family?"

"Maybe. Someone will have to. Once they determine next of kin, we'll see who draws the short straw. Worst job in the world." She gazed outward toward the wreck and beyond. "I hope it's not me."

Nigel arrived home, hardly remembering the drive. He should have been feeling relieved at being done with his dog case and pocketing some change. But the graver mystery of the drowned man in the pickup preyed on his mind like a restless vulture. He needed to shoo it away. He had mind-chewing vultures aplenty waiting at home in the form of a to-do list.

Nigel stepped into a house of strange odors. He'd grown accustomed to the smell of paints, cleaning solutions, and solvents, but this was something different. His nostrils expanded for maximum uptake. This was less abrasive, more pleasurable—not odors, but scents, perhaps, or aromas. Aromas evoking vague memories: friends' homes, aunts' houses, dinner parties, and Christmas meals. *Why the hell,* thought Nigel, *is this stuff wafting around my house?*

He marched toward the kitchen to find Annie, in an apron, chopping a carrot. Annie in an apron? Nigel hid himself while trying to make sense of it. A quick inspection of the place revealed an unprecedented level of activity. Perhaps it was some kind of experiment, maybe a crime scene re-enactment. Or, thought Nigel, his heart pounding, something more sinister. The knife in Annie's hand, laying waste to a potato, was a concern.

"What...eh...what's going on?" asked Nigel from a safe distance. He caressed the edges of a cutting board, which if need be, could act as a shield.

"Cooking," said Annie.

Cooking. The word spilled out casually as if it were some everyday thing. Nigel looked her up and down and wondered what had been done with the woman he married. The fact that she was wearing an apron implied the whole affair was premeditated. After twelve years of marriage, you think you know someone. This was like suddenly discovering an extra toe.

"Cooking?" said Nigel. "Has something happened to cause this...cooking?"

"Sunday dinner," she said, stabbing an onion.

"Ah," said Nigel softly, "Sunday dinner. I see."

He did not see, but he had to tread softly. Somewhere in the back of his mind was the notion that one should not challenge the alternate reality of a schizophrenic. Maybe that was for sleepwalkers. Either way, the idea resonated, especially if a good meal was at stake.

"What's that smell?" asked Nigel.

"You like it?"

"It makes my mouth go juicy. Is it supposed to do that?"

"Drool, you mean? Absolutely. It's the dinner rolls. They're in the oven."

"Dinner rolls? If we're having rolls, then what's all this stuff you're chopping?"

"The vegetables...for the roast," said Annie. She slid Nigel out of the way to retrieve the tray of rolls from the oven.

"Roast? My word!" said Nigel, "Is this, by chance, a gift

from one of those cows you rustled? Because if it is, I'm inclined to say you've found a career worth pursuing."

"Excuse me," said Annie as she rotated Nigel out of the way to access the pressure cooker. "I'll be putting in these vegetables, then I'm taking a break."

"I don't get it. A little choppin', a bit of cookin', some rustlin', some butcherin', throw in the hurricane and some jail time. What do you need a break from?"

Annie added the veggies and went straight to the sofa.

Nigel sat down beside her and picked up a magazine, appearing like someone with nothing to ask before asking, "Are you familiar with a family called the Sandovals?"

"Why do you ask?" said Annie, motionless with closed eyes.

"It seems that Duffy, our refugee dog, belongs to them. And from the conversation of some of the locals, the family might be considered eccentric."

"You mean crazy?"

"To put it impolitely, yes."

"I'm obviously not up on the latest, but I know they're rich. Maybe the richest around outside of Cam Logan." She turned to Nigel. "You know she has a place out here?"

"Yes, I do know she has a place out here. People are very fond of telling me she has a place out here. What I haven't figured out is *why* people tell me she has a place out here. Maybe you could solve that mystery for me. Why is it that people have the desperate need to tell me that Cam Logan has a place out here?"

"She's a big celebrity. Everyone knows her."

"Well, they certainly do know where she has a place. Is there something she's famous for besides having a place out here, or is that enough?"

"She's a country music star. She was on that show, *Nash-ville Dream Factory.* She's had several hits. I'm sure you've heard her before." Annie rubbed her forehead. "There's that song. What's it called?"

"I've Got a Place Out Here?"

"What?"

"Just a guess."

"Bad guess," said Annie, waving her hand as if to rid herself of a gnat. "It's a song about a couple—"

"Couple of what?"

Annie pursed her lips and raised a hand in the air as if to push back Nigel's bad jokes. She waggled her head back and forth, closed her eyes, and moved her lips. Nigel leaned forward and flexed his ears but captured only the faint groan of grinding gears. Annie's body began to rock. Her eyes closed tighter, and her forehead furled. Nigel waited for smoke to appear.

"Work it, girl," whispered Nigel while Annie squirmed like a stage performer, albeit one sitting on a sofa. He wondered if she might be writing her own song.

Her lips moved as if singing a lyric for the deaf. A finger shot upward.

"The Poisoned Pill!" she yelled.

"Glory be! Good show, old girl. I knew you could do it. You've a mind like a steel trap."

Annie emerged from her trance, a little embarrassed but relieved. "So, you know the song?" she asked.

"Afraid not. That was exciting, though. Makes me want to know it. Before we entered into *Name That Tune*, weren't we talking about the Sandovals?"

"What about them?"

"They're rich. Rich and crazy, you were saying."

"Rich and crazy. That's all I know, but I'll tell you who would know something."

Nigel stroked his chin.

"Do you want to know who would know?" asked Annie.

Nigel had the pressured look of a man being offered eternal life for a signature written in his own blood. "Mmm-mmm," he murmured.

"Did you say who? Was that a who?"

"Mmmmmm," Nigel murmured. Shutting his eyes and gritting his teeth, he asked, "Who?"

"Mother! She knows all the gossip from way back. She'll know all about the Sandovals," said Annie, brightening at the prospects of a civil discourse where none had gone before. "It's so convenient. They'll be here for dinner in about an hour—Mom and Stanley. You can talk about it then."

Nigel turned one of the paler shades of white. What had they been talking about? The mere mention of the mother-in-law tended to incinerate preexisting thoughts. There wasn't much room up in Nigel's attic once the mother-in-law showed up.

It should be stated that Nigel was, in general, a defender of mothers-in-law—that much-maligned class not possibly deserving the centuries of vitriol placed at their ample feet. Mothers-in-law were, after all, mothers. They couldn't possibly be the horrible beasts portrayed in media and litera-ture. And yet, there had to be exceptions. Nigel's was one of those.

12

SPEAKING TURTLE, SEARING DRAGON

"Hello, Mother dear, let me help you with that," said Nigel, holding open the door while simultaneously relieving her of an ominous-looking casserole dish. The facsimile of a smile he worked so hard to prop up gave way after several minutes. A left cheek muscle, collapsing under the strain, imparted a slight droop to the side of his mouth. As things turned out, smile muscles would not be needed for the rest of the evening.

"How was your trip, Mo-Mo-Mother?" asked Nigel, following her toward the kitchen.

"It's eight minutes from our house to yours," she said, widening one eye at the expense of the other, examining Nigel as if he were a single-celled creature viewed through a microscope. "If Stanley doesn't crash, the trip is tolerable. He didn't crash."

"Oh, hello, Stanley," said Nigel, successfully distinguishing his form from that of the wallpaper. "Make yourself at home."

Stanley Dillard—unfortunate husband to the mother-in-law, stepdad to Annie, and furniture with a stomach—

tottered to a location most likely to be out of everyone's way. Mother-in-Law was a woman easily characterized. Words such as abrasive, acerbic, acrid, and acrimonious come to mind—and that's just *ab* to *ac*. Her type has been extensively written about (see Lovecraft, H. P.). Stanley, on the other hand, was the type of person no one ever writes about. As descriptions go, it would be hard to improve upon the blank page, but here goes.

Stanley could be described as turtle-like. Pleasant enough, but not much for companionship or conversation. He tended to sit motionless for extended periods, sliding off his log just long enough to obtain food or to maintain a proper body temperature. Nevertheless, he seldom left his shell. Oh, every once in a while, when Mother-in-Law was spewing forth an epic monologue and needed a breath of air, she'd pause and say, "Isn't that right, Stanley?" Stanley would say, "Yes." If he was feeling obsequious, he'd say, "Yes, dear." It was hard to know if he was "in" the conversation or exhibiting some form of operant behavior based on discriminative stimuli. One doesn't know what happens inside a brain like Stanley's. One supposes not much.

After situating Stanley in front of the television, Nigel headed to the kitchen to help with the premeal preparation. He stopped short, however, upon hearing certain exclamations peppered with wicked laughter. While not hearing his name *per se*, he suspected he might have become a topic. His name would not have been mentioned because Mother-in-Law had an inability to remembering it. Why the word "Nigel" should pose such difficulty while words like "imbecile," "lamebrain," or "that nitwit husband of yours" were used with abandon was difficult to fathom. Words of this sort —along with his wife saying, "Mom, keep your voice down" —persuaded Nigel that his help was not needed.

Once the table had been readied, the captives sat down for

a menacing meal of pot roast with vegetables and an assortment of mystery casseroles. In the usual course of such get-
togethers, a strict separation of duties was observed. The
menfolk mostly ate and lightly talked; the womenfolk mostly
talked and lightly ate. If all went well, both sides came away
stuffed with the sustenance of their choice without much
interference from the other. Not only was this the natural
order, but it was how Mother-in-Law preferred it.

Of course, the natural order had not been so clear in the
beginning. Nigel's problem in those early days was that he
tried too hard. It wasn't entirely his fault. A deficiency in his
upbringing had conditioned him to engage in conversation
when seated for long periods of time with family members.
His early, tentative attempts had the effect of throwing sand
on the conversational fire. A few innocuous words from Nigel
transformed the soundscape of animated female voices into a
heart-palpitating silence, which was broken only by the
nervous clanking of silverware and the chewing and sipping
noises of uncomfortably self-aware diners. Moments like
these produced in Nigel a fantasy that fire would engulf some
part of the house, prompting an evacuation.

Stanley, for his part, watched this drama unfold in silent
bemusement. It baffled Nigel that Stanley never offered even
the simplest words of advice to save him from the torment.
But Stanley never did, leaving Nigel like the neophyte
missionary at his first banquet among the savages, wondering
what in God's name happened to his partner while being
urged to sample the local stew. "Awkward" about describes
it. Only much later did Nigel realize that Stanley was one of
those chaps that taught by example.

This Sunday dinner began obligingly enough with a
hearty round of dish passing and many compliments to the
chefs before anything had yet been tasted. Stanley and Nigel
set about gnashing hunks of pot roast while the females

untethered their tongues. All was going according to script when a pause in the tongue-waggling provoked Annie to introduce a new topic.

"Mother, Nigel was asking me earlier about the Sandoval family. Isn't that right, Nigel?"

"Correct," said Nigel, chewing through a gristly bit of beef or—perhaps—the inside of his cheek.

"What was it you wanted to know?" said Annie. "I'm sure Mother has some information."

There wasn't much Nigel could ask without giving away the game. He'd give the old hag a nudge and see how she prattled. "What's their deal?" said Nigel, dislodging a strand of beef—or cheek—from between two molars with his tongue. "I've heard they're eccentric. Anything behind the rumors?"

"You mean the family that bought the golf course? Those Sandovals?" said the mother-in-law, her tone suggesting the topic lacked merit.

"Yes, I suppose."

"They bought a golf course," she said, coldly and clearly, "and now they are living on it."

Nigel nodded and waited for more. The room grew stuffy with silence. Musing that Mother-in-Law may have succumbed, mid-story, to an unfortunate tragedy—like, say, a piece of roast beef lodged fatally in the windpipe—Nigel cast a furtive glance her way. She sat upright, buttering a dinner roll, noticeably not blue. Still, Nigel bided his time and hoped for the best.

"They're a strange lot," said Stanley, breaking his ten-year silence. Three heads swiveled toward him while six eyes widened. They could have heard the drop of a dinner roll, as indeed they did when Nigel's mouth fell open. Six ears extended themselves, awaiting the next pronouncement. Stanley resumed slicing into a potato. As the other diners settled back in their chairs, Stanley sent a quick wink to Nigel.

"Strange, for sure," said Mother-in-Law. "Very quiet, quiet and rich."

Quiet? thought Nigel. New Antigua must have been a different kind of town in those days.

She continued, "No one ever knew what was going on with them. Been around for a long time—seventy years, maybe more. One of them, a girl, was in my class at school—"

"That would be," said Nigel, "the one they call Abuelita?"

Mother-in-Law's eyes expanded, and the whites turned crimson. Everyone else's eyes looked for escape routes. Mother-in-Law had a way of sucking the oxygen right out of a room. That phrase, sucking the oxygen out of a room, has— in the past few years—become a popular metaphor used in various contexts with perhaps different meanings. With regards to Mother-in-Law, it implied a certain action performed during states of exasperation, whereby her back straightened, her jaw tightened, and a massive amount of air whizzed inward through clenched teeth. Humans nearby became woozy and disoriented. Any canaries in the vicinity required immediate evacuation.

Mother-in-Law resumed her response in a well-paced, deliberate manner while her dinner companions gasped. "Me? Abuelita? The same age? Really? Are you insane? A couple of years ago, the paper ran her picture. She looked as if she had been dug out from under a pyramid—one of the really old ones. You know what I'm saying?"

"Yes, quite. I'm sorry," said a blueish Nigel. "I hope you don't think I was comparing the two of you in any way. It's just that some people age quite profoundly, while others manage to gracefully retain their youth. You, dear Mother, I'm happy to say, are in that latter category. You must have some wonderful moisturizers." He stopped talking, overcome by wooziness and disorientation.

"What does that mean?" asked Mother, recoiling like a viper sensing her prey.

"Now, Kayda," said Stanley, breaking his ten-year silence for the second time in ten minutes. "Nigel has observed what I observed earlier today. You seem to get younger and more beautiful by the day. See, dear, I'm not the only one that notices these things."

Nigel noticed Stanley twisting his head ever so slightly in his direction and proffering another quick wink. He interpreted it as a way of saying, "I've given you a reset, young man. Try again." The wink was accompanied by a subtle tightening of the lips, which Nigel interpreted to mean, "Let's not muck it up this time, eh?"

This unexpected lifeline from Stanley had put the old tortoise under a new and decidedly more flattering light. Just moments before, Nigel pondered what manner of log Stanley was a bump upon. But now, the man to his right was not just a chair-filler shoving in the deviled eggs to no good purpose, but a man of substance, reason, and wisdom. Clearly, he had concealed his brilliance until the proper moment. Nigel marveled at the transformation as he watched Stanley, with knife and spoon, disassemble a quarter potato with admirable efficiency and grace. As if that were not enough, his treatment of peas and carrots with a buttered knife left one breathless. Stanley had been holding out.

Nigel reentered the conversation with renewed vigor. "Yes, precisely, that's what I was getting at. What he said. Really, you seem to be aging backward. Why, at this rate, in a couple of years, you and Annie will look like sisters."

The table leaped upward, silverware clattered on plates, and liquids threatened to top their glasses. Nigel massaged his leg under the table with both hands, one atop the knee—

where it had collided with the table—and the other on the middle shin, where it had absorbed the blow from Annie's shoe.

"Sorry about that. So clumsy of me," said Nigel. His eyes played across a landscape suddenly turned hostile. He felt panic: nowhere to turn, no help in sight, and little hope for a timely catastrophe—plane crash, gas main explosion, or earthquake—to bring this dinner party to a happy conclusion. His mind turned to Dunkirk. A strange place for a mind to turn at a dinner party, but it didn't seem so at the time. Nigel imagined himself with those poor sods on the beach facing imminent death by drowning on the one side, or imminent death by Nazi attack on the other. More than a few brave men must have used the brief moments between enemy strafing runs to think back to Sunday dinners with the in-laws. The prospects of one day resuming this weekly ritual would have made their immediate prospects seem considerably less dreadful.

"Nigel? Nigel? Nigel!" The table hopped again. "Nigel, you were staring into the light fixture. You'll fry your retinas," said Annie.

"I was? I'm sorry. Did someone yell incoming? I must have been daydreaming. Is it still daytime?" Nigel looked around the table, noting six bewildered eyes boring in on him. "Weren't we talking about the Sandovals? Mother was talking, weren't you, Mother? We need to stop interrupting and let this lovely woman tell us about the Sandovals. Go ahead, Mother."

"Well, okay, what I remember about this Sandoval girl—I think her name may have been Essie—was she used to wear taps."

"You mean taps like for tap-dancing?" asked Nigel.

"Yeah, like horseshoe thingies on her shoes that made a

click when she walked. She was the only girl I ever knew that clicked when she walked."

"Interesting!" said Nigel.

"I had an aunt who clicked when she walked," interjected Stanley, who was looking less and less like a mute, and more like a slow starter. "That was after hip-replacement surgery."

Mother-in-Law, after wounding Stanley with a withering glance, continued her story—complete with side notes—for the next fifteen minutes. It never got more interesting, and it provided Nigel with loads of inconsequential information about nothing whatsoever. The main gist of the story was that the town had a number of bullet holes in it, and Abuelita had put them there.

"That is quite a story, I must say. It sounds like the Sandovals must have had a run-in or two with some of the local families," said Nigel, hoping to shake out something useful.

"More than one, I'd say."

"You know that to be true?"

"Well, there was that daughter, Essie, ran off with one of the Griesen boys. I doubt any of the parents were happy about that. I don't recall much about it. Essie was my age, but I never saw her once she'd been shipped off to boarding school. The Griesen kid was a few years older, so I never knew him. They ran off together. I think he came back after a few years, but as far as I know, she never did."

"Now, that's the juicy stuff," said Nigel. "Remember his name?"

Annie sent Nigel a quizzical look.

"Not that it matters, I suppose."

"Dolph," she said.

"I'm guessing old Dolph moved away," said Nigel.

"Nope. Still here. Buried up at Sleeping Willow. I remember his name because he died a couple years ago."

"I see," said Nigel, "how all true stories end." Some a lot more interesting than this one.

"Yes, that was an interesting story," said Stanley. Once the dam had been broken, the words just flooded out of him. He sat back in his chair in an expansive posture. With all eyes on him, he twirled a toothpick along the base of a lower molar and said, "Any of it true?"

Mother straightened her back, parted her lips over clenched teeth and made a noise like a vacuum cleaner. Everyone wobbled in their chairs while turning shades of blue. Dinner was over.

Once Stanley had demonstrated the capacity to remove himself from his chair, the in-laws made a move for the exit. Nigel and Annie were, by this time, engaged in the exacting task of resupplying the napkin holders, Nigel aligning and replacing while Annie guided his movements with a series of verbal commands and hand gestures. Stanley exited with a wink and a nod while the Mother-in-Law gave Annie a thumbs up.

It could have been far worse, thought Nigel.

13

NIGEL, THE SHOELESS SNAKE HANDLER

Monday mornings were not Nigel's favorite, even though recently, they weren't much different from Fridays or Wednesdays. That said, the prospects for this particular Monday were dreary even by Monday standards. His pet detective adventure, while an investigative and financial success, had yielded little of what he needed most: thrills, chills, and a diversion. Mostly, it resulted in a grim discovery he could have done without.

Nevertheless, Monday morning it was, and coffee was required to face it. Nigel dragged himself to the kitchen to find a gift from his wife taped to the coffeemaker. It was the crumpled to-do list with an attached Post-it note reading "Stain on ceiling—second bedroom." The to-do list was now receiving updates while he slept.

A demoralized Nigel set off to do yard work. Squatting on the pavement of his driveway and threading line into a weed whacker, he felt a delicate swipe along the back of his arm. He brushed it away. A moment later, he felt a dampness on the same spot. He turned slowly around to see Duffy at his elbow.

"What are you doing here?"

While appreciating the question, Duffy provided no answer.

Perplexing, thought Nigel. The Sandoval place was fifteen miles away on the other side of at least one angry, swollen river. And yet, for a second time, their dog ended up virtually in his lap. It made no sense. It was a mystery, after all. Nigel packed away his despair and prepared for another trip to the Sandoval asylum.

Before returning Duffy, Nigel required some answers. The dog clearly wasn't receiving proper adult supervision. And while Nigel didn't relish playing the part of Dog Protective Services, he also didn't want to be the dog's custodial parent every other day. Before Duffy could go back, Nigel needed to be convinced he had a proper home. After sequestering the dog, Nigel headed back to the Sandovals.

The scene of the drowning tragedy was now devoid of activity. The creek had receded considerably since the day before, leaving the truck only half submerged. Having the place to himself, Nigel parked the car to have a look around before police arrived to clear the scene.

He found a log about four inches in diameter, which he floated into position to act as a walking bridge to the pickup truck. Crossing an eight-foot span of water atop a four-inch log? Piece of cake. He had seen tightrope walkers span a hundred feet on wires no thicker than a thumb, performing backflips halfway across just to relieve the boredom.

The first step was solid as could be. Nigel made a long stride for the second step and felt the log turn under his foot. He whipped his other leg around and launched himself onto the sidewall of the pickup. Landing awkwardly with one foot plunging into the ankle-deep water of the truck's bed, he was safely aboard at the cost of one wet shoe. He sidled up the sidewall to the cab and looked inside. The driver's side window had been shattered, the door was ajar, and the glove compartment hung open. The cab had been cleaned out by the police. Nigel flipped down the window visor and retrieved a folded piece of notebook paper from a clip. It was damp, but maybe still readable. The police had either missed it or left it behind as something of no consequence. Nigel placed it into his shirt pocket and sidled back to the truck bed.

A large toolbox next to the cab, still underwater, was opened to reveal large tools: a sledgehammer, massive metal snips, pliers, and work gloves. Nothing of interest to Nigel. Having seen all there was to see, Nigel perched for a moment on the sidewall of the truck and scanned the scene before him. The birds chirped, and the leaves rustled in the breeze. Dragonflies skittered back and forth over the muddy brown water that gurgled through obstacles on its journey to the Gulf of Mexico. The water that had swept the truck off the bridge, trapping its occupant, was now far out to sea. Nature had moved on.

Nigel's train of thought was broken by a mild splash, maybe a turtle or a bird. He stood up for his balancing act back to shore. He put one foot on the log. The log responded by turning under the weight. The foot slipped off the log simultaneous to the other foot slipping off the side of the truck. His attempt at standing on water was brief, terminated by a feet-first plunge into the soup—awkward, though hardly catastrophic—if not for the log.

The log had not given up on being a bridge. It held steadfast even as the upright and vulnerable Nigel plunged toward it. Wildlife scurried, and birds scattered at the disconcerting thud of crotch hitting wood. Green leaves fell like snow, shaken from their branches by a wild, defoliating yowl.

For a moment, Nigel straddled the log like a triumphant broncobuster. A deception it was, for this was no competition, and Nigel was no winner. The only parts of his body not paralyzed with pain were the tear ducts.

Once the convulsions had faded, Nigel moved himself gingerly off the log. Only the waist-deep water prevented him from curling himself into a ball. Instead, he turned around, placed his hands on the sidewall of the truck, and let loose a series of gurgling yells like some modern Tarzan that had just fallen, crotch-first, onto a log. He stood long after the final yell had gurgled itself out.

He'd have stood there longer still if not for something bumping across the front of his legs. The opaque brownness of the water plus the salty sweat from his brow rendered him effectively blind. He reached down to touch a smooth but somewhat pebbly surface. The texture felt familiar. It brought to mind a purse his wife had owned. He ran his hand around the shape to locate a handle but found none. He ran his hands down the length of it but could not locate an end. Too long for a purse; perhaps a duffel bag.

Nigel then perceived a gentle caress along the small of his back. The reassuring touch produced a warm sense of relief. Someone had heard his screams and come to help. Nigel looked to his left. No one there. He looked to his right. A dark shape hovered in close proximity to his face. Nigel's eyes, still awash from the reflexive tears of blunt force testicular trauma, struggled to focus. His eye sockets performed a series of calisthenics aimed at restoring some clarity to his clouded vision. When Nigel again turned to his right, he was taken aback by a wispy forked object flicking about his face. Behind the object was one jolly giant of a snake head.

"Hold on!" said Nigel.

His eye sockets performed a second set of calisthenics, sparse on the squinting and heavy on the widening. His first impressions having been confirmed, some sort of action was required. Nigel wasn't sure what kind of action, but probably not the kind you spend a lot of time planning. He instinctively reached up and grabbed the serpent just behind the head with his right hand. He had intended to use both hands, but the left was rather tightly clamped against his body. *Snakes are strong*, thought Nigel, as the serpent coiled around his torso and down his leg.

Nigel, hoping to discern the snake's intentions, stared into its face. The snake, not much inclined to care about intentions, stared into Nigel's. Snakes, as a species, are inscrutable. It's hard to know what they're thinking because they don't do it much. This one held true to form. Nevertheless, what Nigel could not imply from her face, he could insinuate from her body, which seemed to be saying, "I want you, and I'm never letting you go." Alas, had Nigel been a better interpreter of snake language, he would have received a message more like, "Rabbit. Where's my rabbit? Give me rabbit."

As bad as Nigel was at interspecies communication, the snake was even worse. Snakes may be inscrutable, but Nigel, at this moment, was anything but. The message on his face read like a highway billboard: "I have a wife, and she's expecting me home to fix dinner." This message sailed over the snake's head like any message sails over a snake's head. The snake continued to flick his tongue in hopes of tasting something resembling rabbit.

Nigel, sensing he might have the intellectual advantage, implemented a plan. Not an elaborate plan, mind you, more like the kind that can be summed up in a word or two. Nigel slogged out of the water and onto the road. He suspected, from the readings of his misspent youth, that this snake was an anaconda. Anacondas prefer the water. Nigel, given a choice, preferred to die on dry land. *Perhaps*, thought Nigel, *the change in environment might even the odds.* He knew it was thin, but plans don't come easily when you're wrapped in anaconda.

The slog to the road, while only about fifteen feet in distance, was not easy. The creek bed was mud that alternated between engulfing and slippery. Nigel made it to shore absent a shoe. The nettles and burrs along the shore's edge were not kind to the unclad foot. Nevertheless, Nigel persisted and burst onto the pavement as a sheriff's squad car screeched to a stop two feet before contact. A trailing wrecker skidded to a halt to avoid a collision with the sheriff's car.

The two deputies opened their doors and stood staring— surprised, one might think—as the snake-wrapped Nigel fell to the pavement. He struggled to his knees before falling again.

"A snake," said the rubber-faced deputy.

Nigel would have liked to raise a hand to indicate that a man was also present, but he didn't have one to spare.

"A big snake," said the female officer.

"We should probably help," said Rubber-Face. "You know about snakes?"

"No," said the female officer.

"We need to be careful then. It could be poisonous," said Rubberface, drawing his revolver.

"Not poisonous," yelled Nigel from the ground.

"That's what you say. Who are you?" asked Rubberface.

"Victim," grunted Nigel, his face a bright red.

"This your snake?" asked Rubberface as he walked over to the anaconda-spooled Nigel.

"No... Please, could you get me...get me out?" grunted a purplish Nigel.

"We're going to have to unwrap him," said Rubberface to the female officer, who squatted on the other side of Nigel.

"We should get a picture," said the female officer.

"Please...hurry," grunted Nigel.

"He's in a hurry. We should get him out," said Rubberface.

"Look. He's missing a shoe," said the female officer.

"Please hurry… Please, Barney." Nigel hoped the personal appeal might result in some urgency.

"What did you call me?" asked Rubberface.

Nigel stayed silent. The tone of the questioner suggested an answer was inadvisable.

"Did you just call me Barney? Is that what you called me? Listen, I don't know who you think you are, but if you want our help, you need to be respectful. You got that? You better, Mister. We're going to get you out of here in good time," said Rubberface.

"A good time would be…now," said Nigel, holding up the snake's head with a palsied hand.

"Are you waving that snake head at me? At me? Mister, you wave a snake head at a Tonkawa County deputy, and nothing good is comin' of it. You keep that snake head to yourself. Do I make myself clear?"

"Yes," grunted Nigel.

Authority having been asserted, the two officers began the task of unraveling Nigel. The lady grabbed the tail end —of the snake—while Rubberface rolled Nigel along the street, unwrapping the huge reptile as he went. Eventually, the three humans found themselves sprawled over the pavement straddling various segments of snake. Nigel continued to hold the serpent's head in an increasingly unsteady hand.

"Okay. You two hold down the snake while I go to the squad car and call this in," said Rubberface.

"I don't know if we can hold it down," said the lady officer. "Maybe I should go instead."

"If you two couldn't hold him down," said Rubberface, "then we two might not be able to either. Look at his face. He's still purple. What's our plan B?"

"We could put it in the trunk of the car and drive it back to animal control," said the officer.

While options were being weighed, the wrecker driver

walked up carrying a giant wrench. "You want me to whop it on the head? Then it's just roadkill."

"I don't think we should do that," said the lady cop. "A snake this size might be worth something."

"*National Enquirer* may want a story on it. Where did this big boy come from, you suppose?" asked Rubberface.

"I don't mean to impose," said Nigel, "but just maybe it came from that truck sitting there in the creek."

The officer pulled at his face, accentuating its rubberiness. "Sir, can you tell me what you were doing here?"

"I have business with the Sandovals up the road. I saw the truck, so I stopped to take a look."

"What's your interest in looking at the truck?"

Nigel felt uncomfortable with the direction of the conversation. "Maybe I wanted to buy it."

"That flooded-out truck? You want to buy it?"

"It'll go cheap. I like a deal."

"You think you're going to buy that truck?"

"Well, not after I've had a look, no."

"Why not?"

"Too flooded."

"I could book you for tampering with evidence. You know that, right?"

"What about the snake?" Nigel held up the snake's head to make his point.

"Book a snake for tampering with evidence? Are you crazy?"

"I mean, what are we to do with the snake? My arm is getting very tired trying to control his head. We need to do something, or I'm going to let it go."

"Okay, we're going to lift this snake up together and take him over to the squad car," said Rubberface. "I'm going to open the trunk, and we'll dump him in. I'll count to three, and then we all lift."

"Shouldn't you measure him?" asked the tow-truck driver.

"Good idea," said Rubberface. "You got a tape measure?"

"No. I thought you might have one," said the tow-truck driver.

"Why would I have a tape measure?"

"You're a policeman," said the tow-truck driver. The deputy and the lady cop rolled their eyes.

"Okay. Everyone, on the count of three, we lift and walk. One...two...three." The three transitioned from a prone position to a squat, and then: *Rip.*

"Not again," said Rubberface.

The lady officer convulsed as the three stood up. Clutching the snake to their waists, they shuffled to the car like a chain gang, whereupon Deputy Rubberface retrieved the keys from his pants pocket. Trunk opened, the snake was unceremoniously dumped. Lady Officer then stepped back, squatted down, and snapped two quick cell phone shots of Rubberface's ripped pants.

"In the car," said Rubberface. "Let's get this thing over to animal control."

14

GALOSHES, 1892 STYLE

Wet, muddy, and one-shoed, Nigel resumed his drive to the Sandoval estate. Before coming within sight of the place, he pulled his car over and popped the trunk. Certain odors wafting through the interior of the car had alerted Nigel that his wardrobe, after a knockdown-dragout with an anaconda, might be sub-optimal for visiting. In his trunk were several grocery bags of perennially back-closeted, misfit clothes waiting for redemption in a recycling bin. A couple of items would now be offered a temporary reprieve as emergency apparel. He found a pair of ill-fitting, almost-never-worn black slacks and a blue, seldom-worn, button-down shirt.

Nigel had no problem recalling why these items had been relegated. The pants were, as he called them, standers-not-sitters. That is, the overly stiff material opposed any movement greater than a stiff-legged walk, and did so with noisy, irksome swishes. The shirt, on the other hand, was built of a fabric that had a talent for pulling wrinkles right out of thin air. Two months stuffed into grocery sacks had not altered their character in the slightest. The pants sprang into action as if they were starched yesterday. The shirt looked as if it had been sewn from the hides of raisins. He could do nothing about the missing shoe except to make up a story.

Nigel drove past the yellow sports car and parked directly in front of the main entrance, hoping to avoid any sort of meet and greet. He bounded up the steps, and to his amazement, he saw a pair of galoshes sitting beside the door as if waiting for a needy visitor. Nigel wasted no time slipping his be-socked foot into one and stomping his be-shoe'd foot into the other. The door opened before he could ring.

"Hello, Mr. Blandwater-Cummings," said Gastrick, the butler. "What can I do for you today?"

"I…ah…just dropped by," said Nigel, trying to recall why. "To…see how the dog was doing. How is the little scamp? Is he around?"

"I suppose. Personally, I limit my exposure to the *little scamp,* so I could not say how he is today. He does not confide in me."

"Does he, by any chance, have a long history of escape?"

"You mean running away?"

"Precisely, running away."

"He has tried on occasion but not been as successful as one might hope."

"He might be better than you think," said Nigel.

"Improvement is always possible. If you would like to have a continuing conversation on matters regarding the dog, perhaps you would like to speak to Mrs. Sandoval. She is, after all, the dog's keeper."

"That would be excellent," said Nigel. As he stepped inside, the galoshes squeaked with each movement on the exquisitely polished floor.

"You're wearing galoshes," said Gastrick, staring downward with raised eyebrows.

"Indeed."

"Would you like to remove them, please?"

"I would prefer to keep them on, actually," said Nigel. He shifted his galoshed feet as Gastrick glared at them in an unnerving way.

"Interesting. I have a pair of galoshes remarkably like those."

"Well, you know," said Nigel, "galoshes are pretty much the same all over. If you've seen one galosh, you've seen them all."

"Not my galoshes," said Gastrick, moving his head around to examine the footwear from a different angle. "Mine are one-of-a-kind, passed down to me from a great-great-uncle."

"Heirloom galoshes. Maybe they should be in a museum," said Nigel, shuffling his feet.

"Perhaps," said Gastrick, bending at the waist for a better look. "He was an anthropologist, a foremost authority on the Iniki-Kutati people of northeastern Siberia. The galoshes were an initiation gift commemorating his first kill."

"Whale?" asked Nigel, stepping backward.

"Missionary," said Gastrick distractedly. He jutted his head forward toward the galoshes, and then pulled back, all the while rubbing his chin like an art critic examining one of those Rembrandts that turn up at garage sales. "Where did you get your galoshes, Mr. Blandwater-Cummings?"

"Oh, some shop. Secondhand, I think. Probably London," Nigel replied, moving whichever foot the butler had taken an interest in behind whichever foot he hadn't.

"What are they made of?" asked Gastrick.

"What are yours made of?" asked Nigel.

"Walrus hide," he said, jamming a monocle into his eye.

"Walrus hide? Imagine that." Nigel was examining the

galoshes for the first time himself. They did appear to possess certain qualities consistent with the hide of a blubberous creature exposed to wind, saltwater, and sub-zero temperatures with limited access to moisturizers. "Mine," continued Nigel, "are probably imitation walrus hide."

"I'm not so sure about that," said Gastrick. He was in a deep crouch, sniffing at the galoshes. "Mine are authentic walrus hide, but not your ordinary, authentic walrus hide."

"No, of course not."

"In 1892, they were vulcanized in an attempt to make the world's finest pair."

"I wasn't aware they could do that to walruses. Did they get the ears right?" asked Nigel as he paced around the room, trying to maintain a distance from the shoe-sniffing butler.

"The process was technically successful," continued Gastrick, "but would have been too expensive for commercial application. They would have cost $1200."

"Twelve hundred dollars, eh? Somebody might pay that."

"That's in 1892. They'd be about sixty grand today."

"Precious."

"If you would please remove them, I'll see that they're safely stored," said Gastrick, eying the footwear like a bride-to-be eyes her engagement ring on the finger of a slippery niece.

"I prefer to keep them on, thank you."

"Please, it would be better to remove them. Mrs. Sandoval is very particular about her floors."

"Oh, very well. If you insist," said Nigel. The galosh on the shoeless foot dropped off at the touch of a finger. The other galosh could not be removed until Nigel spent a good two minutes seated on the floor, wedging it off. When it did come off, it came off with the shoe still inside. Gastrick hovered all the while like a vulture with a hankering for aged, vulcanized walrus-hide.

Nigel shooed him away. "I'll hang on to these, if you don't mind. They've got my shoes inside." He clutched the ghastly objects to his breast.

"It's quite all right. I assure you, they'll be kept in a safe place."

"They certainly will," said Nigel. "Right here with Papa. They're holding my shoes—shoes that never leave my sight, even when I sleep. They're very special, these shoes, given to me by a great-nephew, a prize-winning chemist. The only shoes in existence made of pure corbomite—and not just any corbomite, mind you. Plasticized corbomite."

"Very well," said Gastrick, his shoulders drooping to match the corners of his mouth. He directed the stocking-footed, galosh-cradling detective toward a side room housing Mrs. Sandoval. Since the last visit, she had updated her fifties teenybopper outfit to something more modern. Think sixties beatnik, complete with sunglasses. Nigel waved from across the room but received no response.

Between Mrs. Sandoval and the sock-footed Nigel lay fifty feet of the smoothest, cleanest, most frictionless surface to be found outside a freshly Zambonied hockey rink. As Mrs. Sandoval and the easy-striding Gastrick watched and waited from across the room, Nigel made his way with a series of stiff-legged baby steps. The rapid swishes of his pants echoed through the noiseless vacuum. Halfway through the trek, his impatient left foot set sail on its own accord, leaving a confused right foot to deal with the consequences. If not for the heroic actions of an exposed pinky toe applying frictional pressure through a fortuitous hole in his sock, all dignity would have been lost. As it was, Nigel pulled himself up from a half-split and swished his way to the sofa with no more damage than a strained left groin.

"Mrs. Sandoval, so nice to see you again," said Nigel, dropping the galoshes to the floor and extending his hand.

"Mr. Nigel was it?" said Mrs. Sandoval, giving his hand a dainty shake.

"Close enough. I'm sorry to trouble you again, but I had a few questions."

"You're wearing socks, Mr. Nigel."

"Indeed."

"Do you care to explain?"

"I always wear socks. A habit. Mother insisted."

"But you're not wearing any shoes!"

"You've caught me there," said Nigel. "I can't deny it."

"Why?"

"They're in the galoshes. The galoshes have my shoes, and they refuse to give them up."

"Why were you wearing galoshes? It's not raining."

"A very good point," said Nigel, noticing Gastrick's prominent nose peeking from behind a doorway. "It's an interesting story about why I was wearing galoshes, but I'm a bit short on time just now. I would prefer to get to the matter at hand. Now, if I may ask you a couple of questions—"

"Gastrick, two shots of tequila, please," barked Mrs. Sandoval.

"None for me, thanks," said Nigel.

"Two shots of tequila, Gastrick. Make it snappy," yelled Mrs. Sandoval.

"How long have you owned your dog, Duffy?"

"Do you own an iron, Mr. Nigel?"

"What?"

"An iron. Do you own one? It doesn't look as if you do. I suggest you get one and learn how to use it. You look as though you've been in a fight with a wild animal," she said, fingering the collar of her black turtleneck.

"Yes. Very perceptive. You are quite right. I shall go out and buy an iron and learn how to use it. Now, how long have you had Duffy?"

"Two years."

"Has he escaped often?"

"Only twice, to my knowledge."

"And do you know where he is now?"

"He's enjoying escape number two."

Mrs. Sandoval seemed surprisingly complacent about it. Perhaps the dog's previous return gave her confidence the dog would find its way back, or perhaps she was already on her tequila drip.

Gastrick returned with two long, slender shot glasses of tequila.

"Do you have a theory on how, or why, Duffy has escaped?" Nigel asked.

"I would guess because someone left the gate open," she said, slamming down round one and finishing it off with a side-to-side head waggle and cobra-like hiss that would have produced an uproar had there been an Indian elephant in the room.

"Who would leave the gate open, Mrs. Sandoval? Who would do that multiple times?"

"Someone who drank tequila, possibly." She slammed down the second round, after which she formed her mouth into an oval and sucked air until her cheeks bulged, followed by an exhale with flapping tongue. "I hate to confess this, but it was probably me. Gastrick told me that I must have left the gate open." She removed her sunglasses. Probably steamed up.

"You believe that to be true?"

"Why shouldn't I? I'll confess something to you, Mr. Nigel. As painful as it is for me to admit, I sometimes drink too much."

"Really? Are you sure?"

"Yes. I admit it. Sometimes I have a nip or two, and when I do, I'm not at my best. Actually, that's not true. With a nip or two, I probably am at my best. But after three, four, five, six and seven, I'm not at my best. So I have to believe that I let the dog out. It is well within my capabilities.

"I wasn't questioning your capabilities. However, I've located your dog twice in the same place. Both times in the far eastern reaches of the county. That's more than fifteen miles from here and across the river. Do you have any idea how, or why, your dog would end up there?"

Mrs. Sandoval widened her eyes. The pupils rotated upward and to the left, then to the right. She swiveled her head in a wide circle before leaning toward Nigel and whispering, "Extraterrestrials?" She sat back in her chair. "Ooooo-oooo-oooo," she sang while holding the two shot glasses on her head like antennae. She dropped her head and then yelled, "Gastrick! Ice cream. Mint chocolate chip. Thank you."

Nigel returned to the questioning, hoping it wasn't too late. "Mrs. Sandoval, do you or anyone in this house keep snakes?"

"Yes, I have a whole room full. I'm sure Abuelita has some as well—"

"Really? A whole room full?"

"Of course. I've traveled quite a lot, you know. And whenever I go to a new place, I bring one back. Something new, something exciting—something I don't have in my collection."

Amazing, thought Nigel. He wouldn't have thought she was the type. "Do you have large ones? Really large ones, I mean?"

"The one I brought from Borneo takes up the entire corner of a room. It must weigh 500 pounds. I had to have it shipped."

"My goodness! You have it in the house? It's here? Now?"

"Of course it's here. Why wouldn't it be here? You think it would just crawl away? You're that imbecile, aren't you?"

"Aren't you worried about having such things in the house?" said Nigel to the lady who couldn't keep tabs on her dog.

"What are you driving at? Why should I be worried about having them in the house? Where else would you have your keepsakes?"

"Did you say keepsakes?"

"Of course, I said keepsakes. That's what we were talking about—my keepsakes."

"No, not keepsakes," said Nigel. "Keep snakes. You know, legless reptiles; serpents. I said, 'Does anyone here keep snakes?' "

"Stefanie!" shouted Mrs. Sandoval, waving to someone passing toward the entrance. "Stefanie, can you come in here?" said Mrs. Sandoval. "There's someone I want you to meet."

In walked an attractive, sensibly dressed woman who might have passed for Mrs. Sandoval's sister had she not been young enough to be her daughter.

"Mr. Nigel, whatever you wanted to ask me, you can ask her. I must eat my mint chocolate chip ice cream while it's still cold," said Mrs. Sandoval. She leaned back and shouted toward the kitchen, "Gastrick! Ice cream!"

Nigel turned to the newcomer. "Nigel Blandwater-Cummings. Glad to make your acquaintance."

"Stefanie. Glad to make yours. You're not wearing any shoes, and your shirt is frightful. What happened?"

"I'll spare you the tedium of that story, if that's okay. A more pressing matter is—as I was just inquiring—do you keep snakes here at the house? On the property, I mean."

"Keep snakes? Here? You mean like some kind of zoo?"

"Not many snakes, but maybe just one. A large one, perhaps?"

"What interest would we have in keeping a large snake?"

she asked, as if never before considering the possibility. She then seemed to have an idea. "Abuelita, maybe in her younger days, but I don't think she could manage it now. No, no snakes in this house, I'm afraid. Why in the world would you ask such a thing?"

"I happened across one on my way up. Wondered if it might be connected with someone living here."

"I don't know how long you've lived here, Nigel, but there's no shortage of snakes on the property, especially down by the creek."

"Not like this one, I should think."

"What was special about this one?"

"It was twenty feet long, for a start."

"For a start?" she said. "I'd hope that would be an end. I've never heard of a snake that size in Texas."

"Not native, I'm sure. South American, I should think. An anaconda, I believe."

"What would a South American snake be doing here? Is it dangerous?"

"No longer. Me and the local law enforcement captured it, and they carried it off to Animal Control. You have nothing to fear, I'm sure."

"Gastrick, another shot of tequila!" yelled Mrs. Sandoval.

Stefanie leaned in close. "Please excuse my mother. Once she gets going…well…she gets gone pretty quickly."

"It's quite all right. You have an interesting family, if I do say so. The other day, I met your grandmother."

"You mean Abuelita. She's a twelve-gauge personality for sure. Not my grandmother, though she might as well be."

"Not your grandmother? She's a great-aunt then?"

"No. I don't think there's a name for what she is to me. It's not conventional, let's say."

"But she's related in some way?"

"I'll give it to you straight. Abuelita was once married to a younger man. My mother, seated on the floor behind you, was later married to an older man—the same man. So, I'm the product of that second marriage. Abuelita is my father's first wife, but not my grandmother."

"I see."

"So, Abuelita is not officially related to me, but she was like a grandmother growing up."

"So, what's unusual here is the living arrangement," said Nigel, trying to grasp the layout. "In my experience, ex-wives generally don't mix except at funerals, weddings, and murder-for-hire parties."

"Yeah, well, my mother is not exactly conventional, and Abuelita doesn't know what conventional means. The story goes that my dad left Abuelita because he had an interest in my mom, who was a maid at the old Sandoval house. I don't know if that's true. Parents don't talk about such things with their kids. People say when the breakup became public knowledge, the police department stationed officers outside the house 24/7. To everyone's surprise, the split was handled amicably. Only two shots fired, and that was at a pair of boots."

"Abuelita didn't care?"

"You might say she made a soft landing. Word was that she already had a love interest with the gardener, a guy called Guapo. Plus, Abuelita, as it turned out, was a shrewd businesswoman. She'd already obtained most of the family wealth in her own name. From that point on, her wealth expanded while father's dwindled. As far as calamitous events in her life, the divorce probably wasn't in the top five."

"She's had some adventures, has she?"

"She certainly has. To see her now though, it's like the fizz has gone out. You know how she met Dad?"

"I'm guessing not at a church cotillion?"

"He saw her in a burlesque show in Laredo."

"In Laredo. Imagine that." Nigel was trying not to imagine that—and having a difficult time of it.

"She had this act. She wore a vest—no shirt, just a vest—a pair of six-shooters, and chaps. There are posters if you don't believe me."

"I believe you."

"She was known for plucking cigarettes out of the mouths of audience members with her bullwhip. One night, it must have been in the fifties, Dad was one of those audience members. On this night, Abuelita—or as she was known at the time, Sola Pistola and her 45s—was off the mark. The whip caught him on the lower lip. Have you ever had your lip flicked with a bullwhip, Mr. Nigel?"

"If I have, I don't remember."

"Anyway, it knocked Dad right to the floor. Apparently, Sola Pistola knew what to do. Dad said in his wedding vows, 'She administered first aid in ways not administered before or since.' They were married before the swelling went down."

"That is quite the love story."

"Isn't it? But it wasn't all whiskey and bullwhips. Abuelita already had a daughter when they were married—"

"That would be Essie?" said Nigel, recalling the mother-in-law's story.

"You know that? What else do you know about her?"

"Ran away very young with a Griesen boy."

"Well, you know everything. I've never even met her. She was gone before I was born. They also had a son who died young, then they were divorced. Dad married Mom, and then I happened."

"Gastrrrrrick! What did you put in that last tequila? It tasted horrible," bellowed Mrs. Sandoval while Gastrick collected the dishes and glasses.

"You must be referring to the glass of water I brought with your ice cream," he answered.

"Glass of water? What was in it?"

"Water."

"It's gone flat. No more of that, Gastrick, or I'll throw you to the snake."

"Looking forward to it, ma'am."

Stefanie looked at Nigel with an expression that was two parts exasperation and one part embarrassment.

"But how, if you don't mind my asking," said Nigel in a low voice, "did you, your mother, and Abuelita end up living together? It seems an odd arrangement."

"Mom, even though she was marrying Abuelita's husband, was just too valuable as a home administrator for her to let go. It was kind of a custody agreement. Dad could have her as a wife as long as Abuelita could keep her as an administrator. Mom not only got a husband but a big raise, which was great because we needed the money."

"I thought the Sandovals were rich," said Nigel.

"So did Dad. He lived like it long after we weren't. He disappeared while on an anthropological expedition to the Amazon when I was five. He'd financed an outfit hoping to uncover lost ruins. At some point, he became separated from the expedition and was lost in the jungle. Abuelita put up money for a search, which turned up a flask, a sock, and a few dodgy witnesses. One said he'd gone native in the jungle. Another said he'd been kidnapped and killed by drug traffickers, and another claimed he was the last known victim of tribal cannibalism in South America. I think that last story was concocted to make us feel special."

"And what do you believe?"

"I believe it was suicide in some form or other. The expedition wasn't exactly sponsored by *National Geographic*, you understand. These guys were looking for a payday, and once it became clear that wasn't going to happen, I think Dad decided not to come back. We had to sell off our house just to pay the debts. Given our situation, Abuelita took us in, and we've been living under one roof, a small dysfunctional family, ever since."

"That's quite a family history. It's fortunate you get along so well."

"Isn't it? Except for the two, or three, or four times a week when one of us tries to murder one or the other of us, we get along great. Of course, taking away Abuelita's pistols was a step change for home safety. Now Gastrick has time to intercede before the fatalities mount up. 'It's not the time,' he'll say. I'm waiting for that day when he grows tired of the whole mess and says, 'Okay, ladies, it's time.' "

"Life here must be a non-stop merry-go-round," said Nigel while thinking of a cuckoo's nest.

The family history was interesting but didn't explain the giant snake. Nor did Mrs. Sandoval's reasons for Duffy's escapes explain the dog's appearance at Nigel's place. Perhaps Stefanie, the household's only level head, might provide a better explanation. "My actual reason for coming today was about your dog, Duffy. He's in my possession, again—"

"How do you keep finding our dog?"

"A good question. Equally good is, 'Why do you keep losing him?' "

"To that, I have no answer. I have little to do with the dog. Mother is the owner." She nodded in the direction of Mrs. Sandoval, seated barefoot on the floor, whistling a rousing rendition of the *Bridge on the River Kwai* theme while conducting with her own slippers. "As you can see, with her, anything is possible."

"She seems to think she let the dog out. I have my doubts about that, but he's been escaping somehow. I don't want to sound demanding, but before I return him again, I'd like some assurance that he'll be properly kept. Bad things can happen to stray dogs wandering about the countryside, especially when they look like Duffy. I have nightmares of one day walking into some Believe-It-or-Not museum and seeing Duffy, stuffed, behind glass, presented as the mythical hound from hell. Gives me goosebumps. Can you tell me that won't happen?"

"That won't happen," said Stefanie, laughing. "Rest easy. I'll put Gastrick in charge of the dog's security."

"Gastrick? Duffy doesn't seem to like Gastrick."

"Doesn't matter. Gastrick will do his duty. He's very efficient."

"I'll take your word for it," said Nigel, gathering his galoshes. "I should be going. I've taken enough of your time."

"Very well. Abuelita will be down soon, and Mother will be back up."

"Give my regards to dear Abuelita when you see her. I'm afraid she doesn't much like me."

"She threw something at you?"

"Not a physical object, but—"

"She likes you fine then. Since we took away her guns, she always carries a few projectiles. If she didn't unload on you, then you're on her good side."

"I'm glad you took the guns away. You're a responsible parent."

"Someone has to be," she said over Mrs. Sandoval's snoring.

With that, Nigel turned to face the treacherous fifty feet of polished marble floor between him and the exit. Once, at a corporate management retreat, he had walked barefoot across twenty feet of smoking hot coals. The exercise was intended to infuse him with fearlessness. What he recalled was the number of extinguishers, firemen, and burn medications they kept on hand. He wondered if the Sandovals kept a supply of inflatable casts and smelling salts.

Gastrick waited by the door with crossed arms and tapping foot. Nigel prepared himself mentally and physically for the voyage. He took one galosh in each hand, hoping to emulate the counterbalancing poles used by tightrope walkers.

He took a baby step—swish. He took another—swish. After twenty more—swish, swish, swish—he was within leaping distance of the door.

"What's that pervert doing here?" a voice cackled. An approaching electric whir signaled trouble. Nigel shuffled his feet to make a 180-degree turn.

"Hello Abuelita, so nice to see you—"

The wheelchair—with a full head of steam—cracked into Nigel's shins. His stockinged feet, as if riding atop two air hockey pucks, slid backward while his arms—galosh in each hand—slowly windmilled. The hollow double-thud of galoshes impacting the floor drowned out the sound of Nigel's kneecaps hitting marble and the flump of Nigel's head onto Abuelita's lap.

The spacious atrium shook with an unholy, blood-curdling screech—the screech of a victim being drawn into damnation's eternal hellfire. For miles around, nerve endings in animals, vegetables, and minerals cowered and quivered until Nigel's lungs gave out.

Then it was Abuelita's turn. She unleashed a blasphemous barrage that, had it been intelligible, would have turned long-shoremen to stone.

For Nigel—entombed in the dark, hostile environment between Abuelita's thighs—the invectives reverberated through canyon and crevice, around fleshly folds and through porous bone matter, spinning into something eerie and horrific. As distasteful as the current predicament was, "facing" Abuelita was hardly more palatable. Not only was he being verbally abused, but his head was under assault from what felt like a cloud of malnourished bats. Nigel looked up from the deathly hollow.

"Hello, Abuelita—"

The cloud of bats dispersed just before Nigel's head went peanut-shaped beneath the thunderous clap of an open hand on either ear. Nigel wobbled to either side before falling to the left.

After smiting the death blow, Abuelita rose from her wheelchair for a victory jig. "Maniac!" she yelled before letting fly a surprisingly spry kick to a vulnerable part of the body.

"Abuelita, don't kick our guest," interceded Stefanie.

"He's a fiend. Last time he tried to kiss me. You saw what he did this time. In my day, someone who did that without so much as a 'Howdy, ma'am' would be thrown under a train."

"Abuelita, you know it was just an accident. This man is here about our dog."

"Mangy mongrel!"

"No, no, no. We love our dog," said Stefanie.

"I wasn't talking about no dog!" she said, shaking her fist.

"Nigel," said Stefanie, addressing the tightly-curled body, "perhaps you'd better go. Abuelita's feeling cranky."

"Very well," said Nigel, raising his head just enough to see Abuelita. "I hope you feel better soon."

"I feel great right now. That ass-kickin' did wonders. You come around here again, and we'll have another go." She turned and motored away while gleefully tittering.

Feeling the storm had passed, Nigel got to his feet and swished his way to the door. "I'll bring the dog tomorrow, if that's all right."

"That would be fine," replied Stefanie. "I'll try to keep Abuelita in her cage."

"I would not want to meet her in a cage."

Nigel slipped on the galoshes and limped out the open door to his car. As he circled the drive, he noticed Gastrick pacing the porch, looking down at one side and then the other while scratching his head.

15

FORTY-SIX, PART TWO

The oddities emanating from the Sandoval estate were piling up: the unexplained drowning, the teleporting dog, and now, the big snake. Were they connected? Was anyone, other than Nigel, even considering the possibility? Even if the conundrums didn't add up to one big mystery, it was all certainly mysterious. There was an allure—a pull, as it were—to solving these riddles that painting baseboards just couldn't compete with.

After refreshing himself at home, Nigel headed into town to quiz the local populace on the subject of monstrous snakes. No way was this morning's wrestling partner a local boy, and New Antigua wasn't known for attracting foreigners, human or reptile. Someone must know something.

First stop was the animal shelter. As much as Nigel wanted to leap inside and talk snake, something restrained him. He would have liked to believe otherwise, but the source of the blockage was clear: A possible encounter with Unsurpassed Beauty Number 46.

This common schoolboy malady—the fear of the beautiful woman—might be expected to diminish with advancing age due to life experience, falling testosterone levels, and a jack-booted wife waiting at home. But for Nigel, not only had it persisted, it had worsened. Advancing age had merely compounded the effect with added layers of the kind of pitiful self-loathing that overtakes a middle-aged, married man who's been left dumbstruck by a siren less than half his age. The Germans probably have a word for this. Nigel didn't know the word, but he knew the feeling as well as any German ever could.

At times like these, Dora Hart—Unsurpassed Beauty Number 1—came upon him like a fever. It was autumn term —year three of primary—when Nigel first laid eyes on her. It was love at first sight, though Dora failed to notice. There was no mistaking the passion, as demonstrated by an entire semester of Nigel's furtive glances from across the room.

Then, at the start of spring term, as if through divine providence, seats were reassigned. Nigel found himself seated beside Dora, the love of his life. Not as good as being marooned together on an island, but a darned good opportunity, nonetheless. Nigel spent weeks crafting an irresistible opening line and then waited patiently for the perfect circumstance in which to unleash it. While the details have faded, this devastating opener had, at its core, a clever compliment of Dora's unrivaled pasting skills.

Each new school day began with high excitement yet ended with a gnashing of teeth as the perfect setting for Nigel's line failed to materialize. Finally, with just one week left in the term, the opportunity presented itself. Dora wielded her paste wand like a young Michelangelina. Nigel wiped the snot from his nose and leaned in to deliver the most seductive line ever heard in Oatlands Primary.

But before the first syllable had been uttered, Dora turned to him, and referring to his latest work, she said, "I like your clouds."

Nigel's stomach dropped to the floor. What the hell was that? After all the waiting and all the work to deliver the perfect line at the perfect time, she steps in and tramples it. Nigel was stunned. A proper rejoinder would take months to develop. "Oh," Nigel said in a rather abbreviated, choked manner.

He may have appeared calm on the outside, but inside, he panicked. His destiny—a life of cartoons and firefighting with Dora Hart by his side—was swirling like a dead goldfish down the toilet. Within seconds, his opportunity would be gone forever. But Nigel recovered himself. This shaken eight-year-old found, somewhere deep within, the courage of a lion. Nigel turned to Dora, looked her in the eye for the first time, and said, "Want to see me eat paste?" Nigel had never eaten paste, but he'd seen his brother do it. It was a show-stopper, and his brother was still alive.

Dora crinkled her nose as if someone had popped a tin of anchovies under it. The cuteness embodied in her expression of disgust could not hide her disdain. She turned away. Nigel never recovered. He had learned just how unpredictable the opposite sex could be.

With a beginning like that, it's no wonder that Nigel's interactions with beautiful women had been fraught. Typical encounters began with Nigel feeling diseased and ended with him feeling trampled by a thousand stiletto heels. He girded himself for the upcoming battle by engaging in a heart-to-heart with his life-coaching self.

Coach Nigel: *What is your problem, man? Get it together. That girl in there means nothing to you. You're sweating like a pig in a sauna, and for what?*
Nigel: *Stop yelling. You know as well as I do, that girl is trouble. You remember Dora—*
Coach Nigel: *Stop! Stop! Stop with the Dora! You know how you*

are. It starts with Dora, and then it's Penelope, and then it's Emma, and two hours later, you've presented the full production of My Sorry Life: A Calamity in Forty-Six Parts. But you know what? None of that has anything to do with that girl in there. Nothing. Nada. Zero. Zip. This is a whole new ballgame.

Nigel: *But you've seen that girl. You know what I'm up against. Devastating. Too, too devastating.*

Coach Nigel: *She is, isn't she? I'll give you that. Feel good about your taste. It's impeccable.*

Nigel: *Listen to you! Must I remind you, we're a happily married, middle-aged man. We don't need to be thinking of how incredible she is. You're making our skin crawl. Come on now, we've got to stick together on this, or we have no hope. You're supposed to be logical. Feed me some logic.*

Coach Nigel: *Logical? Me? I thought you were the logical one.*

Nigel: *Okay. Try this logic on for size. To that girl in there, we're her father's age, and probably less attractive. That's what she thinks of us: repulsive versions of her father.*

Coach Nigel: *What if she has a thing for older men?*

Nigel: *I knew it! You're the cause of all this. You're harboring a deep-seated conceit that she might somehow find us attractive. That's ridiculous. Look at her, then look at us in a mirror. We might as well be a toad.*

Coach Nigel: *You never know, man. You never know.*

Nigel: *Okay, say she finds us somewhat more attractive than a toad. What does that do for us?*

Coach Nigel: *It's a boost to the self-esteem. We could use that.*

Nigel: *If Annie found us thinking like that, she'd give us a boost all right, and not to the self-esteem. Hey! That's an idea. The wife. She can shut down pretty much anything. What if she were here?*

Coach Nigel: *Ding-dong. Telegram. She ain't here.*

Nigel: *She could be, Coach. She could be. Hey, look who's coming? Speak of the devil.*

Coach Nigel: *Yikes! I'm outta here. Three's a crowd.*

Nigel: *Later, Coach. I'll take it from here. What's up, Annie? Have I got a job for you.*

Nigel sauntered into the animal shelter with Annie, the figment, alongside. Imaginary Annie commented incessantly about the wall decorations, the shaggy little puppy, the boy fingering his nose, and pretty much everything that Nigel laid eyes on. This ghostly strain of Annie had a jabbering streak the real one could not have tolerated. Spirit Annie performed so well in her appointed role that Nigel wondered if she might be persuaded to talk to Annie the Real about a certain to-do list.

Figment Annie was commenting on the ductwork as Nigel edged toward the counter. Miss Unsurpassed Forty-Six was at the counter, bent down over a cage. Figment Annie commented she might be entertaining a kitten.

Nigel took a deep breath. As he was about to speak, Annie appeared behind the girl in full cop uniform. One hand caressed her holstered sidearm, ready to draw. The other hand held a pitchfork at launch position, aimed at Nigel's heart. Exactly the kind of encouragement he needed.

"Excuse me, ma'am, I—"

The gorgeous young siren turned toward him. Nigel staggered back slightly as the exquisite young face rounded into view. Figment Annie bared her teeth while holding up a noose. Nigel stood tall and then noticed the young girl's lovely, bare arm held away from her body with bent elbow. Crawling upon that delicate appendage was the largest, hairiest, most menacing tarantula Nigel had ever laid eyes on. Annie had vanished.

"I'm sorry, I was just giving Legs some exercise. I didn't mean to startle you," she said, stroking the prowling spider.

Nigel, while not particularly fearful of spiders, was growing weary of these unexpected encounters.

"Always a creepy creature," muttered Nigel. "You, eh, do this for sport?"

"No, but I'm one of the few at the shelter who doesn't mind working with them. Most people here like dogs and cats, but when it comes to the reptiles, arachnids, and vermin, they back off. I believe every creature needs a place in the world."

"Yes, certainly. That place must be your arm. Fortunate creatures." Nigel looked for Annie. She was across the room looking at puppies. He decided to leave her be.

"Legs was a secret pet for a fourteen-year-old boy until his mother found him in the dirty laundry. Someone had to go, so Legs ended up here."

"Mexican redknee?" Nigel squeaked out. He was doing okay. Plenty of symptoms—rigid jaw, sweating like Niagara, tongue like a dead ferret—but he was holding together.

"Wow! You know your spiders!"

"Mostly from books. I used to read them as a youth. I mean, I used to read about them—spiders, I mean—in books. I never had one to play. Spiders, I mean. I had books." Nigel noticed how her crystalline blue eyes highlighted her pearlescent complexion—the girl, not the spider. Annie was nowhere to be seen. "I have a question, and you seem like the one to ask."

"Sure, what?"

"Have any snakes come in? Big ones?"

"Well, we have Indigo. He's the only snake we have right now."

"Nothing bigger?"

"How big?"

"Twenty feet, maybe," said Nigel.

"Twenty feet? That's crazy! Are you serious?" she asked with obvious enthusiasm.

"Maybe twenty-two. Who knows? I didn't measure," said

Nigel, noticing an outstanding array of dimples breaking across the girl's incredulous face.

"What do you mean you didn't measure?"

"Didn't bother to measure the, eh, anaconda I captured this morning."

"You captured? How? Where?"

Nigel placed his hands on the desk and leaned toward the enthralled girl. "In a creek south of here. I wrestled him out of the water. Touch and go for a while, but I got the better of him. A couple of police showed up later to haul it off to animal control. That's where it is, animal control. The snake, it's there—animal control."

"An anaconda? That's amazing. I've never heard of such a thing."

"One does what one has to do," said Nigel. He gutted out a smile, thinking how cool he was in the eyes of this impressionable snake-loving lass.

She smiled back.

Annie must have drifted outside.

"That is so cool!" said the girl. Her dad probably didn't fight snakes.

Nigel reflected for a moment on what a fine afternoon it had turned out to be. "Do you like toads?" asked Nigel.

The lovely waif giggled endearingly. Nigel was strangely at ease. What a joy—no, joy wasn't the correct word, relief—it was to find common ground with such a charming young lady. A sense of warmth pervaded his soul. His radiant mood was reinforced by a series of gentle, affectionate pats on his right hand as it rested on the desk. He could not help but smile at the finely-featured girl cradling her delicate chin with her smoothly sculpted hand while the other folded back her silky, blonde hair. Nigel felt the soft stroke of dainty fingers on the back of his resting hand.

Hold on! he thought.

Nigel looked down at his hand. What he saw was a Mexican redknee tarantula the size of a dinner plate. Had Annie—the real one—been there, she would have done something heroic, like put five bullets through it. Annie, the figment, was nowhere to be seen.

Giant spiders, especially in contact with bare skin, promote quick decision-making. So it was with Nigel. He reclaimed his hand, and he reclaimed it fast. So fast that, had his arm not been so firmly attached at the shoulder, the whole assembly would have made a handsome dent in the ceiling. As it was, the shoulder, arm, and hand whipped upward to max extent, then fell back into place, cleansed of tarantula.

A substantial number of Nigel's university days had been spent studying the basic laws of motion. Most of that knowledge had long been displaced, but he still recalled something about *"an object in motion tending to remain in motion,"* and so forth, and so on. Legs, the tarantula, had no university training, but in short order, he had become intimate with the concept. He fulfilled his role as *"the object"* with surprising aplomb, whirling through the air like the emancipated blade of a circular saw. A Mexican redknee tarantula spinning at high velocity is a rare and handsome sight. The sound, a delicate whirl, is also not altogether unpleasant.

Nigel, had he the inclination, might also have recalled that the object in motion tends to remain in motion *"unless acted upon by an external force."* The *"external force"* in this case was the fleshy forehead of a heavy-set mother of three named Thelma Phlegmbocker. Thelma was an intelligent woman, judging by the sound of tarantula striking forehead. A firm "thwud" indicated solid mass through and through. The brainy Mrs. Phlegmbocker had enjoyed a satisfyingly eventful life to this point, having visited both Canada and Mexico. However, her energetic reaction at being struck in the forehead by a whirling tarantula suggested it was, for her, something new.

She let loose a high-pitched screech, which brought to standing attention every hair on every mammal in the place. Mrs. Phlegmbocker's wail soon developed an oscillation, correlated to the frequency with which she bounced up and down. When a woman of Mrs. Phlegmbocker's stature bounces up and down, a lot of things—on her person and in the vicinity—bounce up and down with her. Coal, a two-year-old black Labrador retriever, was delighted to learn that his new owner was the "bouncing up and down" type. Between bounces, Coal spotted an object on the seismically active floor resembling a glove. He had learned from his previous owner that gloves were a form of chew toy sometimes worn by humans. Had Coal possessed a more refined mathematical sense, he would have noted entirely too many fingers, but arithmetic wasn't his thing. Knowing that dropped gloves often led to exciting games of tug-of-war, he went for it. Coal quickly realized he'd found himself not a glove, but a tarantula.

By this time, Mrs. Phlegmbocker had been settled down by a bevy of concerned bystanders who gathered to inspect the pink whirling-tarantula imprint on her forehead. This moment of tranquility was interrupted by gagging noises as Coal ejected the slimed and disoriented source of trauma. Following a preamble of pointing and stuttering, Mrs. Phlegmbocker resumed the wailing and the bouncing. Intent on stopping the calamitous display, a large, ample-bellied, Stetson-lidded man stepped forward. The body of the arachnid disappeared under the well-aimed heel of his size-thirteen cowboy boot loaded up with 280 pounds—290 with belt buckle—of triumphant Texan. The memory of Legs the spider will live on—not so much as a spider, but as a stain.

Nigel watched helplessly as the tragedy unfolded. Half

the populace consoled the traumatized woman while the other half patted some part of the massive back of the big cowboy. The only two not in the mix were Nigel and the lovely Forty-Six. Nigel turned to face the girl, who moments earlier, had showered him with metaphorical rose petals as the great snake-conqueror of Tonkawa County. His eyes met hers for a fraction of a second, long enough for him to feel showered by the metaphorical opposite of rose petals.

"I'm sorry," said Nigel. As an expression of sympathy, it was weak. Given the facts of the situation—the newness of their relationship, the freshness of the tragedy, the deceased being a tarantula, himself being the killer—one could see the situation was difficult. Even an old pro like the pope, should he have found himself in such a situation, would have been at a loss for words.

Nigel stood for a moment at the desk, hoping he might receive some sign of forgiveness from the stunned blonde. She managed a grimace while shaking her head from side to side. Her tightly drawn lips, Nigel noted, revealed near-perfect teeth. Then, from behind the grieving beauty, appeared Figment Annie in marine camouflage, clenching a Bowie knife between her teeth and wielding a flame thrower.

"Too late," muttered Nigel. He turned for the exit.

———

"I bet you had a busy day," said Nigel, poking his head into the animal control office. Leslie Dole stood at her desk in the later stages of filleting a largemouth bass. Of course, Nigel wouldn't have recognized it as such. One, because he didn't know what one was, and two, because of the deconstructed nature of the thing. On one side of the desk were two slabs of fish flesh. On the other was a wet pile of largemouth bass components minus two slabs of fish flesh.

"Not as busy as you from what I hear," she said, using her forearm to sweep bass parts into a bucket.

"You mean that little episode with the tarantula? Well, those things happen. Unfortunate, really."

"A tarantula? I was talking about the snake. What's this about a tarantula?"

"Oh, the snake. Yes, the snake. That was an adventure, indeed."

Of course, Nigel was there to inquire about the snake, but with so many exploits underfoot, how was one to keep track? Between the dog, the snake, the tarantula, the galoshes, and the to-do list, he needed a spreadsheet.

"It's the talk of the town," said Leslie, sponging up bass juice. "You're a local celebrity: the Englishman squeezed by a snake. It's headline gossip—that and Alma Stoppelschuk's bowel blockage."

"So Alma has a bowel blockage, does she?" Nigel hadn't met poor Alma, but in a small town, unfamiliarity seems no impediment to gossip. "Now that I've resolved the local snake problem, maybe I should head over to Alma's and see what I can do with a bowel."

"So, you're good with bowel blockages?"

"Never know until you try. When I woke up this morning, I didn't feel I had anything to teach a snake, but there you go. One thing leads to another, and now I'm your go-to giant snake wrangler."

"Just to make you aware," said Leslie, drawing closer as if imparting a word to the wise, "the story I've heard is that Deputy Winjack—you know, the Barney guy—was the wrangler. You were more like the bait."

"The bait?" said Nigel, extending his neck.

"Maybe bait's not the right word. More like damsel in distress."

"Damsel in distress?" said Nigel, extending his neck still

further.

"Not that you were a damsel by any means, but in distress. And then Barney, Deputy Winjack, shows up to save you. That's what's going around anyway."

Nigel's head shot up on its stalk, jerking and swiveling like a turkey's after hearing a chop. "Oh, it is, is it?"

"'Tis."

"I really don't care who plays the hero," said Nigel, pushing an index finger repeatedly into the desktop. "But when that rubber-faced deputy arrived, I had the serpent's head in a death grip. I was deliberating on a place to dispatch the animal. If Deputy Droopyface saved anyone, it was the snake."

"I believe you. Thunder-stealin' is just the kind of a thing that deputy would do. To hear him tell the story, he and a fellow officer were proceeding to location in their squad car when out of the creek staggers a weak, flaccid Englishman wearing one shoe and covered in anaconda. Struggling Englishman, face turning blue, collapses in middle of street. He and fellow officer jump into action, unwind said snake, saving life of ungrateful, bluish Brit. That's the story I heard," said Leslie, "several times now."

"Flaccid?" said Nigel.

"His word, not mine. If you want the story told with style, get in touch with Luke, the tow-truck driver. He puts the mustard on it. He's over at the Blowout most evenings. He might be charging admission by now."

"Flaccid?" said Nigel.

"If you've got the real story, you go right ahead and tell it your way. I'm here to listen, and I'll help pass it on," she said, dropping bass slabs into an ice chest.

"I might hold on to it," said Nigel, "for publication rights."

"If that's the way you want it."

That wasn't the way he wanted it, but he figured he'd lost any chance to shape the narrative. "I came about the snake," said Nigel. "Is it around?"

"If you wanted to visit the snake, too late. Already shipped out."

"To where?"

"The Houston Zoo."

"You got a zoo to take him just like that?"

"Not exactly. The zoo were rightful owners. He's microchipped, so it wasn't difficult to track down. The mystery is how he ended up here. He was supposed to go to the zoo about two months ago but never showed up. The delivery van was stolen somewhere east of Houston, and the snake goes missing. Then he turns up here a hundred miles away. I don't think he crawled here. Someone must have brought him. How, or why, is anybody's guess."

"You said twelve foot. You measured it?"

"Yep, twelve foot, two inches."

"Are you sure? I would have thought at least fifteen."

"People exaggerate the size of their snakes," said Leslie. "It's unbelievable. Luke probably has it at fifty by now."

"Will the police investigate?"

"The size of the snake?"

"The snake abduction."

"I doubt it. It's a snake, not someone's grandma. Why do you ask? Expanding your business into lost snakes?"

"No. Just curious. Once you've wrestled a snake, you feel like you've got a stake."

"What about your lost dog?"

"Found him twice."

"You must be good. And that tarantula? Another runaway?"

"If it's all the same to you, I'll keep that to myself," said Nigel. "Publication rights."

16

DUFFY BACK, ANNIE OUT

The next morning, Nigel drove to the Sandoval place with Duffy in steerage. Crossing over the creek, Nigel saw no signs of the recent tragedy except a deep set of tire ruts between the creek and the road. Sunlight, shining through the tree cover, dappled the languid, brown water. The cicadas buzzed, birds sang, and frogs croaked.

All appeared normal, yet a pestilence of butterflies in Nigel's gut told him things were not as they seemed. He was, after all, approaching the Sandoval house to return Duffy, their dog that had inexplicably appeared on his own doorstep fifteen miles away. Not once, but twice. And then there was the sad death of the Griesen youth on the Sandoval estate. It seemed an odd place for a Griesen youth to die. What was he doing there? And if the Sandoval estate was an odd location for a Griesen youth, what about an anaconda? Even the place itself seemed strange—a former golf course and country club occupied as living quarters for three women.

Did this confluence of oddities justify an investigation? No one else seemed to think so. Maybe none of this was wacko after all. Maybe this was all pretty average stuff in a

Texas town, and poor Nigel, trapped in his suffocatingly conventional lifestyle, just didn't know what normal was.

What would Annie think? The weirder things got, the more Nigel could use her opinion. But Annie was off limits. Explaining the Sandoval situation would force Nigel to explain himself. A blue chill gripped Nigel as he imagined confessing that he'd hijacked her agency for a dog case. Annie might morph into her mother on the spot.

The Sandoval property looked eerily empty as Nigel parked next to the ever-present yellow exotic car. He was set upon by Gastrick as he opened the car door.

"Hello, Mr. Blandwater-Cummings."

Nigel had known families with butlers back in England. Butlers produced in Nigel an uneasiness, not unlike the discomfort some people feel around dentists or clowns. The trouble with butlers was their presumed superiority. It had been Nigel's observation that butlers were at least twice as smart as the people they worked for. You would think, as members of the servant class, they would conceal this fact. On the contrary, they emphasized it—not as normal people would, by spouting facts and correcting the stupid—but by saying nothing while raising one of those imposing eyebrows they all have. If Nigel needed a dose of humility, he needed only converse with a butler while watching the eyebrow.

This butler, Gastrick, while about half as haughty as the average English variety, was of their ilk. He had the cultivated eyebrow and seldom passed up an opportunity to show you his nostrils. He spoke with a strange affectedness, like those actors from old movies who pretended to be from someplace midway over the Atlantic Ocean.

"Hello, Gastrick. I've brought Duffy home once again." Nigel opened the rear door, where Duffy awaited with a galosh in his mouth. Nigel pulled the boot close while blocking the view from Gastrick, who was stretching himself for a peek inside. Duffy, always up for a tug-of-war, growled and pulled. Nigel and Duffy discovered together that vulcanized walrus hide, apart from being premium galosh material, was the stuff of tug-toy dreams. The gleeful dog—his teeth buried in the gnarled folds and wrinkles—took to the game with the vigor of a prizefighter practicing uppercuts against his sparring partner from the Last Sunset Retirement Home.

"Come on, boy. Release! Let go. Drop it. Stop, please," said Nigel, hoping for the magic unclamping combination.

Gastrick, meanwhile, did his best giraffe impression, trying to glimpse the action through the front windshield.

Once Nigel remembered the leftover dog biscuit in his pocket, the game was over.

"I'm sure Duffy is glad to be home again," said Nigel.

Gastrick didn't respond, as he was busy peering over the open car door and onto the floorboard, where Nigel had dropped the slobbery galosh.

"Yes, I'm sure," he said, attempting to peer over Nigel's shoulder as the leash was pressed into his hand.

"Weather's not too bad today," said Nigel.

"Not if you enjoy hot and suffocating," said Gastrick, raising an eyebrow.

"Is Stefanie around?"

"She is out. I don't expect her back before evening."

"I see. Tell me, have the police said anything about the person who drowned in the creek?"

"Not much. They were more intent on asking than telling. What I know is that he was a young man named Griesen. Apparently, he was involved in some petty crimes, thievery, drugs—things of that sort. He probably wasn't on a good path, from what I understand. He had gone to Houston for a job but came back jobless. No one knows why he was on our drive. Probably made a wrong turn. If he did know where he was, it was probably for bad intent."

"It sounds like a sad end to a sad life."

"I suppose. You never know what might have been."

"Will they do anything about that road?"

"It's a private drive. I don't think they have to. They didn't the last time."

"The last time?"

Gastrick gazed down the road, as he had been since the conversation turned to the accident. He spoke in a standard butlerish tone—calm, measured, and unemotional. "Thirty-some years ago, when this property had just opened as a golf course, there was a drowning in that very spot."

"A drowning? There? Do people know about that?" asked Nigel.

"The people in this house know about it very well. It was Abuelita's son."

The soup thickens. All these occurrences *felt* as if they had significance, yet nothing obviously connected. Was this what investigations were like? Or was Nigel's overactive imagination transforming innocent clouds into sinister objects?

"Abuelita's son? I had heard about him," said Nigel. Thinking aloud, he continued, "So Abuelita bought this property after her son died on the grounds? That seems odd. Why would she do that?"

"Your guess is as good as mine. There were all kinds of rumors and speculation. Some people thought she did it to communicate with his spirit, like he might be haunting the place. Others speculated she did it for revenge. She may have felt the golf club was somehow responsible. If you believe the rumors, she promised to keep the club open, but then closed it as soon as the papers were signed. There are still quite a few golfers in town that would like to wrap a nine iron around her neck."

"That seems a bit hostile."

"You don't play golf, do you, Mr. Blandwater-Cummings?"

"The game haunts me, but no, I don't."

"You'd be safer standing between a mama grizzly and her cub than between some of these golf crazies and their game."

"Do the police know about the old accident?"

"The police? Why would they care about an accident from thirty years ago?"

"Don't you find it strange that there's a death in the same place thirty years later?"

"It's tragic. I don't know that it's strange," said Gastrick. His tone, still butlerish, had taken on a harder edge, as if he were growing tired of the conversation.

"It seems beyond tragic for a single property like this to have two such similar deaths. I don't know what to think about that."

"I would suggest you not think about it. It's not for you to sort out. You've brought us back our dog, and you shouldn't have anything more to do here." He pulled out his wallet and counted out five twenties. "Here, I'm sure Mrs. Sandoval would want you to have this for your trouble."

"Thank you. Tell her I appreciate it. I really wasn't doing this for the money."

"Nevertheless, it's appreciated," he said, sounding not terribly appreciative.

"Enough to eat, dear?" said Nigel, taking away the dishes.

"Stuffed. Thanks for fixing dinner," said Annie, pushing herself away from the table. "This kind of work is boring enough. At least I won't be hungry."

"So, what kind of work is it?"

"Just snooping."

"You'll be gone all night, and that's all I get? Just snooping?"

"You know I don't bring my business home. I will say I'm getting paid good money for this one. A gig like this every week, and I could retire early."

"That'd be great. I'm already making your to-do list," said Nigel, pulling her close.

"Don't start. I've got to get going."

"Just reminding you of what's waiting at home."

"Yeah? What's that?"

"A handsome man."

"Where? Under the bed?"

"On second thought, you best run along," said Nigel. "Rest assured, should you come to deadly harm, I will continue to work on the to-do list, and won't remarry for an appropriate amount of time. Be safe." He dropped an orange and a couple of granola bars into a brown paper bag before holding it at arm's length. Annie took the bag and embraced him.

"I love you," she said.

"How could you not?"

He chose to ignore the eye rolls. With Annie out the door, it was his turn.

17

A PLEASANT EVENING'S STROLL

Finally, some real detective work, thought Nigel. The first order of business was to find proper stakeout attire. Black—hopefully comfortable, ideally expendable—but definitely black. His closet was packed with non-black clothes. The whole operation teetered on the precipice until he recalled the old clothes in the trunk of his car. More specifically, he recalled the swishy pants. Noisy perhaps, but unfailingly black. Now he needed a top.

Nigel foraged the closets until stumbling upon a giant garbage bag full of Annie's future goodwill donations. He tore into the black plastic, and within minutes, he recovered an over-sized knit number in the desired color. He recalled his wife wearing the garment, which had prompted him to comment on the giant folds of fabric hanging loosely about the neck, whereupon she informed him it was a style known as a cowl neck, whereupon he said "Mooooo," whereupon she made it known that he was a fashion moron.

Nigel, checking himself out in the full-length mirror, would have preferred something more military and less chic. The outfit was ludicrous without question, but it didn't matter. No one would see him in it. That was the idea—to not be seen. He pondered for a moment, thinking of the unhappy ramifications should he be found dead while swathed in the pathetic get-up. Nigel resolved to not be found dead.

Nigel pulled his car over some distance short of the Sandoval house, parking his car behind some hedges. As it was already close to midnight, no one was likely to pass this way before he'd return in the wee hours of the morning.

He stuffed his swishy pants pockets with a granola bar and a few dog biscuits. He opened a flat, round can of brown shoe polish and smeared the paste on his face, hands, and forearms. Even under the modest glow of a half-moon, he could see the shoe polish didn't blacken his skin so much as toast it. Before starting his trek to the Sandoval mansion, Nigel retrieved the galoshes from the floorboard of his car. A clandestine return of the heirloom footwear would be an added bonus to his night's surveillance work. He considered taking his cell phone but thought the risk of losing it far outweighed its usefulness in such an operation.

The plan was to watch the Sandovals' dog enclosure from a concealed location. It seemed bloody obvious that Duffy wasn't escaping just to enjoy a fifteen-mile stroll to Nigel's place. He'd been transported there, twice. The old brain muscle scarcely needed to work up a lather to see the hidden hand of a dognapper at work. Duffy had been stolen and moved to a secret lair. A lair that was likely in Nigel's own neighborhood.

Even more tantalizing was the question of *why* he'd been snatched. A ransom, possibly, but none had been demanded. Foiled perhaps by Duffy's elusiveness. But Nigel looked toward an even darker motive. The night of Griesen's death, Duffy was not on the premises. Was this a coincidence or a plan? Could it be that Griesen, the young ne'er-do-well, came to the Sandoval property for a purpose? And could it be that

Duffy had been removed from the property to facilitate that purpose? Just maybe, Duffy's removal was a preemptive action—to make way for a burglary or something else.

The dog snatcher had already demonstrated some persistence, having struck twice. Nigel hoped he'd take another swing tonight when he'd be lying in wait. If not, a night's sleep was lost. The potential benefit, to solve a great mystery, outweighed the risk. This, thought Nigel, was what semi-retirement should be about.

Nigel marched cross-country over the former golf course, with its artificial hills and dales interspersed with groupings of trees. The half-moon provided just enough light to cast deceptive shadows, obscuring the many small ditches and rises along the way. Nigel's feet were repeatedly flummoxed by the ground's ability to be where it shouldn't. Jarring missteps followed stomach-in-the-throat moments Nigel could have happily done without.

As if the dodgy footing wasn't disconcerting enough, a surprising variety of creatures made an unsettling number of noises. Frogs and crickets, the distant yelp of canines, and unidentified buzzings and flappings kept Nigel's nerves sizzling. If hearing these sounds was bad, not hearing them was worse. With each step, the white noise of Nigel's swishy pants masked the sounds of the night, leaving Nigel both blind and deaf to any deadly beasts or murderous fiends lurking in the shadows.

What Nigel didn't know was that swishy pants were pretty darned effective at warding off nocturnal creatures inhabiting derelict golf courses. As for fiends, even in the club's glory days—when all manner of them paraded up and down the fairways swinging their metal clubs—swishy-pants were shunned. Cowl necks, especially on men, would not have been popular either.

As the Sandoval mansion came into view, Nigel walked

an indirect path, keeping to the shadows and away from light sources. Exercising an abundance of care, he stepped slowly and deliberately. The last thing he needed was an errant step into a gopher hole to send him head over heels while he unleashed one of those desperate yells that couldn't be helped. Such a tumble could spell disaster. Thus, each foot was indulgently encouraged to secure an understanding of the local terra firma before accepting his full weight. This methodical technique advanced Nigel for a dozen well-placed, if laborious, paces—until his right heel, having secured proper go-ahead, sunk itself into something squishy. The sinking feeling of his heel was matched by a sinking feeling in Nigel's gut. He retracted his right foot with enough zeal to send him pogoing forward on his left foot. An encounter with a gopher hole sent him tumbling head over heels, unleashing one of those desperate yells that couldn't be helped.

Nigel came to rest on his hands and knees. His body remained intact, but his thoughts had scattered. Before he had time to collect them, he saw before him, at some distance, an apparition. Within the dim confluence of light emanating from the house and the moon stood a womanly figure in a flowing pink gown. She faced Nigel, perhaps as startled as he was, and then vanished. Not vanished as into thin air, but into the shadows.

Nigel wasn't sure what he had just seen. The vision had lasted but a second. If he had just seen his dognapper, it was a disappointing experience. He could describe the figure as a pink dress and dark hair—minimally informative and negligibly trustworthy. He wondered if his imagination had gotten the better of him. Maybe amidst the tumble, the darkness, and the poor lighting, he had caught a glimmer of some common object that he'd hallucinated into something uncommon. Possibly the result of an over-stimulated imagination, like the squish underneath his shoe that had started it all. Nigel smiled at his own foolishness and reached down to his right shoe. His muscles went rigid as he felt moisture. He worked a wet sliver from the tread of his sneaker, and with trembling hand, held it aloft under the available light. The shredded form suggested something mangled. He reluctantly sniffed it. Tomato!

Feeling relieved that the worst must be over, Nigel prowled his way toward the house. The front was well lit, but the grounds were deader than a tomb. The only noise, aside from crickets, came from Nigel's pants as he crept onward. He was eager to dump the galoshes that, by this time, pulled on his shoulders like lead anchors.

Nigel reached a point in front of the house close enough to fling the galoshes to the side of the porch—a spot plausibly close to the location of discovery, yet credibly hidden. He took the two boots into his right hand and prepped himself with two long underhand sweeps before letting them go on the third. One might suppose that two boots thrown in such a manner would have traveled along similar trajectories. Such a supposition could not have been more wrong.

Vulcanized walrus-hide galoshes may be the ultimate in retro wet-weather foot protection, but when it comes to flight dynamics, they were no Mexican redknee tarantulas. The two boots, once free of Nigel's guiding hand, demonstrated a frightening degree of independence—perhaps recalling happier times escaping killer whales in Arctic waters. One boot, expending vast energies whirling in tight rotation, gyrated flatly into some hedges twenty feet short of the target zone. The other boot, rotationless, went vertical. Having failed to obtain escape velocity, it plummeted downward, not to earth, but to the roof of the house, where a bounce and a slide left a toe dangling over the edge. The location of this galosh would have been difficult to explain. Nigel resolved never to do so.

Free of the onerous galoshes, Nigel crept to the rear of the house to look for a concealed vantage point near Duffy's enclosure. Much to his chagrin, the area was exceedingly prowler-unfriendly, being well-lit and devoid of comfy hiding places. The best he could do was a shallow drainage ditch some twenty feet away. To avoid alerting the dog, Nigel crawled to the trough and prostrated himself in its shadow. Spending the night splayed against the bare earth for hours on end was not what Nigel had envisaged.

He needn't have worried. Within a few minutes, Nigel noticed a stinging sensation near his belly button. He may have been lying on a burr. Or given that the pain was both spreading and intensifying, he may have been lying on a bed of fire ants. Nigel hopped up with an accompanying expletive and performed a kind of fire-ant exorcism dance to a complex rhythm of improvised slapping and swishing.

Duffy, having awoken to this impromptu performance, could hardly contain his excitement. He ran from one end of the enclosure to the other, muttering encouragements and barking his approval.

Aware that his cover was being blown, the ant-pecked Nigel had to calm the dog posthaste. He ran to the fence. "Ssshhh, boy. Quiet, Duffy. Sssshhhh."

The dog added a series of whines to his yelps while jumping at the fence. Duffy was not to be calmed until Nigel either left or scratched him behind the ear. If he didn't do it quickly, the entire household would be out with flashlights and clubbing implements.

Nigel made his way to the gate and slipped himself in. The dog was on him like a rash, his sensitive nose detecting goodies. In no time, Nigel was on the ground with Duffy's head half inside the front pocket of his swishy pants. First out was the granola bar. Nigel protested, but after observing the hound's enthusiasm, he opted not to make an issue of it. He emptied his pockets of the dog biscuits, which calmed the hound.

With Duffy now acclimated to his presence, Nigel tried to let himself out of the enclosure. The gate, to his profound disappointment, was distressingly difficult to open from the inside. In fact, it was proving impossible. Unless one possessed the arms of a six-year-old girl capable of squeezing through a chain-link fence, the gate could not be opened. Nigel scratched his head and stroked his chin. He sat down and rubbed his temple. No matter what body part he massaged, he could not think of a way out.

His best hope for escape was the dog snatcher. If anyone showed up to steal the dog, Nigel would be afforded an opportunity to break free as soon as the gate opened. Not only would he escape, he'd also learn the thief's identity. Such a scenario would accomplish the mission's objective in high dramatic fashion. How great would that be?

Nigel took his place inside the doggie mansion to await the arrival of the dog snatcher. The mini-mansion, while fairly spartan for a human guest, was plenty spacious for both dog and man. A pair of blankets were provided, one comman-deered by Duffy, and one used by Nigel as a cushion.

The doggie mansion held one more surprise—a doggie door into the house. It was quite small—maybe too small for Duffy—possibly installed with a different dog in mind. Could Nigel use it as an escape? Possibly, but only as a last resort. For now, Nigel primed his ears for the sound of an opening gate. The hard walls and floors, along with the discomfort of sitting upright, would keep him up and alert for his vigil.

It seemed as if no time had passed before Nigel awoke to a metallic clang.

18

FROM THE DOGHOUSE TO THE SNAKEPIT

The clanging noise alarmed Nigel like the rumbling of Vesuvius alarmed the Pompeiians. He jerked upward like a marionette called to action, then immediately fell like a marionette whose strings had been cut. In between those puppet-like actions had been a blow to the head imparted by the doghouse's five-foot ceiling. Despite a blackness filled with twinkling lights, Nigel bolted on all fours toward the closed gate. Under the light of a pitiless moon, he watched the figures of a man and a dog recede into the night.

Nigel wasn't the type to spend his idle time in the dark abyss, but had the dog enclosure possessed one, he'd have leapt into it. And had there been a chasm at the bottom of that abyss, he'd have flung himself into that as well.

The situation appeared hopeless. He sat crestfallen. He searched his memory for a source of illumination in this black and desperate hour. A movie came to mind about two men stranded on a life raft and drifting for months on the open ocean. These two unfortunates, as he recalled, were down to their last cracker. Each improvised a speech to the effect that in the whole history of men stranded at sea together, no finer mate had ever existed with which to pass the time on a raft with than the fellow sitting opposite nibbling on half a saltine. After these moving tributes, the two men demonstrated their undying support through a manly embrace, affording each the opportunity to assess the amount of meat left on the other's bones. Exactly what happened after that, Nigel couldn't recall, but one of the blokes—the one with the criminal past—survived. The story didn't inspire in nearly the way he'd hoped. He didn't have a half cracker, or a criminal record, or anyone to hug.

Nigel chimp-walked himself back into the dog mansion to take a more probing look at that doggie door. If he did manage to get through it—a big if—then what? He would be a prowler in a dark house. Nevertheless, the more he thought about the dearth of alternatives, the more practical the plan appeared. Of course, it all depended on him getting through that tiny door.

Nigel removed the vinyl entry flap and poked his head through to get a look at what waited within. Cabinetry blocked the view in one direction, but the other side opened to a large space flanked by a refrigerator and a sink. A kitchen entry point was perfect, provided there were no early morning snackers among the residents.

With nothing to lose, Nigel poked his head through the doggie door and began kicking at the ground to propel himself forward. The first four inches could not have gone better. The pace was brisk, the movement smooth, and the enterprise had gained momentum. The operation hit a snag when it came to the shoulders, however. Nigel's shoulders were to the doggie door what a cork is to a wine bottle.

He had no choice but to back out. Corks don't often remove themselves from wine bottles, and Nigel learned why. However, with enough kicking, flailing, grunting, and cursing, he was able to retract himself, breaking off a small piece of framing in the process.

The experience left him panting in a deep, cold sweat. Nigel quivered like a lump of Jell-O being pecked by birds. In his shaky hand, he held the piece of broken plastic from the doggie door. The opening was now larger by the size of the piece. He thrust one arm through the door, then put his head through and began pushing himself forward. Nigel had grown tired of thinking; he now entrusted his primitive reptilian brain to put him through. He squirmed forward like a mad lizard. Soon he was stuck once again. This time, one full arm, his head, and the top of one shoulder were fully inside. He had injected himself with such force that he could now scarcely move in any direction.

In a stalemate, Nigel had no option but to withdraw. He performed all the moves of his prior escape and then some. He kicked and flailed, wiggled and wobbled, grunted and groaned, breathed in and breathed out—all to no avail.

By this time, the sharp edges of the enclosure were making themselves known to some of the deeper tissues of Nigel's shoulder and armpit. His position—one arm extended over his head and the other pinned under his side—was profoundly uncomfortable. Both arms were tingling in a blood-deprived sort of way. Nigel's reptilian brain had no suggestions other than to wiggle. Nigel's human brain, had it a body to communicate with, would have shaken its head, rolled its eyes, and said, "I told you so." Nigel had never in his life, except last Monday, experienced such physical desperation.

"Arrrgh," grunted Nigel as he swung his free arm upward to grab hold of the cabinet, which might provide the needed leverage to pull himself through. On the first attempt, his hand slid along the surface before dropping into nothingness.

"Uuuunghh," grunted Nigel, flailing his arm upward. The

tips of his fingers touched the top edge of the counter. He caterpillared his straining fingertips onto the surface, but his arm could not maintain its awkward position. His fingers lost their grip, sliding along the edge of the counter and brushing against a loose object. The object—a small metal mixing bowl —spun off the counter and onto the tile floor, producing a clang that shook the pulp in Nigel's molars. After several nerve-splitting bounces, the bowl came to rest with that metallic, echoey noise that metal bowls make when coming to rest on tile floors.

Nigel would have hoped the sound of one dropped mixing bowl in such an expansive house would have passed unnoticed by the sleeping occupants. It might have if not for Paco, Abuelita's thirteen-year-old Chihuahua. A largely ignored member of the household, this well-kept Chihuahua had endured all the indignities common to the breed: tramplings, baby talk, groveling for bits of food, and the list goes on. Though Paco had conquered many inner demons while learning to tolerate life's minor outrages, there was one transgression never to be tolerated. The one unpardonable sin guaranteed to spark a holy hullabaloo was any interruption of his beauty sleep. Sadly, the bowl had hit the floor at a particularly inopportune time, coming as it did around the eight-hour mark of Paco's sleep time, with yet another eight to go. Paco could sleep through many loud noises, but as it turns out, the clamor of a metal mixing bowl bouncing on a tile floor was not one of them.

Since Nigel had never visited during one of Paco's rare waking hours, the yapping dog was an unwelcome surprise. But given his recent run of luck, he was grateful it wasn't a leopard. From the increasing volume of yaps and the clicking of dog paws on the tile floor, he determined this to be one of those pesky types that made it their business to announce every stranger they came across during the night.

The trapped Nigel, whose nose was at the same level as the Chihuahua's, saw the yapping little beast scamper into view some six feet dead ahead. Upon seeing Nigel, the dog skidded to a halt and traded in his yaps for an anemic growl.

The dog edged closer, one step at a time. Nigel played dead, though he'd have preferred the dog do it. Sizing up the scrawny little beast, he thought at worst, he could lose a nose —maybe just the tip. The dog seemed unable to growl for ten consecutive seconds without stopping to cough. It was during one of these stoppages that Nigel detected new and ominous sounds. Muffled voices filtered in from the far reaches of the house. The growling dog became backlit as a new light source filtered in from some adjoining room. The human occupants were astir.

Worse yet, Nigel heard an electronic whir, and it was getting louder. He closed his eyes and played dead with his one free arm shielding his face from view. Nigel heard the collision of wheelchair against cabinetry, followed by a whir, followed by another collision, followed by a whir. From underneath his arm, Nigel could see the bottom of the wheelchair positioned about eight feet away.

Something plunked against Nigel's arm. The small pellet ricocheted off and landed on the floor somewhere behind him. Another object soon hit his exposed forehead, and another landed in his hair. Soon, they were landing in rapid succession—some hitting, some not. A few of the objects accumulated on the floor in front where he could see them: two almonds, a macadamia nut, and a Brazil nut, which was soon to be joined by another almond, another Brazil nut, and a pecan. He was being assaulted with fancy-grade assorted mixed nuts—minus the cashews. The dog seemed content to growl, yap, and cough from a distance.

Soon, Nigel could see the feet of various other people

arranging themselves in front of the wheelchair. He heard Gastrick's voice.

"The police should be here in a few minutes."

"Where's my pistol? This is why I need a pistol," cackled Abuelita.

"Now, Abuelita, you've got your knife. That's good enough," replied Mrs. Sandoval. "Should we check to see if he's alive? I haven't seen him move."

"I would not advise it, ma'am," said Gastrick. "I once heard of a young boy who had picked up the severed head of a rattlesnake only to be bitten."

"He has a rattlesnake?"

"No, ma'am. I'm merely suggesting that it is better, in these uncertain circumstances, not to tempt fate."

"You're quite right. We don't want to tempt fate," said Mrs. Sandoval, "but what if I give him a poke?"

"Best leave him be," said Gastrick, "and keep your gun on him. Aim at the heart."

"Both barrels?"

"Presumably. Leave the forehead for me."

"What about me?" yelled Abuelita.

"If it should come to that, the throat," said Gastrick.

Nigel listened to this heartening conversation from his doggie-door entrapment. He hid his face with a covering arm, but he could see, from underneath his armpit, some members of the crowd. Abuelita was making stabbing motions with her foot-long knife.

"No, no, no," said Gastrick. "Horizontally. That's right, Abuelita, like a saw."

Yet more people entered the room, as evidenced by more shuffling and more muffled conversations. The home's occupants conversed in whispers. *Very suspicious,* thought Nigel, *they have something to hide*. The occupants were mostly entertaining themselves with fanciful speculations regarding the motives or methods of the man at their feet. *They could,* thought Nigel, *simply ask.*

Besides the wheelchair, Nigel could see five pairs of human feet. Two pairs too many by his reckoning. He would have preferred to keep the gathering as intimate as possible, but it was too late to influence the guest list. The five pairs of feet reshuffled themselves as the sound of an approaching siren wailed. Within minutes, two new pairs of feet joined the assemblage.

"Now, what have we here?" asked one of the officers, ending with a chuckle that Nigel thought unprofessional.

"A burglar," said Mrs. Sandoval.

"A rapist!" shouted Abuelita.

"An intruder," said Gastrick.

"Looks like half an intruder to me." The officer chuckled.

Nigel could see approaching shoes bending as the wearer squatted. "What do you think you're doing here?" said the officer, leaning over him.

Nigel was becoming uncomfortable in the extreme for many different reasons. He certainly was not in the mood for an interview.

"Appointment," gargled Nigel.

"What did he say?" asked Mrs. Sandoval.

"He said—" The officer paused to collect himself. "He said he's here for an appointment."

"Termites?" asked Mrs. Sandoval.

The room became silent.

Nigel felt momentary relief as eyes turned from him toward Mrs. Sandoval.

"We have an appointment with the exterminator."

"You the exterminator, are you?" asked the officer, clearly enjoying himself.

"Please, remove me," pleaded Nigel, speaking into his armpit. "Please?"

"Sure thing," said the officer. "Can't kill many bugs like that, now can you?"

While the inquiring officer situated himself to manipulate the upper half, he instructed the other officer to go outside to work on the leggy portion. The two of them locked on to Nigel from different ends and pulled, then pushed, then pulled again. When that didn't produce results, they conferenced through the wall, deciding that one side should push while the other side pulled. That, along with some creative twisting and wrenching, proved successful. Once a second arm had worked itself through the opening, Nigel alligatored himself into the house.

Feeling the strain of the ordeal on various parts of his body, Nigel would have liked nothing better than to stand up and stretch himself, but instead, he opted to maintain a fetal position with his back to the audience. He hoped the officers would take control of the situation like they did in the movies: *Everyone, on your way. Nothing to see here. You can all go back to bed. On your way, now.* Then with the room cleared of idle oglers, he could have a heart-to-heart with the officers, share a few good-natured laughs, and be on his way. The kinship he felt with law enforcement—what with his family connections and his own investigation—should help resolve the situation with minimal fuss.

"Let me cut 'em off!" Abuelita cackled.

Nigel listened for someone to put Abuelita in her place. He heard the policeman chuckle...wickedly, in his estimation.

"Okay now, could you sit up, sir?" requested the officer.

Nigel reluctantly complied.

"Turn around and face me," said the officer.

Facing the officer also meant facing the assembled vigilantes.

Highly undesirable, thought Nigel. He shuffled himself around. Dead silence pervaded except for the swish-swish-

swish of his pants, which to Nigel's ear, resembled the passing of a freight train as heard by the newest member of a chain gang. Nigel angled his head downward in the manner of a five-year-old after being rightly accused of setting an aunt's bed aflame.

"Look at me," said the officer.

Nigel would have liked to refuse, but he knew in his heart that it was more of a command than a request. He lifted his head and faced the mob.

The crowd rocked backward, as crowds do when faced with a thing both surprising and repulsive. Nigel felt a rush of air past his ears as the gallery gasped in unison. This was followed by a less unified, "Unnngh?"

"Mr. Nigel, it's you?" said Mrs. Sandoval, speaking for the panel.

Nigel would have liked to refute the inference, but he lacked supporting evidence.

"That's an attractive cowl neck you're wearing," said Mrs. Sandoval. "And what's happened to your face? Is that? It's not...is it?" said Mrs. Sandoval, moving her head around to obtain a view from various angles. Nigel didn't know what she was talking about until he glanced down at his own hand.

"Shoe polish," he said, igniting a few giggles.

Nigel looked at the inquisition arrayed against him. From left to right, there was the cop, a burly man who seemed to regard the whole episode as a happy diversion. Just behind was his smaller junior partner, who'd already had his way with Nigel's lower half but had yet to say a word. To his right, Abuelita—in her wheelchair—wielded a knife in such a way as to suggest the presence of grim fantasies. Just behind her was Mrs. Sandoval, wearing a negligee hinting at grim fantasies of a different sort, who held a large-bore side-by-side shotgun under her armpit. Beside her was Gastrick in a velour bathrobe, clutching a tiny revolver—just the kind of gun you would expect of a butler. To the right of him stood Stefanie and an unidentified man, both wearing matching silk pajamas embroidered with tigers. Just beyond them, almost hiding in a corner, was…

Hold on! thought Nigel.

Could not a man do a little bit of spy work, get himself hung in a doggie door, and deal with a home invasion charge without his wife making an appearance? Whatever happened to privacy? Didn't she have a stakeout of her own to attend? Nigel needed to head this off before things got out of hand.

While he was taking his measure of the panel, the panel did the same to him, mumbling to each other, pursing their lips, and swiveling their heads. All but his wife, that is, who opened a direct conversation—not with words, but with eyebrows.

What the hell? she said with a brow so knit it could have been a sweater.

What the hell, me? What the hell, you? said Nigel with his own downward-arching brows.

I'm working. Remember? I have a job that doesn't involve breaking into people's houses in the middle of the night, said Annie, her eyebrows hopping upward before making an angry dive toward the bridge of her nose.

Okay, said Nigel's widened eyes, *we can discuss when we get home. For now, just don't blow my cover. Deal?* he implored with two upward shifts of the brows; the left slightly higher than the right.

You have cover you haven't blown? said Annie with a scrunched nose and a leftward tilt of the head.

No need for sarcasm. Trust me. Please, said Nigel, plunging his right brow with a forward head thrust.

Why are you wearing my cowl neck? asked Annie with a tilt of her head and a curled upper lip.

Please, said Nigel with a lowering of the head and pursed lips, *we can talk about it later.*

"Mr. Nigel," interrupted Mrs. Sandoval, running a finger up and down the barrel of her shotgun. "Could you please explain what you're doing here stuck in our doggie door?"

"We would all like to hear that," said the large cop.

Well, Mrs. Sandoval, first let me just... Nigel noticed a puzzled look on the inquisitors' faces, prompting him to reboot his reply in verbal mode.

"Well, Mrs. Sandoval, first, let me offer my humble apologies regarding this little disturbance. I realize it's somewhat irregular, and I assure you it is not standard operating—"

"Enough talk!" screeched Abuelita. "Are you going to arrest him, or am I going to start my own standard operating procedure?" She held her knife vertically in front of her face as if imagining Nigel's head atop it.

"Let's hear him out," said Mrs. Sandoval. "But before you continue, Gastrick, please pour some tequila shots—no, on second thought, make it vodka. Save the tequila for sunrise! Vodka shots for everyone." The crowd, as a group, waved off the offer, but Mrs. Sandoval did not rescind the order. "Please continue, Mr. Nigel."

"As you know, I had been contracted to find your dear pet, Duffy." Nigel's eyes slid over to his wife to gather her reaction.

Contracted you? Are you nuts? Annie screamed with bulging, glaring eyes and exposed teeth.

Get a grip. I'll explain later, said Nigel through rapidly blinking eyes.

You bet you will, said Annie with a cascade of facial twitches and a sideward jerk of the head.

"Are you okay, Mr. Nigel?" said Mrs. Sandoval. "I mean, physically okay? You seem twitchy."

"A little too much drama for one night, I suppose."

"If you don't tell your story, and tell it quick, there's going to be a lot more drama," said the big cop.

"Very well," said Nigel. "Where was I? Ah, yes, about getting stuck. Why was I stuck in your doggie door was the question, yes? It was because…I was too big."

"Too big?" repeated Mrs. Sandoval.

"Yes, too big to fit. That's why I was stuck," said Nigel.

"That sounds right," said the previously mute small cop.

"That is not a satisfactory answer," said the stranger in the silk tiger-print pajamas. He dramatized his point with a downward-pointing finger, causing the dog to scramble for a nonexistent treat.

"Stefanie," interjected Mrs. Sandoval, "who is that man? Why are you wearing the same pajamas?"

"You know who that is," said Stefanie through clenched teeth.

"Is *he* the exterminator?"

"No, Mom. That's my husband, Rob. Remember the wedding? Three months ago? He's been away for a few weeks on business—returned last night."

Mrs. Sandoval continued to look perplexed.

"I'll introduce you tomorrow," said Stefanie, her hand on her forehead.

"The beverages," announced Gastrick, placing a tray of vodka shots on the kitchen island.

"Everyone, have what you like. There's plenty more where that came from. We don't get to entertain very often," said Mrs. Sandoval, taking one of the long narrow glasses for herself and passing one to Abuelita.

"You better continue with your story," said Big Cop. "And," he added, scratching his cheek with a spare handcuff, "make it good."

Nigel sat on the floor before the inquisition, sweat collecting on his brow and teeth chattering beneath his lips. The collective gaze of thirteen eyes—fifteen if you counted the dog—cut into him like laser beams. The sixteenth eye, Abuelita's sloppy one, fell on Nigel's foot. The foot shuffled to avert its spell.

"As I was saying, I was hired as a detective to find the Sandovals' dog. And find him I did. Not once, but twice," said Nigel. "Each time I found the dog in the same location, far away from here. An inconceivable distance for the dog to have walked unaided. I believe someone has been stealing the dog and transporting him to that area. I came tonight on a stakeout to find out who was taking the dog."

"And did someone take the dog?" asked Mrs. Sandoval.

"Yes! Absolutely," said Nigel with a finger pointing upward, "the dog was taken."

"Who took the dog?" asked Big Cop.

"I don't know," said Nigel, retracting the finger.

"You saw him, but you don't know who took the dog?" said Big Cop, twirling his handcuffs.

"I saw him from a distance, and it was dark."

"Didn't you think to confront him, or at least get a license plate?"

"I couldn't. I was locked in the cage."

"You were in the dog's cage, and you didn't see who took the dog?" said Mrs. Sandoval.

Nigel sensed an uncomfortable turn in the inquiry.

"No, I didn't get the chance."

"You could have nabbed him," interjected Big Cop. "Why didn't you nab him?"

"It was too late to nab him."

"How could it be too late? You were in the cage. The dog was in the cage. Someone takes the dog out of the cage. What were you doing?" said Big Cop.

Nigel had always held law enforcement in high esteem,

what with his wife being a cop, but this guy was getting on his nerves. "Sleeping," said Nigel.

"Sleeping!" said at least three voices, none of which sounded impressed.

"The dog should have awoken me. I mean, what dog wouldn't bark with someone prowling around his cage? No wonder the dog gets stolen," said Nigel.

"Crap!" yelled Abuelita. "It's bullcrap!"

"What?" said Nigel.

"Anybody can see what's going on here. It's a racket. This pervert gets a hundred dollars every time he brings the dog back. 'Oh, I just found the dog miles away,' he says. 'Someone must a stole him,' he says. Yeah, right. Now the dog is missing again, and he's found stuck in the doggie door," yelled Abuelita, thrusting her knife repeatedly toward Nigel. "I don't think we have to look any further for our thief. He's right here in this room."

"Who?" said Mrs. Sandoval, reaching for another shot glass.

"Look at that little worm," said Abuelita, pointing and twisting her knife. "Stealing dogs wasn't enough for him. Now that he's cased the joint, he was onto bigger, better things. He knew what he was doing. He's been after my body ever since he laid eyes on me."

"Grandma," said Big Cop, "you had me convinced up until that last part."

"You can't believe the rants of a crazy old woman over me," protested Nigel.

"The part of your story I don't get," said Little Cop, "is about getting locked inside the dog cage."

"What do you mean?" asked Big Cop.

"I was just in the dog cage. There's a latch to let yourself out from the inside. A moron could find his way out of there."

"Ah! But what about an imbecile?" said Mrs. Sandoval.

19

LAYING DOWN A BIG ONE

"Okay. That's enough for me. We have a clear case of breaking and entering with criminal intent," said Big Cop.

"Breaking and entering?" said Nigel. "What entering? I was trying to leave. You guys pulled me in here. If that's the crime, then you're accessories. Breaking and entering? You can't be serious."

"Home invasion *is* serious. I'll tell you this, mister," he said, pointing a beefy cop finger at the sitting Nigel, "before we arrived, any one of these folks could have blown your head off, and the courts would have said, 'Good for them. Justice served. Next case.' "

"No. No. No," protested Nigel. "These are my people. They'll rush to my defense. You haven't heard them out. They don't want to press charges. These are all friends of mine."

"Lock him up!" screeched Abuelita, "and throw away the key. Let him rot."

"Friends, eh?" said Big Cop, hovering over Nigel as if he were about to spit. He pulled out a pencil and a notepad. "I'll need to get names and addresses for everyone here, as well as statements, if you wish to file charges."

"Please, everyone. Please," said Nigel, addressing the congregation. "There's a much larger story here if you will let me explain."

"Explain what, you pervert?" yelled Abuelita. She punctuated her remarks with a series of underhanded knife thrusts aimed at Nigel's neck. "Look at 'em. I'll bet he stole that top too. It doesn't even fit."

"Everyone," shouted Stefanie. "I think we should calm down and let the man speak for a few minutes."

Finally, some empathy.

"We needn't rush to judgment," she continued. "The courts will do that. We have before us a disturbed individual —maybe mentally challenged, twisted perhaps—in ways we can't fully understand. But as Christians, loosely speaking, we'd be remiss not to give this man his say. I would hate to think we put a man behind bars, sitting in a barren cell day after day—possibly for decades—thinking he never got a chance to get things off his chest." She turned toward Nigel. "Five minutes."

Nigel stood up. "May I?" he said, reaching for a shot of vodka. It went down smooth—a top-notch brand, no doubt. "Thank you. I will try to get to the point, but please, hear me out before making any judgments."

It dawned on Nigel as he spoke that he was now the centerpiece of a grand performance—a one-man show. It instilled in him a yearning for four more vodkas. Unfortunately, with every eye on him, save one, and every ear poised for his next word, he hadn't the time. His heart pounded, and sweat filled every pore. His predicament brought to mind the ancient Persian tale of the storyteller, Scheherazade. But the Persian tales would have to wait. He had his own tail to worry about.

"As everyone now knows," he said in his best rendition of a lawyerly tone, "I took this case to find the Sandoval's missing dog. And find him I did. Had that been the end of the case, I would have been in clover, as they say."

"Who says that?" said Mrs. Sandoval.

"They," said Nigel, not wishing to belabor the point. "But as it turned out, that was not the end of the case. No, this was the case that refused to die. Perhaps someday, I will write a book about it, and that will be its title."

"*That*?" said Mrs. Sandoval.

"What?" said Nigel.

"*That*. You said *That* would be its title. *That* is a strange title for a book. I once saw a movie called *Them*, but *Them* is a better title than *That*. What would your *That* book be about?"

"You misunderstood. My book would not be called *That*. My book was to be called… I can't remember. Where was I?"

"Which one?" said Mrs. Sandoval.

"What?" said Nigel.

"*I Can't Remember* or *Where Was I*? That's two titles. Or is it the two of them together? *I Can't Remember, Where Was I?* I kind of like that. I can relate. What's your book about?"

"We've gotten sidetracked," said Nigel. "Where was I?"

"The case that wouldn't die," said Stefanie.

"Now that would be a good title for a book!" said Mrs. Sandoval.

"Okay," said Nigel, fluffing his cowl neck. "Getting back to the discussion at hand, I found and returned the dog. That should have resolved the case. However, not only did the dog go missing again, but I found him in the very same place many miles from here. It is my contention that this was no simple act of escape.

"Where did you find him?" asked Big Cop.

"Where is not important. Many miles from here."

"Well now," said Big Cop. "Being the officer that is about to arrest you, I believe the location may be of some importance."

Nigel believed that most any detective would have welcomed with open arms a missing person that happened by their place while engaged in routine yardwork. No shame in that, but it wasn't the kind of thing to burnish the reputation. If Sherlock Holmes had such a case, it didn't make it into a book. Besides, the coincidental nature of the thing made it darn near unbelievable. Not the kind of material you want to volunteer.

"Okay," said Nigel, "the location was the municipality of No Way at 3514 Corrigan Drive, or thereabouts. Immaterial, however."

"Hey," said Small Cop. "Cam Logan has a place out there."

"If the dog ended up there," said Big Cop, "it must have some significance. What's at that address?"

"There is no significance to that address. I know because it is my own house." With this, Nigel put his nose high in the air, as he imagined a lawyer would, to discourage further questions.

"Ha," belched Big Cop. "Ha ha," he scoffed. It was followed by, "Hahahaha."

Nigel detected a note of skepticism in Big Cop's commentary. It made him want to scoff in return and storm from the room. On the verge of doing just that, he realized he could not storm. Any attempt to storm would result in a police takedown, and a scoff without a storm got him nowhere. So, as was his habit, Nigel ingested the scoff, later to be excreted as waste product along with chewed-up bits of his soul. Another day in the life.

"Let me get this straight," said Small Cop. "You had a contract to find this dog, and he shows up at your house? Wow! You're good."

Big Cop slapped his forehead.

"Exactly as described," said Nigel. "And that's just a start. Hear me out."

"Haven't we heard enough?" said the man in the silk pajamas.

As a class, Nigel didn't trust men wearing clothes made by worms—this current encounter a case in point. The embroidered tigers, though possibly not worm cloth, did nothing to bolster the man's credibility. However, unbeknownst to Nigel, the man in silk had a similar prejudice against men in cowl necks. The fact that the specimen sitting before him had been extracted from a doggie door in the middle of the night by two policemen was also, in his opinion, a case in point.

"You haven't heard anything yet," protested Nigel.

Big Cop, puffing himself up like a rooster ready to crow, shoved his notepad into his shirt pocket and nodded to Small Cop. Nigel saw the two advancing in a pincer movement.

"You haven't heard," said Nigel, hoisting a quivering eyebrow, "about...the murder!" He stuffed that last word, "murder," like an English Christmas goose.

"What?" said Big Cop.

"Muuuurder!" expectorated Nigel with more juice than a French kiss between Winston Churchill's bulldog and Alfred Hitchcock's St. Bernard.

"Did he say murder?" asked Mrs. Sandoval.

"He did say it. He said murder," said Mr. Silk Pajamas.

"Murder?" said Stefanie.

"I thought he said Mordor. You know, Middle-Earth," said Small Cop.

"What's this about a murder?" said Big Cop, irritated that his arrest had been put on hold.

Until now, the idea of murder had been more idle speculation than a hypothesis, but desperate times call for desperate crimes. "Over the past few days, this property has been the site of some very strange happenings," said Nigel.

"You're the strangest happening I've seen," said Abuelita, twisting her knife into some imagined organ.

"A few days ago," continued Nigel, "a young man died on this very property."

"You're talking about the Griesen kid," said Big Cop. "That was an accidental drowning."

"Perhaps. Perhaps not," said Nigel. "Consider some of the other incidents. For example, an anaconda was found in the vicinity of the death."

"An anaconda? You mean, a big snake?" said Small Cop.

"Yes, a giant, non-native snake. What was a giant snake doing there? Could it have been for some nefarious reason? And of course, there is this disappearing dog. Could that have a tie-in to the case?"

"Why would a missing dog have anything to do with that case?" said Big Cop, frustrated by a lack of physical confrontation.

"You are, no doubt, familiar with the Sherlock Holmes case of the dog that didn't bark."

The members of the congregation examined the floor, scratched various body parts, and avoided each other's side-eyed glances. Small Cop raised his hand sheepishly.

"My uncle had a dog that didn't bark. A snake bit his tongue."

"Very well," said Nigel, flaring his nostrils. "In the Holmes story, the fact that the dog was not heard to bark, even when a suspect was nearby, turned out to be an important clue to solving the case. Why would a dog not bark?"

Nigel examined his fingernails while the members of the panel shuffled their feet and acted as if they'd not heard the question.

"Because he had no tongue?" said Small Cop.

"Other reasons," said Nigel. "Maybe the dog knew the suspect, as in the Sherlock Holmes story. Therefore, he felt no need to bark. Alternatively, the dog did not bark because he was not there. Could it be that the Griesen kid's destination was this very house, and the dog had been removed to prevent its bark? Perhaps the Griesen kid's location that night was no accident, and the missing dog was no coincidence? Furthermore, could it be that the death was no accident?"

The crowd, as if descended upon by a smelly gas of unknown origin, fell silent and withdrawn. Heads cast themselves downward, feet shuffled, and eyes darted to avoid contact with other darting eyes. Nigel glanced at Annie sitting silently in the far corner. He had avoided looking in her direction. When angry, she had a way of glowering, which caused his brain to collapse. Now she was docile, occupied by some deep inner thoughts. Perhaps she was developing theories based on the facts as he had presented them, and not—as he feared—plotting to make his life a living hell.

"Eh? Anyone?" said Nigel, calling the class to order. "You see what I'm getting at, eh? I believe that solving the mystery behind the missing dog may solve the bigger mystery. As an investigator, I follow the clues wherever they may lead. Any questions?"

"I have a question," said Mrs. Sandoval, holding up an empty shot glass. "Have you consulted with the detective, Annie, over there? You work for the same agency."

Annie popped her head up like a turkey hearing the word Thanksgiving. She glared at Nigel; Nigel looked away. If Annie hadn't quite figured things out before, she had now. The news that her one-woman company had a home invader working in it must have been a shock.

"Well, just," said Nigel, scrambling for damage control. "I mean, we work for the same firm, yes, but we work in different divisions. I mean, I've seen her around, coming and going and whatnot. I mean, who wouldn't notice such an attractive lady, but we've not been formally introduced, I don't believe." Nigel stretched his neck and waved toward the corner. "Hi there, my name is Nigel. What's yours? Ann? Annie? Maybe we can do lunch sometime. Discuss the case. That'd be nice."

Nigel didn't have many in his corner, but this woman's disdain for his overtures elicited an unspoken pity among all those present.

"You work for the same detective agency, but the two of you don't know each other?" said Big Cop.

"It's a little uncomfortable to talk about, but it's like this," said Nigel. "I'm in the pet division, you see. She is on the people side. It's not something we're proud of, but there's a frightful amount of office politics in our agency. You know, silos, departmental rivalries, deep state, all of that. I'm sure it's the same for you guys down at the precinct, like, between murder and vice. Same at our office between pets and people."

"Really?" said Big Cop.

"Absolutely. You know," said Nigel, lowering his voice and drawing closer to the officer, "we don't even attend the same company Christmas parties. Sad, really."

The officer, perhaps recalling his own internecine squabbles, cast his gaze downward while curling his massive lower lip. The rest of the crowd looked lost, like a school of codfish after swimming too close to a depth charge.

"My point is that we have a mystery on our hands," continued Nigel. "A mystery which, sad to say, will not be solved by the local police force. In fact, if I am taken into custody by these county mounties, this case may never be solved."

Big Cop's chest popped forward as if he was about to get something off it.

"Bull crap!" yelled Abuelita, disrupting the chest inflation.

"Beg your pardon?" said Nigel.

"Bull crap! Everything you said was bull crap. I know why that boy was coming to the house. I know what he was doing, and I know who sent him. There weren't no murder. This detective—if you want to call him that—this so-called detective," she said, indicating Nigel while caressing the side of her face with the long blade of her knife, "couldn't figure out who farted in a phone booth."

Nigel felt rather strongly that he could and wanted to prove it. But he understood the PR perils of confronting a delicate old person, even if she was, in fact, a hideous, indestructible she-demon.

"Abuelita, dear Abuelita, I was not aware you had such information," said Nigel as graciously as possible while holding a quart of bile in his mouth. "Please, by all means, fill us in. Please explain to us why the young man was coming here, to see whom, and to do what. What can you tell us? Go ahead. Explain," said Nigel, opening his arms to indicate an open floor.

"I will, if you'll shut up," she said. "That man was coming to take my picture. He was hired by my boyfriend—"

"Boyfriend?" said Mrs. Sandoval, putting a word to everyone else's gags.

20

ABUELITA'S MIDNIGHT CONFESSION

"My boyfriend," affirmed Abuelita. "He hired a photographer to take my picture."

"Wait a minute. My head is swerving," said Mrs. Sandoval. "Gastrick, bring another tray of vodka. Now, Abuelita, where, pray tell, did this boyfriend come from?"

"The internet. That's how it's done these days. You think I spend all my time playing solitaire? I don't think so."

"Why have we never met this *boyfriend*?"

"You been to Chicago?"

"No."

"Well, that's why. He lives in Chicago. He's a business-man. A damn fine businessman, too."

"Gastrick!" shouted Mrs. Sandoval.

"Coming," said Gastrick, arriving with a tray full of shot glasses and a bottle of Absolut vodka.

"What business is he in?" said Mrs. Sandoval, throwing back a shot before Gastrick had set down the tray.

"All kinds of business. He has vineyards."

"In Chicago?"

"He just winters in Chicago," said Abuelita, "to watch the

Bears. Otherwise, he'd be in Argentina, or maybe Sonoma. He goes wherever he wants. You can do that when you got the do-re-mi. He sent me a postcard from Paraguay."

"Why has he never come here?" asked Mrs. Sandoval.

"Are you kidding? Him, come to this little rathole? That would blow everything. When the time is right, he'll send a limo and take me to some far-off place, and we'll be married."

"Abuelita, I don't want to be a Debbie Downer," said Mrs. Sandoval, holding her head while trying to enunciate, "but don't you think he might be after your money?" Exhausted, she licked the rim of her shot glass.

"Are you nuts? That's why I got me a rich man. What would he want with my money? He wants me for my body."

The vodka shots, heretofore standing at attention, suddenly found themselves being upended.

"This is a charming little back story," Nigel interjected, "but what does it have to do with the drowning victim?"

"That man was a photographer hired by my boyfriend to take photos of me," said Abuelita. "Tasteful photos. Pure class."

"We knew nothing about this," said Mrs. Sandoval. "You were just gonna wait 'til he showed up to tell us?"

"Nope. He was to come straight to my room. I'd let him in through the French doors. You'd never know a thing."

"Let me get this straight," said Mrs. Sandoval. "Without us knowing nothing, you'd just fling open your doors and let loose a 'Come on in' to a man none of us never met?"

"It's my house, you know. Besides, wouldn't be the first time."

Upon hearing Abuelita's story, faces in the room registered surprise wrapped in disbelief accented with disgust. Reactions would have been similar had someone opened a cupboard revealing an eight hundred-pound tuna left there to ferment. While the story seemed plenty fishy to Nigel as well, he saw an opportunity. He called for attention by tapping a pen against a shot glass. Little good it did, producing a dull "thunk" instead of the desired "ting."

"Everyone, please," said Nigel. "Please, everyone, I believe that Abuelita has just provided us with evidence suggesting an attempted homicide."

"Did you say attempted homicide?" said Big Cop between vodka slurps.

"He did say homicide," said Small Cop. "Before he said murder. He's changing his story."

"Yes, homicide," said Nigel. "We have new information which makes for an even stronger case of foul play. I daresay, we could have teased out the truth to this sad episode some time ago had my investigation not been so rudely interrupted."

"Excuse me," said Big Cop. "We didn't interrupt an investigation. We interrupted a home invasion."

"Hear me out," said Nigel, thunking the shot glass. "After I'm finished, I'll let you decide for yourselves the merits of my investigation. May I kindly ask our local law officers to recite the list of items found with the victim in the submerged truck."

"I can't," said Big Cop.

"You can't because you are not allowed to disclose the information?" asked Nigel.

"I can't because I have no idea. It's not my case."

"I see. In that case, I will describe what was found at the scene: one drowning victim, Oscar Griesen, deceased; one bouquet of roses—freshly cut, hand-picked—"

"How thoughtful," said Abuelita.

"One bottle of supplements from Wylie's Drugstore—"

"What kind of supplements?" asked Big Cop.

"Something called Vita-O, a kind of…female supplement…libido enhancement."

"Not needed," said Abuelita, picking her teeth with the butcher's knife.

"One bag of high-end photographic equipment and—oh yes—one fifteen-foot anaconda," said Nigel.

"Twelve-foot," said Big Cop.

"That may be the official measurement, but as anyone dealing with large snakes can tell you, official measurements tend to de-exaggerate a snake's true length. At any rate, one massive, constricting reptile. Also note that at the time of the flooding incident, the dog, Duffy, a usual resident of these premises, had gone missing for unknown reasons. The dog," said Nigel, pointing at the ceiling with an index finger, "which could not bark. Given what we've just been told by Miss Abuelita, I believe we have all the information we need to piece together an entire murder plot—a murder plot where no one died due to an untimely death, but a murder plot, nonetheless. I trust you can all see the obvious."

Nigel had laid out an orderly array of dots ready for connecting by any third-rate mind. Nigel looked upon this array of slack-jawed toe-gazers, and—Annie excepted—failed to see a third-rate mind among them. Suddenly, a divine look of enlightenment flashed across the face of Mrs. Sandoval.

Aha, thought Nigel, *a convergent thinker.*

She smacked her lips and flicked her tongue, indicating a vodka shot had hit its mark. Frustratingly, Nigel would have to do the connecting, and he wasn't sure how to go about it.

"Okay," said Nigel. "To get to the point, I believe the photographer was sent here to kill Miss Abuelita."

A buzz arose within the gallery. The vodka was doing its thing.

"No!" yelled Abuelita, plunging her knife down by her side, where it penetrated the sandal of Silk Pajama Man between first and second toe.

"Yes!" yelled Nigel. "The dog was stolen so that he could

not alert the residents to any intruders. The hitman, young Oscar Griesen, was then to arrive with an anaconda to be used as the murder weapon against the frail Abuelita."

"But why a snake? Why not a gun, a knife, or a blunt object?" asked Big Cop.

"A clean kill. A snake," said Nigel, pausing to grope for an explanation, "leaves no fingerprints, powder residues, or bloodstains."

"What about snakeprints?" said Small Cop.

"A big snake," continued Nigel, "may be the most perfect murder weapon ever devised by man to snuff out a little old lady. The anaconda, a silent killer, both dispatches the victim and disposes of them, all in one go. No mess, no fuss. Abuelita, with her powdery bones and fading musculature, would have been a mere midnight snack to the beast."

Nigel staggered backward as the shot glass ricocheted off his forehead before skittering toward Silk Pajama Man, who was removing the butcher's knife from his sandal.

"Fading musculature? I'll show you what fading musculature can do!" shouted Abuelita.

"What about the photographic equipment? If he was just going to kill her, he didn't need photographic equipment," said Big Cop.

"I beg to differ," said Nigel. Differ he did, but it required a moment to figure out why. "Hitmen," he went on, "like photography. They *need* photography to document their successes for their scrapbooks." The onlookers didn't look very convinced. "Oh!" exclaimed Nigel, nearly jumping out of his swishy pants, "and they must provide visual evidence. Who would trust a hired killer based on mere say-so? Not me. I'd require evidence, high-quality photos—a standard part of the job."

"But what about a motive? I never trust a crime scenario without a motive," said Big Cop.

"What are always the motives for premeditated murder? Passion, greed, jealousy, hatred, the thrill of the hunt. Looking at poor Abuelita, we can rule out passion."

Nigel dipped to his right to avoid the shot glass whizzing past his temple.

"Abuelita, please!" said Stefanie. "You could have hit a policeman. You don't want to get arrested, do you?"

"That jackass don't know nothing about what he's talking about. Not a thing. That man didn't want to kill me. He wanted to take my picture, just like I said before."

"If that's the case," said Nigel, "then please explain why a photographer would bring an anaconda to a photo shoot? Help with the lighting, perhaps?"

"No, smartass. The photographer was going to take pictures of me with the snake. That was the plan all along."

"You and the snake?" said Nigel. "The photographer… coming here? To take pictures of you and the snake? Were these to be before and after photos? Or maybe a compare and contrast? Why would a photographer come here to take pictures of you and a snake?

Before she could answer, Mrs. Sandoval yelled, "Gastrick!"

"You shouted?"

"I screamed for ice cream." She laughed. "Ask our guests if they'd like ice cream."

"Mrs. Sandoval has insisted that I ask if any of you would care for some ice cream," announced Gastrick.

"Two scwoops of Fwench navilla," said Mrs. Sandoval.

"Very well," replied Gastrick.

"Abuelita," said Stefanie, "tell us why you would take pictures with a big snake."

"My boyfriend wanted 'em. I told him about my act, and he got all excited—"

"You are referring to your Burlesque act, Priscilla Pistola and her 45s?" said Nigel.

"No. Why would I need a snake for that? This was the act before that act: Serpentina, Snake Lady from Amazonia. Me and a snake—and seven veils. I start out with kind of a belly dance of the seven veils. By the end of it, the snake was covered with veils, and I was covered with the snake, if you can picture that. Fritz couldn't, but he wanted to. I told Fritz that if he loved me, he'd make it happen. That's why he sent a photographer with a snake."

"You would re-create the dance for pictures? Don't you think you're a little old for that?" said Stefanie.

"Babe, whatever they wanted back then, I still got. Besides, you know what men lose when they get old? Eyesight. Fritz is near-sighted, far-sighted, and astigmatized. The secret to capturing an older man's heart is knowing the proper distance to keep 'em at."

"Aren't you afraid this man will try to take advantage of you?" asked Stefanie.

"I'm more afraid he won't."

"More shots!" shouted Mrs. Sandoval, who—not having received her ice cream—was licking the barrel of her shotgun.

"I was thinking financially," said Stefanie. He hasn't asked you for money, has he?"

"Gracious, no. He's got money up the wazoo. He don't need any from me. As soon as we get the paperwork together, he's gonna take me away from here, and we're gonna do it."

"Get married?"

"That too. You can help with the wedding dress."

21

THE IGNOMINIOUS EXIT

Big Cop, having gained more than enough insight into the love life of an octogenarian, stepped forward with his thumbs in his belt. "This has been interesting, but we need to get on with our business. This man here," he said, pointing at Nigel, "was found breaking and entering. Apparently, he's known to everyone here, and he has offered an explanation, ridiculous though it is, as to why he was here. Officer Golic and I need to know if you wish him arrested and held on charges. Otherwise, we'll have to let him go."

"Put him on the sex offenders list!" said Abuelita.

"Not unless he's convicted of a sex crime. We don't have that here."

"Damn. Whatever happened to justice? Just look at that sick-ass prowler," she said, waggling her knobby finger. "Cowl-neck blouse, and brown grease all over his sorry self. Can't you at least give him the business?" She gazed imploringly at Big Cop with her vulture eye. "You know you want to."

"No, ma'am. We're not allowed to engage unless ..." said

Big Cop, grinding a large fist into his palm. "Unless he were to resist or make a run for it."

"Officer," interjected Nigel, "rest assured, I have every intention of cooperating."

"Coward!" shrieked Abuelita.

"I think, under the circumstances," interrupted Stefanie, "that you can let him go. Gastrick will show you out."

As Nigel and the officers were ushered toward the door, Silk Pajama Man pulled Big Cop aside.

"If you did want to rough him up a little," said Silk Pajamas in a low, but easily heard voice, "you know, teach him a lesson, I'm sure no one in the house would be watching through the windows." He slipped the officer a packet of some sort and slapped him on the butt as he walked away.

While being escorted out, Nigel glanced back at Annie, who had maintained her silence throughout. Her profession-alism did not permit shows of emotion, but she could not have been happy with the night's developments. Nigel yearned to place his head under her foot and plead for forgiveness, but supplication and humiliation would have to wait. Perhaps it was for the best. Such delicate discussions required extreme levels of earnestness and humility, not to be attempted wearing her cowl-neck top and slathered in shoe polish.

Nigel waited while the officers made calls to the station. Already, conversations had turned to more mundane matters, such as get-well gifts for Mrs. Stoppelschuk's bowel blockage party. Nigel wished he could trade places with Mrs. Stop-pelschuk. Such wistful thoughts were shelved when he felt a bump to the leg. Nigel looked down to see Duffy looking up. *How did he get here?* The night had come full circle. Actually, more of a downward spiral.

Once the officers had concluded their administrations,

Gastrick showed Nigel and the two officers out through the main entrance.

"Keep walking," said Big Cop, his hand on Nigel's shoulder.

"Okay, that's far enough," he said once they'd crossed the main drive, fifty feet from the door. "The folks in the house are desperate for some justice, so we're going to give them a show."

"A show?" asked Nigel, envisioning the officer performing a pantomime.

"You ever watch wrestlin'? We're about to create our own version. Nothing to worry about, but it'll give the folks inside a warm feeling. Now you stand there, and I'm going to airmail a swift kick to the backside. You need to make it look good, see, like you've sustained real damage. Got it?"

"Is this standard procedure?" asked Nigel.

"No. Standard procedure is three to five for breaking and .entering. We're taking the short cut. You ready?"

"I hardly think this is necessary," protested Nigel. "Couldn't you write me a ticket instead?"

"They don't want to see note writing. They want good, old-fashioned American justice, and that means a butt kickin'. Bend over, and we'll get this over with."

"Very well," said Nigel, bracing himself and closing his eyes. His teeth locked tight at the sound of size thirteen shoes on a cement drive positioning themselves for a kick. He discerned the sound of a backswing converting into a powerful forward motion. The shoe whizzed upward, just scraping his trouser-covered derriere.

"Hop to it," said Big Cop as his foot reached its apex.

Nigel lifted himself off the ground a good six inches and came down, rubbing his sparsely afflicted rump as if urging out a hesitant genie. To enhance the effect, he limped around in a big circle with a hop here and a shaky leg there. For

someone expressing such strong reservations moments
before, he had taken to the spirit of the thing in a hurry.

"Okay," said the officer. "That was good. Academy Award
stuff. Now, one more and you'll be free to go."

Nigel once more assumed the position only to encounter
an unexpected delay.

"Excuse me, officer. I've been sent by the lady of the house
to offer my assistance."

What possible assistance could Gastrick offer? pondered
Nigel.

"She has requested that I be permitted to do the honors.
With all due respect to the excellent job you're doing, Ms.
Abuelita has expressed her belief that such disciplinary action
should be exacted by a member of the household. She has
sent me to act on her behalf."

Alarmed, Nigel turned to see the officer gesturing toward
his rump as if it were a tray of desserts.

"Hold on," said Nigel. "You're not going along with this,
are you?"

"You would prefer to be charged?" Gastrick interjected.

Nigel turned to the officer, who held his palms to the sky
and curled a lower lip.

"I doth protest!" said Nigel.

"You *what*?" said the officer.

"Doth protest."

An uncomfortable silence followed. The officer gave a
blank stare while the crickets sang a sprightly tune.

"I suggest we proceed," said Gastrick.

"*You* suggest we proceed? This is highly irregular, I must
say. That's my official statement, highly irregular," said Nigel.

"I assure you," said the butler, "I will administer the
action in a fully efficient and professional manner. You have
my word on that." He held out a hand.

Nigel looked again at the officer, who raised his palms to

the sky, and—as was becoming his habit—curled his lower lip. Feeling little recourse, he clasped the butler's hand. Nigel had experienced quite a few handshakes in his day, but this one sent a chill. Something about it sent him tumbling into the uncanny valley.

"Hold on," said Nigel, "he's wearing surgical gloves. Look at that. Surgical gloves for Christ's sake! What's that about? I demand answers!"

The officer curled his lower lip.

"You needn't worry," said Gastrick, "it is merely a precaution."

"A precaution? What? Next thing you know, he'll be pulling out a gas mask. What do you mean, a precaution? I knew a doctor once—"

"They are not for you. Nothing to do with you."

"Nothing to do with me? You mean there's someone else? So, after you've whomped me one up the backside, you've an appointment to remove someone's appendix? What do you mean they have nothing to do with me?"

"Nothing to do with you, sir. They are for the boots."

"The boots! The boots?" Nigel looked down at Gastrick's feet. "Holy crap! What's he wearing? Look at those things," he said to the officer curling his lower lip. "Those aren't his shoes. Most irregular! Don't you have any normal footwear? What are those? Special arse-kicking boots?"

"Authentic World War II paratrooper's boots worn by my great-uncle during his service with the 82nd Airborne. He liberated France in these boots."

"Did he? And to think, his beloved shoes that once kicked Nazi booty are now being unleashed on the backside of an ally! Your great uncle, dare I say, must be spinning in his grave!"

"I think not. He's looking down upon us now with great satisfaction."

"Oh, he is, is he? You should be ashamed. Ashamed. Justifying your sadistic impulses in the name of a dear, departed loved one."

"My great uncle is ninety-six years old and quite alive. He's looking down from there," said Gastrick, pointing toward a lighted upstairs window. "While he was in Europe, receiving three Purple Hearts, his girlfriend back in England was carousing with an Englishman—an ally, as you say. My uncle kept these boots all these years for the sole purpose of one day kicking that Englishman's ass. When I asked to borrow his boots to kick an Englishman's ass, he asked if I had finally found the British bastard that stole his girl. Regrettably, I told him I had not."

"At least there's some decency in you."

"I told him you were his son. You should have seen the old gentleman's eyes light up. He danced a jig."

"Splendid! Just wonderful. So the gloves were for him?"

"No. The gloves were for handling the boots. They are, after all, treasured heirlooms. I could not allow them to come in contact with bodily fluids or residues."

"Oh, I see! The boots cannot be allowed to come in contact with bodily fluids or residues, but they're perfectly okay to be sent hurtling into my ass."

"Well, I hardly think a good thump to your trousers exposes them to bodily fluids or residues."

"You might be surprised."

"Shall we get this show on the road?" said Gastrick.

Nigel was heartened by Gastrick's use of the word "show." Perhaps he was in on the game after all. *He must be,* thought Nigel.

"Make it convincing," said Nigel, nodding his head with a wink.

"Rest assured," said Gastrick.

His somber, solemn tone did not reassure. *Is he just digging*

into his role? wondered Nigel. Perhaps he needed to be explicitly informed. As Nigel opened his mouth to speak, there
came the distant sound of rapping on glass. Looking toward
the house, Nigel saw Abuelita at one of the windows moving
her arm in a motion suggestive of kicking.

"We best get on with it," said Gastrick.

"Right," said Nigel. "You understand this is an
exhibition?"

"Indeed."

Reassured, Nigel leaned forward at the waist, bending the
knees slightly to position his butt for a swiping blow. He
heard the shuffling of boots on pavement readying themselves for the performance.

"An exhibition," said Gastrick, "as in the days of the
public executions."

The popping sound of Nigel's eyes as they pushed past
their sockets was obscured by the swoosh of a paratrooper's
boot rocketing toward its destination. The operation occurred
with such speed that Nigel's remembrance would forever be
preserved in a single image—the tip of a shiny black boot
peeking out from between his legs and heading upward at an
enormous rate of speed. Once contact was made, sensory
perceptions other than agony ceased. Nigel felt his entire
body catapulted upward, some parts catapulted more forcefully than others. As his body yielded to the downward pull
of gravity, some parts yielded less than others. The senses
returned, and Nigel heard what sounded like applause,
though it may have been something flapping loosely
inside him.

"Let's get out of here," said Big Cop.

The officers jumped in their car and drove off.

Nigel stood himself up before squatting again—a
maneuver repeated several times. He gasped and gulped for
air until his mouth filled with a sticky, cottony sensation that

—after clearing—appeared to be the remains of a moth. At least, he hoped it was a moth.

A quarter-mile from his car, Nigel resolved to get himself back as quickly as possible, a decision lamented by a multitude of nocturnal creatures from land, sea, and air. Though he didn't know it, Nigel provided the finest moving feast these parts had experienced in a dog year. This "feast," from Nigel's perspective, was barely noticed at the time, but—like so many insults suffered that night—would need a few hours to fully fester.

As bad as the night had been, it was the future that troubled Nigel. He worried that what Gastrick had done, Annie could do better, and repeatedly. She had been quiet throughout the ordeal, but there are sayings about calms before storms, and Annie was a stormy woman.

Nigel tried not to think about it. Not an easy task, but achievable with an iron will. Therefore, as he drove away from the Sandoval estate, his mind was actively unoccupied with thoughts of what his wife was thinking at that very minute. As he waited for a traffic light to turn green, his mind was staunchly not consumed with thoughts of what his wife might say upon her arrival home. As he drove up the driveway of his house, his brainpower was not wasted preparing words for his defense.

As Nigel laid his head gently on his pillow, no thought crossed his mind regarding the mood of his wife in the coming years. Nor did it enter his head that if he were sleeping when Annie arrived home, he might never be permitted to wake up again. If that last thought had been allowed to permeate, he would have slept better.

22 BREAKFAST IN THE LION'S DEN

Nigel sprung up in bed, awakened by the opening and closing of the front door, followed by a groan. If his dreams could have extended into reality, the groan would have been from a brain-eating zombie. The unfortunate sound of keys landing on a coffee table dashed that possibility. Not quite ready to face what lay in store, he headed to his quiet place, the bathroom, for a sit-down pee.

Nigel set about convincing himself that he had done nothing wrong—at least not suicidally, homicidally wrong. He talked to himself about the person he was: a person of worth, a person to be respected, and an equal partner in marriage. He repeated these affirmations, and his confidence climbed. The more propaganda he spouted, the more he believed it. In his growing enthusiasm, he stood up and thumped his chest three times. The realization that he hadn't finished peeing knocked him down a notch.

Nigel entered the living room feeling like one of those guys marching into the Roman coliseum to face the lions. Not the athletic types sent out to entertain on Saturday after-noons, but one of the scrawny specimens paraded into an empty arena on Tuesday mornings to teach the lions how tasty humans were. Annie was stretched out on the sofa with her eyes closed. Nigel saw no weapons within her reach.

"Good morning," he said. "I just woke up. Must have gotten three hours of sleep. Three hours more than you, I suppose. Want to go to bed?"

"Need to eat first," she said without opening her eyes.

"What can I get you?"

"Cereal."

"All righty, cereal coming up," said Nigel. "How was your day? Anything interesting?" Nigel slapped a hand across his mouth. Old habits are hard to break, even ones that can get you killed.

"No."

No? She said no? Was this a trap? Was she toying with him like a spider with a fly?

"Same here," said Nigel, pouring multi-grain Cheerios into a bowl. He noticed he still had some shoe polish on the back of his hand. Rubbing it off, he began to feel better about his chances. Perhaps, having had several hours to reason out the situation, Annie had developed a thoughtful perspective on last night's escapades. Perhaps he'd inadvertently advanced her cause, whatever that was. Or maybe she'd seen him take one in the nuts and given herself over to some previously unrevealed well of compassion. Whatever was happening, Nigel had to encourage it.

He filled a small glass with orange juice, noticing as he poured what a splendid orangey color it was. Remarkably orangey. He placed a bowl silently on the table and accompanied it, just to the right, with a neatly folded napkin underneath a shimmering silver spoon. Just beyond the bowl, off-centered to the left, he placed the delightful orangey glass of juice. The arrangement as a whole was, he thought, as handsome a place setting for a bowl of Multi-grain Cheerios as he could ever expect to be a part of. Nothing was too good for his forgiving wife.

Nigel stood for a moment admiring his own handiwork before ruminating on relationships. Much has been written in literature regarding the grace, patience, and forgiveness inherent in the female character. Nigel, while not doubting the literature, would have—if forced at knifepoint—confessed to not having seen it much. At least, not as an adult, and not from his wife. Annie had many great qualities—qualities Nigel admired without reservation. But grace, patience, and forgiveness? That's why they needed a dog. But coming into the morning, Nigel had every expectation of being eviscerated, possibly in his sleep. And yet ten minutes had passed with not a single angry word. Could it be that those female traits—grace, patience, and forgiveness—had been secreted away in some hidden chamber, just waiting for an opportunity to surface?

The more he thought of this, the more his Annie—his dear let-bygones-be-bygones Annie—reminded him not so much of a woman, but of an angel in womanly form. He was certain that one could search high and low across God's green Earth and never find a more divine spirit to scarf down a bowl of multi-grain Cheerios. It came to him in a flash that she also deserved toast with strawberry jam.

"Breakfast is served, dear."

Annie rolled herself off the sofa with a groan and trudged to the table. With leaden eyes, she navigated to the first available chair—not the chair where Nigel had placed her cereal.

"Your cereal is over here, dear," said Nigel, gesturing like a model on *The Price is Right*.

"Why?" she said.

"This is where you always eat, so this is where I placed it," said Nigel.

"Why would you do such a thing?"

"I just thought you would want your cereal in your usual place. I can—"

"I don't mean the cereal."

"Oh? You mean you wanted coffee instead of orange juice…angel?"

Annie let out a deflating gasp. He had once heard a similar gasp when he'd presented her with the second half-gallon of laxative in preparation for her colonoscopy. Nigel's vision of Annie as an angel in womanly form took a serious hit.

"We need to talk," she said, using the phrase the way all women use the phrase.

Nigel shuddered at the phrase the way all men shuddered at the phrase.

"After your breakfast would be good. You need your nourishment," said Nigel.

"Now," she said. Her eyes remained three-quarters shut, and her head held in a single direction as she spoke. The body language conjured images of zombies, the kind that joylessly feasts on hearts.

"Maybe you would prefer to take a nap first, dear. I know you must be tired."

"No nap. We need to talk."

"Okay. If you prefer. I'm concerned for your health, but if you want to talk, we can talk. There's nothing I like better in this world than talking to you. I don't know if I've told you this before, but I consider you one of the world's great conversationalists. My world, anyway. I've often thought it an absolute shame that you and Willie Shakespeare never got together. You'd have hit it off—"

"Nigel, what were you doing at the Sandoval place?"

"You mean last night?"

"There have been others?"

"No, not really. I had been there a couple of times during the day, working on my case."

"Your case? What do you mean, your case?"

"You didn't catch it from the discussion last night? I thought I'd jolly well described it. The Sandovals, you see, had contracted me to find their dog. Not much of a case, of course, but that's why I took it—because it wasn't much of a case. If it was a real case, I would have shipped it straight to you because you're the real detective—an expert. You know your stuff. Any real case would go to you, believe me. Missing dog cases—that's more my speed."

"Why would they contract you?" said Annie, coming straight to the point. "How did they know you were in the dog-finding business? I mean, I didn't know you were in the dog-finding business, and I live in the same house. Funny how they should know and not me."

"Isn't it? Funny that you should say it was funny because it *was* funny. They called for a detective, and of course, that would be you, but when Mrs. Sandoval explained the case was about a missing dog, well, I knew that wasn't a case for an expert detective such as yourself, so I volunteered my services."

"You volunteered? So you're not getting paid?"

"Yes, of course I'm getting paid. That is, I get paid if I crack the case. I cracked it, twice, in fact. Maybe I'll crack it three times. If we're all done here, I best get crackin'."

"How much did you get paid?"

"Two hundred dollars."

"Two hundred dollars? You took a case for two hundred dollars contingent upon solving it?"

"Plus expenses. I got paid expenses."

"Expenses for what?"

"Lunch."

"Two hundred dollars and lunch?"

"Actually, I made three hundred dollars and lunch. I found the dog twice."

"And you ended up breaking into your client's house in the middle of the night. You're lucky you didn't get shot."

"That wasn't luck, actually. The only one likely to shoot was Abuelita, and I knew she didn't have her pistols."

"Fine. The luck was you getting stuck in their doggie door. I saw plenty of guns around, not to mention knives, skillets, and croquet mallets. There were endless ways for you to be killed. But that's not the worst of it."

"It's not? I was thinking it might be."

"No. It's not," said Annie. "I'm trying to build a reputable detective agency in this town, and my husband—my clueless, amateur, dog-detective husband—takes a case using the name of *my* agency and botches it to no end. It's devastating to my brand. Completely embarrassing for you, for me, for the agency. When I first answered the phone regarding her case, Mrs. Sandoval said, 'I'm so glad it's not that imbecile.' I had no idea what she meant, but now I get it. Everything I've accomplished in the past two months could be undone in a minute by your thoughtless actions, parading around as if you were a private eye. Did you ever think about that?"

"Not in those terms, exactly. I did hide the fact that we're married."

"This is a small town, Nigel. People will find out, especially if you're running around like a chicken with his head cut off."

"That's a disturbing image."

"Not as disturbing as a bullet in the forehead. Is that what you want, Nigel, a bullet in the forehead?"

Trick question, thought Nigel, but he knew how to handle it. "I want what you want, dear."

"Oh, you do, do you? Well, a bullet to the forehead isn't sounding so bad just now. Did you think that crawling into the home of my client in the middle of the night, with greasepaint—"

"Shoe polish."

"Shoe polish smeared all over you, in my cowl-neck top—and what was the deal with the cowl-neck top? Is that something new? You're dressing in my clothes now?"

"I needed it—"

"You needed my cowl-neck top?"

"For the ensemble. I needed it for the ensemble."

"The ensemble? What? You're putting together ensembles? You mean like for your fall collection? What are you talking about?"

"The ensemble for the stakeout. I needed black clothes for the stakeout. I didn't have a black shirt, but your cowl neck—it's black."

"Okay," said Annie. "Enough about the details of your little escapade. The point is this. I'm trying to start a business here. Not only that, but we also have to live here. It's not like Houston, where you can do all kinds of stupid things and still be anonymous. It doesn't work that way here. One little incident can create a reputation you can never live down."

"Is this the point in the conversation where I can say how terribly sorry I am?"

"If you intend to stay alive for the next twenty-four hours, then yes, now would be a good time."

"I am very sorry. I can see I've put you and your company in a difficult spot, and that's the last thing I wanted to do." Nigel wasn't adept at making puppy dog eyes, but he did his best.

"I haven't talked about my business much because I don't like to bring work into the home, but it's been hard getting the business up and running. The kind of jobs I expected haven't materialized, so I've had to take jobs like that Gilbert gig for a lousy sixty bucks an hour."

"That's pretty good."

"That's pretty good for a dog detective, not a human one who likes to eat human food and live in a human house."

"Have you cracked the Sandoval case?" said Nigel, hoping there might be good news to brighten the diatribe.

"Suffice to say I've still got some work to do, but I don't think it'll be difficult."

"What's the case about?"

"Nigel," said Annie with an incredulous expression, "my investigations are confidential between me and my paid clients. I am not going to discuss my cases with you, especially not that one."

"Can't you just tell me what they hired you for? I know some things about the family. Maybe I can help."

"Okay. Here's the deal. I'll tell you why they hired me, but in return, you must promise that you will have nothing more to do with them, that you will stop the detective work, and that you'll get on to your real job, which is fixing up this house. Also, I need to know everything else about your so-called detective activities. Are there any other cases?"

"No. No other cases," replied Nigel. "Now, what about that Sandoval case?"

"Well, the old lady in the house, Abuelita, has an estranged daughter who hasn't been seen in decades. So, a couple weeks ago, Abuelita gets a strange phone call, and for some reason, she thinks it's from her daughter. Then last week, she claims to have seen a woman—her daughter—lingering outside the house in the middle of the night. She even says the woman threw pebbles against her window to wake her up."

"What was she wearing?"

"Abuelita?"

"The woman outside the house?"

Annie looked at Nigel as if he were a diarrheal strain of E.

coli. "Why would you possibly care what she was wearing? What possible interest would that be to you? Maybe after putting so much thought into your own prowling ensemble, you wish to compare notes with your fellow prowlers. Is that it? You want the fashion lowdown for this season's night crawlers at the Sandoval Estate? Sorry to disappoint, but I'm not providing fashion reports."

"So, you were hired to find the lady?"

"I don't know that there actually is a 'lady,' as you say. We're dealing with someone who might be verging on senility. My job is to locate the daughter. They've also had a few things go missing around the house. They want me to look into that as well."

"What kind of things?"

"You're getting into details I don't like to discuss. Just some papers and documents, and believe it or not, a pair of old galoshes."

"Galoshes?" said Nigel, tightening his jaw muscles to prevent his mouth from flopping open.

"Yes, like rain boots. Now, that's all I'm going to tell you. It's your job to forget about the Sandovals, forget what I've told you, and get back to your work."

"Can I give you a hint about something?"

"What?"

"For the galoshes, look in the bushes about ten feet to the right of the porch. If you should find something there, look up."

"Look up? What will I see looking up?"

"A galosh, perhaps."

"In the sky?"

"Just a hunch."

"A hunch? You have hunches?"

"It's how I roll, Sugar."

Except for the four hundred bug bites layered over his

body demanding to be scratched, Nigel was beginning to feel better. He would see another dawn. His wife, while perhaps short of saint status, had not been the multi-headed, fire-breathing beast he so feared. Perhaps there was a bit of angel to her after all.

"Nigel?"

"Yes, dear?"

"Where is the to-do list?"

"What?"

"The to-do list. Where is it?" asked Annie.

"Could be anywhere, dear. Why would you want it?" said Nigel. Unless she hoped to start a fire, he considered its location classified.

"I want to see what progress you've made, and what's left to do."

Nigel scratched his ankles, then the back of his neck. Of all the things he would have wanted to hear, Annie asking for the to-do list would have been at the bottom, right after the sound of Krakatoa erupting beneath his feet. "Not seen it for a while," he said. "Committed to memory. It's all up here," he said, pointing to his head as if something were there.

"Isn't that it?" said Annie, pointing to an end table.

"Couldn't be," said Nigel.

"I think it is," said Annie, snatching the paper while Nigel was busy trying to scratch inaccessible places on his back. "Wow!" she said. "You've made good progress."

No doubt she had noticed the many items with slashes through them and had assumed those tasks were complete. This was an oversimplification. Nigel had already instituted his program of slashing out two items for every item accomplished. So the slashes did not represent completed items, but items Annie was expected to forget about *over time*. Therein lay the problem. The well-established hole-in-the-wall phenomenon required time to establish itself. Annie's premature inspection of the list put Nigel's strategy—and by extension, his physical well-being—in grave jeopardy.

"New drawer pulls in the kitchen," said Annie. "You've done those? I didn't even notice. Let's take a look."

Nigel's face went white, or perhaps crimson. No video exists, so maybe it flashed in alternating colors like a cuttlefish contemplating a messy divorce. Nigel scratched his belly because nothing more constructive came to mind.

"Wait a minute!" said Annie. "These are not new pulls. Why is this marked off the list?"

"Inadvertent?" offered Nigel.

"What else is *inadvertent*?" asked Annie.

Nigel might have assumed the question was addressed to him but chose not to answer.

"The vent with the smoke stains on it—you've replaced that?"

Nigel considered the question rhetorical, as she was headed straight for it.

"No! Not done. Nigel," she said, pausing for painful effect. "What. Are. You. Doing?"

At the time, he was scratching underneath his left knee but declined to go with that as an answer. "What do you mean, dear?"

"I mean, what is going on with this list? All these items marked off, and you haven't done the work. You agreed to take on the task of putting this house in shape, and it looks like you're just going through the motions. What's going on?"

"You misunderstand, dear," said Nigel in a businesslike voice. Maintaining a cool demeanor gave him the best chance of making a break for it if things went postal. "The items are not marked off because I have done them. Is that what you were thinking? Really?"

"Okay, I'll bite. Why are they marked off?"

"They're marked off because..." Nigel spoke slowly to

allow himself time to think. "Those are the items I have committed to memory. They're on, what I call, the short-term list. I keep the short-term list in my head. Some of the items on the short-term list have been done, and some haven't. You apparently *assumed* that the crossed-off items were completed items. I guess someone *could* make that mistake, but shall I remind you what happens when you assume?"

"No, not necessary. I will *assume* these crossed-off items will get done and get done soon. Is that a safe assumption?"

"Yes, dear. You may assume it," said Nigel, scratching underneath his left upper arm while exhaling a morning's worth of hot gas.

"Good. Now, I'm going to eat my cereal and then go to bed. You can do whatever you want as long as I don't hear a peep for the next seven hours."

"I'll be as quiet as a church mouse," said Nigel. "A dead one, if it makes you happy."

One reason dead church mice can be so quiet is their refusal to work on to-do lists, an appealing attribute. From now on, if Nigel told his wife he'd be like a dead church mouse, then a dead church mouse he'd be like, right down to its whiskers. If the past few days had taught him anything, it was that freelancing, personal initiative, and independent decision-making were a recipe for hot Nigel soup. From this point forward, he resolved to be his wife's little genie. Her wish would be his command. Free will was a thing of the past. Having taken to heart the life of a slave, a great weight fell from his shoulders.

With that out of the way, Nigel sat down for a game of Candy Crush. The computer screen came alive with a local news feed featuring a funeral announcement for the local drowning victim, Oscar Griesen. Nigel's attention was more specifically focused on an accompanying high school yearbook photo. The picture was enigmatic. The forever-frozen face radiated kindness, intelligence, weariness, and distrust, along with a multitude of other contradictory attributes, if one chose to stare long enough.

It's a haunting thing, a photo of a recently departed stranger. The unknowing beholder can't help but slap a personality on it, to build a person from it, to interpolate a life around it, all from one tiny, singular, two-dimensional moment. Nigel felt himself drawn into the game even while understanding the absurdity of it. And yet, he felt a connection with the photo on his screen. He imagined the face in life: moving, talking, living. He heard a voice, an open, generous voice. Nigel slumped as he recalled the living face, Oscar Griesen, offering assistance from the window of a white pickup truck. He shuddered as he recalled meeting Oscar with just a few more hours left to his life, then he slumped as he remembered discovering the lonely site of Oscar's last breath.

Nigel's impression of the victim, based on a couple of sketchy discussions, had been of a ne'er-do-well—a sort of drifter or petty criminal. A churning in his soul suggested that narrative was incomplete, if not totally wrong. His gut, a merciless enforcer of conscience, began tying itself in knots as he recalled how he had—just hours before—implicated this boy, this victim, in a murderous scheme. The dead have no defense against rumor and innuendo. Only the living can make that case for them.

Funerals didn't like Nigel. Raw emotions, dead people, living people you don't know, living people you know too well, uncomfortable clothes, clammy handshakes, hugs, thoughts of one's own death, strange locations: it all made for a trying afternoon. Still, trepidation or no, Nigel approached the New Antigua Baptist Church for Oscar's funeral.

This church was nothing like the church of Nigel's youth, which was always a rather impersonal affair. One could slip in and slip out without drawing notice, and at no point in the proceedings was one instructed to contemplate being 'left behind' on an operating table. In fairness, the people were as friendly as you'd ever want to meet if hand-clasping, back-rubbing, and mama hugs were any indication. Still, after a sermon like that, Nigel longed for a stiff drink, and no one was offering that.

The preacher provided few details about the deceased, instead using his death as a pretext to make fervent demands of the mourners. Though not mentioned explicitly, the impli-cation was that the deceased had made bad choices. Nigel's stomach, once again his most empathetic organ, twisted itself into a pretzel. He felt sad and embarrassed for the family whose painful mourning process was interrupted for the sake of delivering a message, which was undoubtedly delivered multiple times a week in that very church. A quiet despair infected Nigel as he waited for the service to end. The source of his despair lay not just with the preacher, but with himself as well. The two of them had committed the same sin of maligning the deceased with insinuations. Nigel ducked out of the service as soon as he could.

Outside the sanctuary, Nigel looked at the names in the registry and noted several Gastricks among the attendees. It seemed unlikely that these Gastricks were not related to the butlering Gastrick, yet that member of the clan had given no indication of any familiarity with the young Griesen. Of course, within a small town's web of relationships, anything was possible.

To the left of the registry table was a poster board with a picture of Oscar presiding over a gallery of large black-and-white photos of small-town scenes, sporting events, and local characters. Nigel was no critic of artful photography, but these struck him as well-composed, professional-grade pictures. The young man's output as a serious photographer bolstered the credibility of Abuelita's wacky story.

As people streamed out of the service, Nigel was swept into a line of mourners inching its way toward the weary, hunch-shouldered parents. Nigel's level of discomfort could not have been higher had he been wearing a cowl-neck top and slathered in shoe polish. He clasped the hands of the heartbreakingly frail mother. Looking into her red-rimmed eyes, he said, "Your son was a generous person." A thank you was returned in the form of a pained grin.

Once the crowd had thinned, Nigel—portraying himself as a family historian—approached two men of Oscar's age. The two accepted Nigel's offer of a free lunch at a place called the Beast Row Grill in exchange for their insight into Oscar, the person.

23

FORTY-SIX, PART THREE

Nigel had not been to the Beast Row Grill before, and he would not be that interested in returning. It was an excellent venue for this meeting, since Nigel wasn't much interested in eating.

The first of the young men to arrive was a tall, lanky blond with a goatee. Nigel had neglected to collect his name and would, therefore, know him as Toothpick. The second young man, more robust in build, arrived a moment later. Beefy was his presumed name.

Waiting for the food to arrive, Nigel opened the questioning. "I don't know much about Oscar, but I heard he'd been in some trouble the past couple of years. You know anything about that?"

"He got arrested for possession of prescription drugs that weren't his. That's all I know. He did no time, though," said Toothpick.

"He was a drug user?"

"It was Percocet, prescription pain pills," said Toothpick. "He was found in possession without a prescription. Honestly, I think he might have taken the rap for someone in his family. Both his dad and his brother had some run-ins with the law, so if either of them had been found in possession, it'd have been jail time. Oscar never really talked about the arrest. As far as I know, he didn't use drugs."

"Weed, maybe," said Beefy.

"Well, yeah, goes without sayin'," said Toothpick.

"Was he working after high school? Did he have a job?"

"He had been working some of the ranches around here. Day labor and handyman stuff. He could fix a lot of things," said Toothpick.

"He fixed my guitar," said Beefy.

"Maybe he did, but anyone that's heard you play would believe it," said Toothpick.

"He had an obvious affinity for photography," said Nigel. "Did you know anything about that?"

"He got into that after taking a course at the community college. He was good. He thought he could make some money with it," said Toothpick.

"He took pictures at the football games," interjected Beefy. "He would sell them to players or to their parents. I know he put on his Facebook page that he was available for assignments. I don't know if he got any."

When the conversation deteriorated into a series of junior high anecdotes, Nigel steered it deftly toward a discussion of pets.

"What about pets?" asked Nigel. "Did he have any pets?"

"He liked dogs, but he didn't own one," answered Beefy, "probably because he was afraid the snake would eat it."

"The snake?" said Nigel, subjugating the urge to say, "Bingo!" "He had a snake, did you say?"

"Did he? One big mother of a snake. I should let Dan here tell you about the snake," said Beefy.

"He thinks it's funny that I don't like snakes."

"That's not what I think is funny. I think it's funny that

you screamed like a little girl at the sight of it. That was funny," said Beefy.

"Hardy-har-har. What he's not telling you is that while I was screaming, he was shittin' his pants. Thing is, he can do that and no one notices. Except he smells better."

"Listen to him. Like he didn't let loose."

"If Mr. Scuzzy Britches is finished," said Toothpick, "I'll tell you the story. One day, Oscar—and this was just after he got back from working in Houston—he brings out this huge plastic container. Heavy, you could tell, but he didn't say what's in it. He said, 'Look what I found.' Like a dope, I walked right up thinking he'd found a crate of potatoes, or a bag of charcoal or something. He opens it up, and this snake —absolutely humongous—raises its head; a head the size of my foot, and it flicks his tongue. I admit I yelled, but mostly at Oscar for punkin' me like that. Jake's laughing about it now, but I remember he was standing beside me one second, and the next, I'm standing beside a yellow puddle."

"I got away from the screaming. But the puddle, my friend, must have been yours. It's okay, though. No one can scream like that without peeing a little. You should own it, bro," said Beefy.

"Where'd he get the snake?" asked Nigel.

"He had this job in Houston maintaining drainage ponds and pumps and things, and—according to him—one day, he saw this snake sitting in the weeds in one of the ponds. He knew it had to have been an escaped pet. He thought there must be a way to make some money with a snake that size," said Toothpick.

"He had it on his Facebook page. Something like, 'Monster snake available for pictures, parties, movies.' I'm not sure he got much interest because he talked about selling it," added Beefy.

"I told him he should release it in places where a giant

snake wouldn't be appreciated. Then he could show up like a snake wrangler for hire to take it away," said Toothpick.

"Like where?" said Beefy. "Chicken farm?"

"Daycare center."

Beefy howled. "Oh yeah! I can see it now. 'Did Bobby come in from recess? Bobby! Where's Bobby?' "

Nigel interrupted the merriment, "Can I ask what Oscar was like as a person?"

The two grew somber.

"He was a good guy. Not the type that would stand out—he wasn't going to be valedictorian or captain of the football team—but he would always be around to help. I trusted him more than most people. He probably wasn't that well understood because he wasn't into, like, the normal stuff," said Toothpick.

"I would say he was smart. He was almost too smart for me, sometimes—"

"Not really a compliment, you know," said Toothpick.

"I mean, he was into some intellectual shit that didn't mark him as cool, but that's who he was. I don't think he got much encouragement from his family," said Beefy.

"Do either of you know what he was up to when he died?" asked Nigel.

They both nodded their head.

"The rumor is he was involved in some kind of scheme, like a fraud or something," said Toothpick.

"You don't believe that?" asked Nigel.

"No way. Not something he would do. Anyone that says that doesn't know him. It's like if someone said I had a secret life as a ballet dancer. It just doesn't fit," said Beefy.

"You're right about Oscar," said Toothpick, "but about your secret life as a ballet dancer, I've always had my suspicions."

"Is that right?" said Beefy. "I've always had my suspicions that you were thinking about me as a ballet dancer."

"Gets you excited, doesn't it? I always knew," said Toothpick.

Nigel was increasingly feeling like an outsider. He thanked the two for their help and headed out.

The conversation confirmed what Nigel felt in his gut—that the thumbnail sketch version of Oscar Griesen was misleading, if not woefully untrue. Nigel did not feel good about himself, having both succumbed to the lie and embellishing it. Worse, he didn't know what could be done about it.

Nigel paid for the pair's meal and transported himself—and his giant Styrofoam cup of iced tea—to the car. His car keys, having been liberated from the pants pocket, took things a step further and ended up sprawled on the asphalt. When Nigel squatted to retrieve them, he noticed a colorful object moving over the cracked pavement. An ant it was, but not just any ant—a bright orange and black woolly mammoth of an ant. Its legs and antennae moved in quick jerks, but the ant itself skittered in one direction then the other, either in no hurry to reach a particular place or in a big hurry to reach no place in particular. Either way, Nigel had discovered a dazzling, if temporary, pet.

Nigel shook out his cup, then guided the little beauty in. He clamped on the lid to create a cozy, if spartan, habitat for the little guy. Though not such an enthusiast as himself, Annie could appreciate a bug of exceptional beauty or cuteness. This little trophy scored well on both counts. What better salve for a marital rough spot than a colossal, furry ant?

Nigel listened to the delicate scratchings within the cup. He wasn't one to name his insects, but if he were, this one would be Lil' Hairy Antkin.

Within two minutes of leaving the Beast Row Grill, Nigel

slammed on the brakes to avoid a collision. He had pushed the accelerator when the traffic light turned green, before detecting—out of the corner of his eye—an object in sunflower yellow approaching from the left at a high rate of speed. He screeched to a stop, allowing the blur to pass unscathed. Having spared the miscreant, Nigel watched the flash speed away. The car was familiar. Absent some enormous coincidence, it was the exoti-car from the Sandoval residence. Nigel turned to follow.

Pursuing yellow sports cars through small-town streets in Ford Fusions is akin to threading needles while wearing mittens. The sports car darted; the Fusion wallowed. Nigel was able to track the sportster by watching pedestrians and drivers crane their necks to see what had just roared past. Nigel's Fusion, on the other hand, would not draw attention if it levitated.

Nigel lost the scent as he entered the old city center. Not ready to give up, he wound his way up and down the streets before spotting his target in the parking lot of the animal shelter. Nigel pulled into a parking space at the hardware store across the street to wait and watch.

Nigel scrunched down in the driver's seat. He wore sunglasses but sadly lacked a fedora to pull low over his brow. He reclined his seat and trained his eyes on the doors of the shelter. Within minutes, the interior of the car had jumped to 110 degrees, even with the windows open. He rolled up the windows, started the car, and maxed the AC. After an indeterminate amount of time, he was awakened by a knock on the driver's side window. A young clerk he recognized from the hardware store was yelling about a new shipment of downspouts. Nigel gave him a nod and a thumbs up. The clerk seemed amused; Nigel was not, particularly.

Now fully awake and shivering in sweat-soaked clothes under the blast of maximum AC, he turned toward the animal shelter to see Gastrick, the butler, rumble away in his sports car. Nigel drove across the street to the shelter.

He had supposed his previous visit would be his last. Given the kind of disruption he had caused, security may have been employed to assure as much. But even if brawny security guards were not on patrol, Annie's restraining order was. Nigel had promised to deep-six the investigation stuff, but things had changed since accepting her edict. A moral imperative and a strange coincidence had placed him in the perfect place to get crucial information. *What was he? A man or a dead church mouse?* The binary nature of the question made answering difficult. But acquiring information is not investigation, he told himself. As long as he was there, he would ask a few questions.

There was still one problem: Miss America, snake-and-tarantula division. Perhaps, thought an optimistic Nigel, she wouldn't be there.

He crept to the entrance, opened the door, and stuck his head inside. The timing was unfortunate. A large schnauzer attached to a small lady expressed a dislike bordering on derangement upon seeing Nigel's bodiless head appear in its path. Nigel popped himself out, but not before catching a glare from the crystal blues of Forty-Six. He stood back from the door, yielding the entire space to the exiting schnauzer. The dog—seeing, for the first time, Nigel in full—appeared emboldened. The little lady, acting as a drag anchor in heels, glared at Nigel as if he were the one with snarling lip and foaming mouth. The irate dog passed as Nigel's left eyelid began to twitch.

If he were to go in, he needed a strategy or distraction of some sort. Devoid of ideas, he got in his car to leave when a plan presented itself in the form of tiny scratchings in a Styrofoam cup. The little guy, collected as a peace offering for

Annie, now had a more urgent mission. The Serpent Queen was just the type to appreciate such a creature.

Nigel entered the building and walked straight toward the desk holding his hands together as if clutching a delicate prayer. He reached the edge of the desk as Forty-Six was directing a tribble-like creature into a small cage. Nigel introduced himself with an "Ahem."

Forty-Six remained bent over the cage for what seemed an inordinate amount of time for caging a tribble.

When her face finally made its appearance, Nigel was struck by the tightness of her jaw and the stony coldness of her relentlessly blue eyes. Only now did Nigel understand the depth of the offense he'd committed in coming between a young girl and her tarantula. She acknowledged Nigel with the dourest of smiles forced through severely drawn lips. If those lips had been knuckles, they'd have been white and knobby.

"Hello again," said Nigel, removing his top hand to liberate his little pet onto the open range of his hand. The critter wasted no time exploiting its newfound freedom, marching in herky-jerky fashion out of the palm and up the forearm. Nigel held his arm out slightly and twisted his wrist to display the charming bug to maximal advantage.

"I found this guy outside," said Nigel through a hopeful grin.

As the lovely ant marched with a feathery tickle up the arm, Nigel observed the girl's face, especially the mouth area. That's where it starts, the earliest signs of joy or delight. He watched, but the mouth did not move. Nigel's left eyelid began to tremble. The girl remained bereft of emotion. She seemed stunned. In awe, perhaps. Awe might work.

"Never mind my new little critter," Nigel said. "I came to ask about—"

At this point, Nigel observed the Serpent Queen clamping

her hands over her ears and corrugating her gorgeous face into a warped mask of horror. A gentleman would have offered concern and assistance. Nigel, under normal circumstances, would've been all over it. But for the moment, he was busy. Busy screaming—contorting his own face into a quivering mass—and grabbing at a forearm experiencing something of an impalement. A simple impalement—say, by a knitting needle—would have been bad enough, but this one felt like a knitting needle discharging fifty thousand volts.

Who can say what goes through a little ant's mind? Not Nigel. Insects are simple creatures with a limited emotional range. Things are either swell or un-swell. Importantly, no matter how un-swell things are, an insect's face does not flush, nor does its brow pull inward, nor does its mandible grind, and nor does it emit curses. An un-swell insect has but one way to express its displeasure. And Nigel's Lil' Hairy Antkin—snatched from its daily routine, incarcerated in a Styrofoam cell, subjected to extreme temperature swings, and finally, displayed like a circus freak to compensate for his captor's pitiful inadequacies—had finally had enough. He expressed his displeasure midway up Nigel's forearm. Lil' Hairy Antkin, after expelling a full sac of venom into his abductor, felt swell once again.

Nigel did not. He demonstrated his discomfort with a series of impressive shrieks and body contortions. The forearm, paralyzed by waves of electrified pain, clenched itself immobile while the body at large flailed, wobbled, and twisted. Eventually, the whole assemblage collapsed in a heap, where it writhed like an earthworm atop a mound of fire ants. Nigel may have blacked out—or perhaps the pain had vaporized time—but at some point, he discovered himself on the ground looking up at an array of faces, most of them human.

"Cow killer," said one of the human heads.

Hearing those words, a semi-lucid Nigel panicked at the thought of the atrocities he may have committed during those lost minutes.

"That's what it was, all right," said a different head, "one of them cow-killer ants."

"I've heard if you pee on the sting, it makes the pain go away," said a woman.

"I'll pee on it," said a round, freckled face. "I'm ready. I got buckets."

"Naw, that's for jellyfish," said the original head.

Nigel forced himself into an upright position before the discussion escalated into a challenge. His further struggle to stand up was rewarded with a scattering of applause.

Though he'd managed to stand, his mind raced to understand what had occurred. It was starting to dawn on him where all that pain had come from. While Nigel was grateful to be alive, his throbbing arm left Nigel to wonder what hideous damage had been inflicted. His eyes dropped downward to assess the devastation but were stopped by an all-consuming dread. The thought of a once-serviceable limb transformed into a swollen purple mass left him trembling. The longer he averted his eyes, the more disturbing the images became. He could wait no longer. Nigel opened his eyes to the carnage.

What the... thought Nigel.

The forearm was not only whole but in its original color. The site of the sting could barely be detected. A mosquito would have done more damage. What kind of a fiendish devil-bug inflicts such misery without so much as a mark suitable for a commemorative photo?

"You ought not mess with things around here unless you know what they are," said Forty-Six.

"Truer words," said Nigel, "have never been spoken."

The black-and-orange ant crawled out from under a sheet

of paper on the desk. The girl fidgeted for a moment before roundhousing a red sneaker onto the bug with an impressive level of brutality. She gazed at Nigel with a self-satisfied look. The girl, not the ant. Lil' Hairy Antkin had been converted into a two-dimensional still life, suggestive of surprise followed by extreme blunt force trauma.

Nigel looked into the girl's eyes. They were as blue-green as the waters of a mountain lake in March, which can only be seen as the ice gives way beneath one's feet. But Nigel felt no sense of panic. In fact, he felt calm. Very calm. Very, very calm. Had he been, at that moment, in a commercial airliner spiraling downward in an uncontrolled descent, having just lost a wing, he would have spent his remaining time gazing out the window admiring the passing cloud formations while clipping his toenails. He was that kind of calm. Imperturbable, you might say.

Determined to put this unexpected bout of tranquility to good use, Nigel addressed the young lady at the desk. The very same young lady who had, just moments earlier, invoked in Nigel a queasiness familiar to blindfolded prisoners being offered a dinner of sausages while trapped in the holds of steamships plowing turbulent seas. That kind of queasiness. But no more. Nigel was calm.

"Miss," said Nigel, "a well-dressed gentleman exited these premises some ten minutes preceding my arrival here. Might you be so kind as to inform me as to the business he may have been conducting?"

"What?" she said, jiggling her head as if to shake the words out of her ears.

This type of response sometimes elicited irritation, but noting that her eyes were reminiscent of the cerulean blue sky opposite the sun as it sets over a field of Cornwall clover in September, a pass was given. With his new-found wellspring of serenity, nothing was likely to get under his skin. He re-formed the question and tried again.

"A short time ago, there was a man in here. A middle-aged man who had a body like a grasshopper and a face like a codfish—"

"You mean that butler guy?"

"Yes. Absolutely. That butler guy, an apt description. May I ask, what was that butler guy doing here?"

"He dropped off a dog," she said, pointing back toward a caging area where, in one of the intermediate-sized prisons, sat a dejected Duffy.

"That is," Nigel said, "the very dog I inquired about a couple days ago. Now, what if that dog already has an owner?"

"They need to pick him up. You know the owner?"

"I think so. It might be a while before I can contact them. If I give you my number, can you keep the dog here and let me know if anyone enquires about him?"

"I suppose," she said, stroking her chin. "I'll put a note in the dog's file. Hopefully, whoever is here at the time will see it and give you a call. Can I put a reason for the note? Are you the dog's former owner?"

"No, I'm a detective of sorts." Nigel noticed the girl sit up. "The dog is possibly germane to my case, but I don't want that mentioned. Just say I'm an interested party." Nigel handed her his card.

"I'll take care of it, Mr. Blandwater-Cummings," said the girl, looking at the card. "Is that really your name, Blandwa-ter-Cummings?"

"That really is my name. You can call me Nigel."

"Okay, Mr. Blandwater-Cummings. You're a defective for hire?" she asked, looking at the card.

"Detective for hire. Detective. It's an inside joke."

"I see, I guess. Watch out for the bugs. Especially the pretty ones."

"Now I know," said Nigel, turning to leave.

Nigel's arm still tingled, but not so painfully. Overall, he felt better than he had in years. His step was deliberate, his mind clear, his nerves silent. The deep serenity would be hard to describe because he'd never felt anything like it. Nigel imagined it must be how one of those Zen Buddhist monks feel after being acquitted of a murder charge. The world just felt right.

Not only that, but Nigel also had a pretty good bead on a dognapping suspect. He would need to contact Mrs. Sandoval before returning Duffy. It might be one of those difficult custody decisions: dog or butler. She would have to make that call.

24

CRAZYTOWN

Once home, Nigel consulted the all-knowing Google about that magical cow-killer ant. He discovered it was not an ant at all, but a species of velvet wasp. The females are furry, beautiful, wingless, and have one of the most painful stings in the insect kingdom. The males, by contrast, are of no particular interest except to the females, and even then, just for the night. The sting of the female, while excruciating, leaves no lasting physical damage.

Nothing was mentioned about the psychotropic qualities of cow-killer venom. So, where did all the serenity come from? Could it be a natural by-product of intense, soul-searing pain? Maybe a kind of ant-based electro-shock therapy that scrambled the brain waves, leaving the victim temporarily free of the jitters. Nigel could see how such an ordeal could leave one a better man, rather like going through one's wedding ceremony. Or, he thought, perhaps he'd experienced what you feel when Dr. Death raps on your skull one moment, only to discover that you've won a staycation the next. There was a span of time for which he possessed no recollection. Perhaps he had drifted toward a warm and loving light, or he could have been abducted by aliens for the testing of skin products. All cool, but he would never know.

So, looking beyond the cow-killer sting, Nigel reflected on what had been learned from his latest travails. Oscar Griesen, the drowning victim, possessed the snake found at the scene. He had promoted the snake as a prop for his photography services. This tended to corroborate Abuelita's bizarre explanation for his location and intentions, but her tale of an online mystery lover appeared sketchy at best. Abuelita must have thought she'd hooked the prize tuna, but to everyone else, it appeared she was the one getting the hook. And she was no prize tuna—more like a hagfish. Now that things had gone awry, was the hagfish off the hook?

And what of the dog? Gastrick, having dumped the dog at the shelter, was now suspect number one without a number two. But why? Is a weekly appointment to stick a thermometer up a mutt's bunghole sufficient grounds for a dognapping? Nigel had not the experience to hazard a guess.

Of course, Annie was in a far better situation to investigate these questions, but was she even looking? She was hired for very different reasons, and it wasn't like Annie to stray from her mission. Information was tantalizingly close at hand, yet if the wife suspected Nigel of having so much as dipped a pinkie into the investigation, New Antigua would have a brand-new murder case on its hands. Still, he thought of Oscar Griesen's parents and the rumors circulating about their son. The need to uncover the truth gnawed at his gut like a swallowed rat. He could not give it up just yet.

Nigel dialed up a Mrs. Rosharon Gastrick, a name he had seen on the funeral registry. After convincing her that his intentions were not evil—no timeshares—he ascertained that her maiden name was Rosharon Griesen, Oscar's aunt and a Gastrick by marriage.

"Is your husband related to the Gastrick that works for the Sandoval family?" Nigel asked.

"You mean Jordan? Yep. My husband's older brother, not that anyone would guess it," she replied.

"You mean he looks younger?"

"Naw, I mean they ain't sociable. Jordan don't powwow, nowhere, for nobody. Once he took that fancy job at that golf course, and grow'd tight with the golf folks, he don't show his face no more."

"He worked at the country club, you say? That would be the Sandoval place now?" asked Nigel, struggling to penetrate the accent.

"That'd be it. Once they bought the place, he stayed right there to run it for 'em. Nobody knows why. They weren't running no country club, and he sure didn't need no money."

"He has money, you think?"

"Seen that ride of his? Yeah, I think he got cash. He was the boss man at that there country club. They paid foldin' money, for sure. That ain't all. If you feed the pigs, you get to eat bacon, you know. And that trough had some pretty fat pigs. Bacon and ham to go 'round, I 'spect. You get what I'm sayin'? I think you do."

"Do I?"

"Course'n, he might a learnt things he wasn't 'post to learn, like which hogs slop with which sows, stuff like that there. Maybe there's slop to be had there, too."

"Yes. Of course. What?"

"I'm just saying. You clean the cats, you get hairballs. He got that scratch some way. Rides like that don't show up at no bus stop."

"Certainly not," said Nigel, thinking it might have been the thing to say.

"Got that right. I knew you was. Say what?"

"What?" Nigel wiped his brow and regrouped. "If I

understand correctly, you think he may have been involved in some quasi-legal activities or inside business transactions."

"I'm not spoutin' about this or that. I say he's a black sheep. Don't graze with the rest. He eyes different pastures, greener ones. After he works for the country club, suddenly he's got *investments*, he's got *properties*, he's got them mobile homes he rents out. But we don't know nothin'. He keeps it to hisself. Tell me, how'd you know Jordan?"

"I did some work for the Sandovals, and I met him in passing. I was curious when I noted that you shared a family name."

"You been up to Screwball's, eh? House chock full of nuts, is what they say. What you reckon?" she said, almost as a challenge.

"Reckon?"

"About the Sandovals. They a bunch a loose bricks or what? Give me the poop, Sweetie."

"Poop? I see—"

"No, you don't see. We're on the phone, so talk."

"Very well. They may have their eccentricities, yes. I'm not sure I would classify them as 'chock full of nuts' as you say."

"Really? They bought a golf course, man, to live on," she said. "And they don't play golf! It's like buying a champeen steer for the milk. Makes no sense. They paid a handsome loaf to get that golf place, and once't they made it not a golf place, it's worth half a loaf. Well, Bubkis, as an impartial observer, I say, chock full 'o dem nuts."

"When you say it like that, it does sound a little crazy."

"Sure as shinbone. At least the old broad ain't shootin' at walkers-by no more."

"I believe they've taken her pistols away."

"And the long guns?"

"I haven't observed any. Not in her hands, anyway."

"Probably the reason you're still with us. Thank the Lord.

When that biddy shut down the golf club, this town went to lockdown. Crazy lady with gun squares off against golf junkies needin' their fix. Extra! Extra! Read all about it. I hid the kids in the storm cellar. Whole town was a sweatin'. Our salvation came in the form of a bolt from heaven."

"A bolt from heaven?"

"Lightning. Struck the old Sandoval house. Up in flames she went. Crazy lady wouldn't come out. Shot a fireman's hat off. Came out only 'cause a certain fireman agreed to carry her out without wearin' a shirt"

"And that was the end of the feud?"

"Golfers scared of lightning. They later regrouped into foursomes, but by then, the old Duffer was an unplayable lie forcing a retreat to the nineteenth hole. Don't hear from 'em nowadays, the golfers. But you see 'em out there pretendin' like they're playing. Swingin' their clubs with no balls and no holes, and sometimes, no clubs. They need a hobby."

"What about Oscar?" asked Nigel, hoping she might have some information about his death.

"A terrible thing, bless his soul."

"Yes, my condolences. Did he have business with the Sandovals, or your brother-in-law, Jordan?"

"Oscar lived in one of those trailers of his. Don't mean he had no business with 'em. Why you ask about the Sandovals? What would he be doing with them?"

"I don't know? He was found out there."

"Out there? In their creek?"

"Yes, on the Sandovals' property."

"On the golf course?"

"The former golf course, yes."

"Oh my God," said the woman, as if realizing something terrible. "There's evil there. One of theirs taken, now one of ours. The score has been settled."

"What do you mean?"

"The Sandoval boy all those years ago in the same place, the same way. You put store in black magic?"

"I've seen David Copperfield."

"The juju. Been a long time, but maybe not too long. What's done is done. Not to be undone. You be gone. I can't talk."

Nigel wrapped up the conversation quickly after that unexpected left turn down Spook Alley. He didn't know quite what to make of it. He wondered to himself if every small town in America was, like this one, a boiling cauldron of stick-in-the-eye crazy.

His phone buzzed with a message from Annie.

Football game tonight. Be ready when I get home.

25

FRIDAY NIGHT LIGHTS, AND LIES

A football game? Nigel had never been to an American football game. Nevertheless, the message indicated a willingness by Annie to scabbard her dagger and curtail the scorching glances. Slow torture was well-suited to the home but not so much to public events like football games. Perhaps the doggie-door incident was already receding into the past, becoming a shared scar rather than an open wound. Nigel could only hope because, as of now, the very thought of it left him feeling like a stomach ulcer soaking in lemon juice.

Of course, Nigel was obliged to accept any directive from the wife regardless of recent events. As he was once told by a guy named Luigi, "Never turn down an invite from the Capo, especially if he knows where your horses are stabled."

Annie arrived home, went straight into the bedroom, and reemerged ten minutes later in a dark-purple T-shirt and a baseball cap styling a Buc-ee's beaver logo. She looked cute.

"Purple is the color, is it?" said Nigel, standing to welcome her in.

"Purple and copper."

"Purple and copper? Hired a fashion consultant, did they?"

"I don't know about the purple, but copper makes sense."

"Does it?"

"If your team is called the Copperheads, it does. We've always had copper helmets."

"Have we? I'll need a wardrobe upgrade. My color palette is lacking in purples and coppers. Anyway, not knowing the proper colors, I went for neutrals," said Nigel, posing like a fashion model. "I don't suppose the opposing team's colors are white and khaki."

"Not unless we're playing West Boresville. Tonight, we play the Green Beast from Southland East. Green and white."

Nigel gave her an up and down look. "I must admit, purple does it for you. Or maybe it's the beaver logo. How about me? Am I suitable for a high school football game?"

"No, but you're what I'm stuck with."

"Sorry about that, but it was rather short notice. Could I ask *why* we're going to a high school football game?"

Annie looked surprised. "Why would we not?"

A half hour later, Nigel stood with Annie by his side at the entrance of the New Antigua High School Football Stadium Complex. *So this is where the money goes*, he thought.

The town of New Antigua, estimated to contain twenty thousand men, women, and children, had constructed a football stadium capacious enough for all of them—plus a few guests. The structure's red-brick facade matched that of the nearby high school except that it was newer, cleaner, and higher quality. The main entrance was flanked by two brick pillars, each with a ten-foot cement inset sporting a three-dimensional relief of a slithering copperhead snake. The mirror-imaged snakes were positioned as if climbing upward on the stadium wall. Each snake's head, with mouths open and fangs bared, were angled downward as if preparing to strike at the incoming fans. At the base of these grotesqueries, hordes of grade-school children gazed upward, thinking high school must be the coolest place ever.

Nigel had lived in Texas long enough to understand the misplaced importance of high school football in these small towns. *Tribalism run amok,* he thought. My town is better than your town because our collection of pimply seventeen-year-olds can beat your collection of pimply seventeen-year-olds in a football game. It seemed a shaky premise. Why not, say, compare economic statistics instead? Admittedly, tickets to that would be a hard sell.

From the surrounding parking lot, droplets of purple spectators rolled in, congealing into a bubbling mass outside the stadium gates. The ticket takers—at several locations—presented choke points, which split the percolating purple flood into multiple streams with counter flows and eddy currents. Nigel and Annie weaved through clots of appropriately attired fans toward the stadium gates. The drummers of a marching band pounded out a martial beat, compelling movement into even the most dedicated idlers. Somewhere in the distance, a cheer went up. "Copperheads bite… Copperheads bite… Bite…bite, bite, bite… Sssssssssssss."

Deep purple is not, in Nigel's estimation, an intimidating color. However, he had to admit that being surrounded by this unified mass of purple-clad humanity was provoking a response within him. Purple banners waved majestically over the seething expanse of purple brotherhood, whose throbbing to an incessantly purple-hued drumbeat seemed to sync with his own reverberating purplish heart.

As the drumbeats grew louder, Nigel felt taller and wished that he, too, were clad in purple. Looking toward the far end of the parking lot, he saw a group of cars and school buses festooned with green and white ribbons amid clumps of sadly green-clad people.

The invaders, thought Nigel, *lambs to the slaughter, the unaware, the unfortunates, and the soon-to-be disillusioned. Pity the poor SOBs growing up in Southland East, unaware of the lesson in humility they were about to receive at the hands of New Antigua's resplendent youth. They have no idea.*

Annie grabbed the distracted Nigel's arm to steer him toward the ticket stand, only to be stopped in their tracks by a pudgy, spotted adolescent. In front of his two giggling cohorts, the freckled-face teen grabbed his own forearm and jerked himself about in a spastic St. Vitus dance. Emergency medical personnel would have been summoned had the performer, between maniacal screams, not been so thoroughly enjoying himself.

Annie looked at Nigel for a clue.

Nigel, feeling looked at, shot Annie a glance that said, *It's your football game. You explain it.*

The boy, whose laughter had overtaken his ability to squirm, looked at Nigel and said, "Do you want me to pee on it?"

Annie, perplexed, looked at Nigel.

Nigel, feeling even more looked at, turned his eyes toward the heavens. Failing to see any sign of a rescuing lightning bolt, Nigel leveled his gaze to see beautiful trouble drifting his way.

Freckle Face and his cohorts scattered, and in their place, dead ahead, was the Serpent Queen in full regalia. Nigel felt so looked at, the side of his face could have toasted buns.

"Are you doing okay?" said Forty-Six, violating Nigel's norms regarding personal-space intrusions by beautiful girls when his wife was in the vicinity. Nigel felt claws dig into his arm as the skin on the side of his face began to blister.

Forty-Six, as it turned out, had maintained a rather dowdy appearance for her day job at the shelter. She dispensed with the librarian façade for football games. It was as if a spectacular butterfly had metamorphosed into a Super-Spectacular Butterfly. She wore a form-fitting sequined top—dark purple, of course—which, by design, left an entire shoulder completely nude. And who would have guessed that those crystalline blue eyes would have popped so magnificently with the artful application of glittery purple eye shadow? Nigel would have. As if that were not enough, a colorful little copperhead snake undulated up the left side of her face, the metallic-copper head—poised with flicking tongue—just above her eye. The snake wiggled far too enticingly whenever she spoke, smiled, or breathed.

"I'm doing fine. Thanks for asking," said Nigel. He made a slight attempt to move past. Forty-Six, obviously not used to that sort of thing, did not retreat.

"I'm surprised you made it to the game after what you went through," said the talkative Serpent Queen.

"You mean that little fall? Really, I'm quite all right. A bit painful at the time, I'll admit, but now everything is okey-dokey. I don't believe I even told the wife about it. Not worth mentioning, really. Forget about it. Thanks for asking. Enjoy the game."

"What about the case? Did you—"

Nigel felt something piercing his bicep. Annie's eyes applied a sort of laser melt to his skull.

"The case?" said Nigel. "Oh, the case. Yes, the case. It was damaged, somewhat. But I managed to get a replacement. No harm done," said Nigel.

"What case was this?" asked Annie to Forty-Six.

"Now, dear," interceded Nigel, "she's referring to the case...the one I dropped...when I fell. Only minor damage. I'll tell you all about it, but right now, I am starving. Let's you and me get a hot dog. If I don't get something in my stomach soon, I'm going to drop." Turning to Forty-Six, Nigel continued, "If you'll excuse us, Miss, we need to be on our way. Thanks for your thoughts. Bye."

The copperhead aboard the goddess's face stretched to its fullest possible length to accommodate the dropping of the mouth and the raising of the brow. Nigel ushered Annie away in a direction perceived to put the greatest amount of distance between her and the Serpent Queen in the shortest possible time.

"What case?" side-lipped Annie as she was muscled through the purple throng.

"Just a cardboard case. Nothing really, dear."

"A cardboard case of what?" side-lipped Annie.

"Beer," said Nigel as they made their way to the ticket counter.

"Since when are you buying cases of beer?"

"Two tickets, please," said Nigel to the ticket jockey.

"Hey! Don't I know you?" said the ticket jockey. A glance upward revealed yet another disturbingly familiar face from the animal shelter. Nigel was quickly getting fed up with small-town life, where friends and acquaintances lurked at every corner.

"Don't think so," said Nigel, obscuring his face by scratching a make-believe mosquito bite on his forehead.

"What about the beer?" asked Annie.

"Do they sell beer here? We can get some if that's what you want."

"No, the case of beer. Why did you buy a case of beer?"

"For you, dear. If you must know, I bought a case of beer for you," said Nigel, moving the couple toward the entrance gate.

"For me?" said Annie. "What? You bought a case of beer for me? Why would you buy a case of beer for me?"

"I say it's for you, dear, but I really mean for us, as a couple. I wanted us to share the experience."

"You wanted us to share a case of beer?"

"Maybe not in a single go, mind you, but yes. It'll do our relationship a world of good. I saw this case of beer, and I thought to myself, that's just the kind of beer Annie would enjoy. And I thought once you opened it, you would probably want to share its foamy goodness with your generous husband."

"So, what brand is it?"

"What brand, did you say?" Nigel scanned the crowd for a suspicious-looking character with a backpack that he could stand beside. Any such character would do, as long as he was packing a bomb.

"Yes, what brand?"

"It's a craft beer. You probably haven't heard of it. I hadn't heard of it, but I thought it would be just perfect for you."

"So what brand is it?" she asked, being mighty persistent.

"I think...I will save that bit of information...for the surprise. It's a rather unusually named beer. Fantastically named, as a matter of fact. It's a part of the experience, you know. I want to see the delight on your face during the unveiling."

"The unveiling?"

"Absolutely! This was all supposed to be a surprise, but you've let the cat out early. I'm thinking now we shouldn't even do it. Perhaps I should just return it."

"You don't need to return it. We can have some tonight."

Tonight? thought Nigel. He had overplayed his hand. "Not tonight," protested Nigel. "Tonight is football night. We can't have football night and beer night on the same night. That would never do. Doesn't make sense."

"Then when?"

"The fourteenth," said Nigel, grasping a number.

"The fourteenth? Let me think. That's a week from Tuesday. That's an odd choice. Why the fourteenth?"

"Valentine's Day," said Nigel, connecting it somehow with the number fourteen.

"Valentine's Day is in February. It's September."

Marriage to a detective can be a burden. Nigel steered her toward an entrance ramp into the stadium. "Do you remember last Valentine's Day?" asked Nigel. Nigel didn't, but one doesn't quibble about what's behind an escape hatch.

"I remember you got me nothing," said Annie sharply. "I remember you called Valentine's Day a trap perpetrated by weak women and enabled by crass commercialism. I remember you saying that women couldn't have it both ways, reserving a date in perpetuity while espousing spontaneity. I remember—"

"I am formally apologizing," said Nigel, as one would after stumbling into the den of a hibernating bear.

"Now? You're apologizing now?" said Annie with a voice like a razor.

"No. On the fourteenth," said Nigel, "you will receive my official apology."

Annie stopped and pulled Nigel out of the purple swirl of traffic.

"Let me get this straight," said Annie. "Your idea of an apology is to open a case of beer seven months after the fact? That's your idea of an apology?"

Put that way, even Nigel could see the idea had its deficiencies. Why couldn't wives come equipped with stingers like cow-killer ants? They could quickly inflict their measure of pain, leaving their stricken husbands to emerge as better men. Instead, what wives had were perfect memories; a terrible thing to bring to a marriage. Nigel once read that elephants are life-long monogamists. However did they manage?

Nigel's well of explanations was starting to run toward the dry side. Annie waited with crossed arms and busy fingers. Without warning, Nigel lunged in her direction, aided by a shove from behind.

Nigel stumbled into Annie, wrapping his arms around her for her protection and his balance. At first, Nigel thought a melee had broken out, and if not a melee, then a fracas, a ruckus, or a tussle. It was nothing of the sort. Creeping past was a large, rowdy knot of people holding cell phones in the air. Annie, standing on her tiptoes, declared that in the center of this throbbing mass was none other than Cam Logan. Nigel, looking deep into the throng, saw a phalanx of New Antigua's finest surrounding a mass of glossy, yellow hair.

Nigel didn't know a Cam Logan song from a bullfrog's croak. He wouldn't know her face if she bit him on the lip, and he hadn't the faintest idea how many husbands she'd had. What he did know was that her timing was impeccable, and for that, he would have kissed her on the foot. Annie wanted a photo, so Nigel held her up, fencepost style, to snap a few with her cell phone. With the proper timing, a photo of police-escorted yellow hair would be hers for the keeping.

By this time, the crowds were pushing their way into the stands. Nigel and Annie followed the purple current as the band played a popular tune recognizable to anyone the band director's age, followed by a cheer from a far section of the bleachers. "Copperheads, Copperheads, we got the fangs; poor Southland East, not worth a dang!" The pulsating streams flowed from the concourse, up the ramps, and into the open air of the stadium. From six entrances, purple spread outward over the stands like grape Kool-Aid on the shirt of a four-year-old. Nigel and Annie opted for a spacious row of open seats, which soon became a jam-packed row of occupied seats.

"Weren't you going to get a hot dog?" Annie asked.

"I was," said Nigel, struggling to remove his hand from

an unfamiliar crevice. "I think I'll wait. I'm probably only half a dog from not fitting into this seat."

Nigel, with just enough space to swivel his head, soaked in the spectacle. The opposite bleachers, hosting the green-clad fans from Southland East, held no more than a quarter of those on the New Antigua side. Nigel estimated the New Antigua side filled to roughly ninety percent capacity. Ticket sales pegged the figure at sixty-five percent, but New Antiguans were known to be resourceful. The Southland East band, seen from across the field, looked far less impressive than the Bitin' Copperhead Band and could certainly not match their volume. When the New Antiguan team, whipped into a frenzy by their adoring fans, plowed their way onto the field through a tougher-than-it-looks paper barrier, victory seemed all but assured.

A cheerleader best exemplified the New Antiguan fighting spirit. She took a nasty tumble when leading the players onto the field but hopped up to perform three cartwheels while protecting a gimpy ankle. She followed that up with a back-flip, ending in a gruesome lower leg injury. Fortunately, the band played heroically throughout, masking the snap and crunch of bones that might have otherwise been dispiriting. Fifteen minutes later, fitted with an inflatable cast, the cheer-leader led yells with her upper body as she was loaded into the ambulance. *This,* thought Nigel, *is Americana.*

Following the invocation, which sounded a lot like a prayer; *and* the national anthem, compliments of the afore-mentioned Cam Logan and her impressive array of hair donors; *and* the two school songs, which sounded like they were written by the same octogenarian composer on the same afternoon in 1934; the ball was teed up for the opening kick-off. The excitement among the New Antigua crowd, had they kept a chart for such things, would have been off it. The Southland East player received the ball on the five-yard line behind a poorly coordinated blocking scheme, which enabled Copperhead players to converge from all angles. The tiny Southland returner would have had to break no fewer than four tackles to escape being pinned deep in his own territory. In fact, he broke six tackles on his way for a touchdown.

As it turned out, the returner on that opening kickoff must have been Southland East's worst ball carrier because no one else had to break six tackles to get to the end zone. The Copperhead defense had pinned their hopes on a technique known as the "arm tackle," which they applied at every opportunity. The Southland East team had evidently gotten wind of this strategy, as they appeared well-practiced in evading such a maneuver. As you might surmise, the Copper-head defense had a rough half. The Copperhead offense, under the guidance of a different set of coaches, fared better. They equaled the number of tackles achieved by the defense and made a first down. The score at the half was thirty-five to zero.

Nigel had been careful not to say much to Annie. Or to look her way. Or to touch any part of her. He figured halftime might be the right time. "Does New Antigua always get beat like this?" asked Nigel, fully aware that he had nothing to hide behind.

"Of course not," she said. "I was just reading we've won ten games—"

"Really? Ten games? Last year, they won ten games?"

"In the past eight years. Ten games in eight years. Before that was a losing streak."

"Really? What about the other team? Southland East? They must be pretty good, eh?"

"Of those ten wins, seven were against Southland East."

The marching band took to the field playing that song from *Titanic*. The football team was nowhere to be seen, prob-ably in a locker room rearranging the furniture. The cheerleaders had also disappeared, leaving Nigel nothing to dwell on.

The second half began on a decidedly more upbeat note with New Antigua returning the ball to midfield before fumbling. Southland East scored on the next play, and lively discussions erupted in the stands, mostly about deer hunting.

The giant video screen at the west end of the stadium had ceased showing game highlights, as it became increasingly clear there were none. Instead, the screen streamed advertise-ments for local enterprises alongside music clips, cat videos, and scenes from the crowd—anything to distract from the carnage on the stadium floor. At one point, the blinding glare from a sideline video camera found Nigel's retinas. He squinted and smiled for the first few seconds, hoping he might get a free teeth bleaching. After a few more seconds, he wondered if he might be able to see his own bones. Minutes passed. By this time, Nigel was mostly trying to shield himself from the deadly rays. While squirming to find a shadow to hide behind, he caught an image of himself on the big screen, a single white blossom sprouting in a field of purple.

Nigel was no Hollywood producer, but a shaky, twelve-minute video of an uncomfortable man in a white shirt struck him as substandard entertainment, even when viewed on a screen the size of Connecticut. Having had quite enough of himself, Nigel turned his attention toward the cheerleaders just as they appeared to turn their attention to the big screen.

"Uncomfortable Man in White Shirt" had concluded its run, replaced by something even less technically accomplished but decidedly more dramatic. Debuting on the big screen, for the stadium's viewing pleasure, was what might aptly be named, *"Stumbling Figure Wrapped in Reptile."* Nigel felt strangely haunted as he watched the video play out. He noted, with some relief, that on the big screen, the species of the partici-

pants were not immediately identifiable. The presence of a snake was fairly well established, but the other creature begged interpretation. The first-time viewer might well ask, "Is that a monkey?" Continued viewing revealed the movements of the stumbling animal to be un-monkey-like. A chimpanzee, perhaps? The squat, waddling motion might suggest so. It was only in the video's final third, when the hapless creature lands on the pavement and looks directly into the camera lens, that a positive ID can be established. At that point, the viewer can determine with certainty not only the species, but the individual.

Nigel, on first viewing, had dismissed the video's entertainment value as meager at best. Perhaps he was too complicit for a fair and impartial judgment. The film was not an immediate sensation. Most fans had lost interest during the interminable *Uncomfortable Man in White Shirt* segment. But with each successive showing, more of the audience caught up with its charms. In fact, the video had—within its twenty-three-second runtime—everything necessary to become a sensation: mystery, intrigue, horror, pathos, relief, and farce. Once the viewer had determined that the victim of this horrific snake attack was not a helpless ape, but an inept, awkward human, the laughter could scarcely be contained. The stadium's occupants unified in a way seldom seen at sporting events. The players and coaches on both sidelines— and at least one referee—were splitting a gut. The New Antigua offensive team, with their backs to the video board, took advantage of the moment to score a touchdown against a convulsing defense. The score tightened to 48 to 7, but the fans scarcely noticed.

Nigel was beginning to feel uncomfortable. He glanced down at Annie several times, but he could see little beneath the Buc-ee's cap. While it seemed unlikely the average stadium-goer would recognize him as the man in the video, the wife was another story. Might there be enough in the video to tip her off? It was a warm night, but he shivered at the thought. He glanced down at her again but was soon distracted by an intense light.

The sideline camera crew once again focused their glaring light on Nigel. His giant image reappeared on the big screen, this time with a caption underneath: "Indian name: Wrestles With Snake."

Nigel, in averting his eyes, noticed various members of the crowd pointing toward him while patting their companions on the shoulder. This regrettable behavior appeared to be growing stadium-wide. Some people, upon finding the white-shirted Nigel in the audience, clapped. Nigel looked down at Annie to see the top of her Buc-ee's cap.

"Maybe we should leave," said Nigel, scrunching down to whisper in her ear. "This game is not going well."

"I would like to leave," said Annie, "in a submarine."

"Maybe I should go first, and you can meet me by the exit gate when you're ready. Take your time," said Nigel, hoping to draw fire so she could make a clean getaway.

Nigel could not help but notice the applause and laughter following him out of the stands and through the exit gate. He was now a celebrity around town. And, he feared, a pestilence at home.

26

NIGEL, THE WORM...OR PISSANT

Nigel attempted conversation with lines such as, "Not much of a football game," "The mosquitos are not so bad this year," and, "Is there anything you'd like to talk about?" Annie refused to bite, though if his jugular became available, she just might. The car traveled through the night like a tomb with a steering wheel.

The home environment did nothing to loosen Annie's tongue. She went to bed without so much as a "Goodnight." Nigel laid himself out in the recliner because he knew he'd be tossing and turning all night. He rose at two o'clock, snuck into the bedroom, and sat in a chair to watch Annie sleep. She could not possibly know what she meant to him. Before he met her, he was a shallow, self-centered creep who cared about no one. Now he was a shallow, self-centered creep who cared deeply for his wife. What a difference she had made.

At three in the morning, he was pacing. The silent treatment was not a standard Annie tactic, even though Nigel had sometimes wished it was. Annie, the former marine, had always confronted her frustrations by attacking. He had grown to understand this and had developed therapeutic, non-injurious methods to handle it. He had a talent for being the punching bag, absorbing Annie's frustration until she regained her equilibrium.

But what to do about a silent treatment? This was something different and frightening. Had he crossed a line? Had there been one too many straws for the camel's back? What deep and serious questions was she mulling over? The doubts pecked at Nigel's deadened mind like a flock of hungry vultures. He tried desperately not to imagine the worst, but the more he tried, the worse he imagined.

Nigel was awakened the next morning by light filling the room, or perhaps by urine filling his bladder. Either way, he had little choice but to start a new day with more dread than promise. He felt as if he'd spent the night on a heavily trafficked railroad track.

A note on the kitchen table read, "Gone to work." Being Saturday, it wasn't expected. Nigel wondered if it might be an excuse to get out of the house. He threw the note away and paced the house like a monkey in a leopard's cage. Keeping busy was the standard prescription for anxiety. The to-do list awaited action, but given his teetering marital status, provided a weak motivation. An odd idea fell upon Nigel like a plummeting vulture. Call Stanley.

A week before, the idea would have seemed preposterous. After all, Annie's stepfather had always appeared as the suckling toad to her mother's fire-breathing dragon lady. But in their last encounter, Nigel had perceived something quite different. Stanley wasn't the gooey marshmallow he'd been presumed to be, but perhaps more of a sly dragon trainer. He'd demonstrated—if not a steel backbone—at least an asbestos skin.

Nigel's situation was like Stanley's in miniature. Annie was her mother's daughter, though more tiger than fire-breathing dragon. Nigel was like Stanley, though—he'd like to think—with human characteristics. Clearly, Stanley had blazed a trail that Nigel was now following. What Stanley had seen, Nigel was now seeing. Stanley was a fellow traveler, a possible mentor, maybe a guru in waiting.

Nigel dialed him up. "Hello, is this Stanley?"

"Speaking," he said above some very loud music. James Brown, if Nigel wasn't mistaken. "Just a minute." The music faded.

"Yes, Stanley, this is Nigel...Nigel Blandwater-Cummings. Annie's husband. How are you?"

"I am fantastic, dude. Could not be better. And you?"

The voice sounded familiar, but not Stanley-like: too strong, too enthusiastic, and panting as if from a workout. The only panting Stanley was known to do was after downing three deviled eggs in quick succession. "This is Stanley? I'm talking to Stanley Dillard?"

"You betcha. Stanley Dillard at your service. What ya need?"

"Yes, well, this is not so easy to talk about, but I thought, with your vast experience, you might be able to help me out."

"Hey, if this is about loans for cloud-based properties, I'm not doing that anymore."

"Oh no, nothing like that. This pertains more to relationship issues between me and Annie. I thought since you've been with her mother for many years now, and Annie being so much like her, that you might be able to give me some opinions. You know, fill me in on how to keep the roses in bloom."

"I'm flattered you called me. I mean, it's nice to know you think so highly of me, but I'm not sure I'm qualified to hand out relationship advice."

"I think you are. I've thought about this, and your relationship with Annie's mother and my relationship with

Annie are quite similar. I can't think of anyone better qualified than you to give advice on the subject."

"Again, I thank you for that, but there's something you
should know. You see, me and Kayda are no longer together."

The news astonished. How often does a turtle shimmy out
of its shell? "Really?" said Nigel. "How long has this been the
case? I mean, we all had dinner just last Sunday."

"Since Sunday, then."

"Really? Maybe you'll get back together. You mustn't lose
hope."

"Lose hope? Lose hope, did you say?"

Nigel moved the phone away to protect his delicate ear
from the roar of laughter. "You seem rather happy about it.
Am I reading that correctly?"

"You are. You are reading that correctly, my friend.
Indeed! You're a good reader."

"May I ask what precipitated this breakup? It seems kind
of sudden."

"Well, I suppose there are a lot of things that precipitated
it. Twenty years of being treated like a turd precipitated it.
But truth is, I owe it all to you?"

"To me?" said Nigel. "But I've only known you for ten
years."

"I mean the breakup. You got the whole breakup thing
rolling. I'm not sure it would have ever happened without
you."

If this were true, Nigel deserved to be sole beneficiary in
his will, but he didn't see how it could be. "Are you sure?
How would I have anything to do with your breakup?"

"That night over at your place. I saw the two of you
together—you and Annie. I always thought the two of you
were a perfect couple, like a pair of lovebirds."

"We are. That's us, a pair of lovebirds."

"She may be a lovebird, but you seemed more like some kind of worm."

"A worm did you say?"

"That's what I said. A worm. And not a pretty one, I might add."

"Are there pretty ones?"

"Well, if there are, you're not one. Now, what was I saying?"

"You were saying I was a worm."

"Yes, of course. I don't mean literally a worm, not physically. I wouldn't go that far, but emotionally, you're a worm, or maybe a pissant."

"A pissant? Is that better than a worm?"

"About the same, I expect. Neither of them has a backbone, and that's my point. You were acting the part of some low-to-the-ground, spineless creature that begs to be stepped on. A slug. You could also be a slug if that's your preference."

"No, I don't think so." Nigel wasn't about to mention it, but when coming up with a spirit creature for Stanley, he had vacillated between turtle and slug. Feeling generous, he had gone with turtle. He was not feeling as generous now.

Stanley continued. "To see a grown-up man throw himself down—happily, it would seem—under the heel of their wife's boot continually, again and again, time after time... Well, it turned my stomach. And of course, Annie. Poor Annie. You can't blame her. What's she to do but grind away? That's what anyone would do living in a house with a worm, or a pissant, or a slug. Now, don't get me wrong. I'm not criticizing you."

"No, of course not," said Nigel. "You're not?"

"Not at all. Not one bit. I absolutely believe in a person's right to make their own choices. If you prefer a life devoid of personal pride, a life of crushing subjugation, then by all

means, live it up. Knock yourself out. Be happy. But what I
saw that night scared me."

"It's scaring me now," said Nigel, fighting off a shiver.

"It scared me because I saw a faint reflection of my own
life."

"Just a faint reflection?"

"I'm ashamed to admit it, but yes I did—a faint reflection.
Kayda has this unfortunate tendency to be dominating."

"Dominating? Kayda?"

"Yes, she does, and it's not a positive. Over the years, I
had grown somewhat accommodating. But when I saw what
you had become, I said to myself, 'Self, if you don't make a
change, that'll be you in ten years.' Just saying that gave me
the shakes. I made the resolution right then and there that I
was not going to let myself be turned into some goldarn dung
beetle."

"A dung beetle? Is that better than a worm or a pissant?"

"Of course it is! But that doesn't mean I want to become
one. So, I put together a list of grievances to be addressed."

"A list? How many items?"

"Twelve items. Originally it was forty-seven, but I consoli-
dated. I sat Kayda down—not an easy thing because she
hovers—and I told her these grievances had to be addressed,
or it was splitsville. I presented her with the list, and do you
know what she said?"

"Whatever you say, darling?"

"After she finished laughing, she said, 'How in the world
did I marry a man with three?' I says, 'What are you talking
about?' and she says, 'I've had two in my pocket since before
we said our I do's. Now you have the nerve to present me
with this? You must have had a third one somewhere. Hand
it over, and forget about your silly list.' You know what I
did?"

"Marbles?"

"I walked straight out of that room! Never felt better. I walked out with three, by golly! Count 'em! Three!"

"I'll take your word for it, if that's okay."

"I've already got a couple of connections on Tinder."

"Won't they be surprised."

"I may not have been under the boot like you are, but I was definitely under a thumb. I've got so much to do. There's the single's cruise to the Caribbean I need to book, an appointment with a hair replacement specialist, and then a planning session with my cosmetic surgeon. I hope this has been a help."

Nothing in the previous conversation could have been regarded as a help. The sooner the whole discussion could be forgotten, the better. Nigel refocused on the pressing issue of conciliating with his wife. But how to go about it, he hadn't a clue.

When people in small towns feel themselves under great pressure, they head to the supermarket. Nigel made like the Romans. He trudged in with no notion of what to get beyond a case of exotically named beer. *What an uninspiring place to build an apology kit.* He selected a small flower arrangement in a vase, a greeting card with a smiling chimpanzee on the front, a bag of dark chocolates, and a double twelve-pack of Love Street Ale. The check-out girl squealed with delight when she recognized him as the snake guy.

Nigel drove to his wife's office and parked out front. Annie's truck was not there. Where might she be? A chill descended as he realized she might be with her mother, the mother whose husband had just walked out on her. He imagined the conversation which might be taking place at that very minute.

Annie: *You're better off without him, Mother. You'll see. I'll help you find someone new. I'll put together some outfits to hide that*

hunchback, and we'll go to a makeup artist to patch up those cracks.
You're still a catch.

Mother: *It was that idiot husband of yours. Everything was fine*
until he entered the picture. I don't know what you see in him.

Annie: *You won't need to worry about him much longer.*

Mother: *You mean… Finally? You've seen him for what he is?*

Annie: *A worm.*

Mother: *Pissant.*

Annie: *Slug.*

Mother: *Dung Beetle.*

Annie: *No. That's too good for him.*

Mother: *You know, that Bronson Studly kid always liked you. He's*
a widower now, and they say he's worth millions.

Nigel examined his meager offerings and felt his blood pressure spiking. He breathed deeply and conjured up his happy place: palm trees swaying in the breeze above an empty beach of fine, white sand. The shoreline stretched for an idyllic mile, but something had washed up in the surf. Was that a body? A limp, fully-clothed body? A drunken cruise-ship passenger with new hair plugs stumbles across the human flotsam, then digs out a wallet containing ID for a Nigel Blandwater-Cummings—a person not reported missing.

Nigel ceased his meditation, a practice which too often ended in highly serene nightmares. He entered Annie's office to leave his peace offerings. He placed the vase and the pouch of chocolates at the center of her desk, moving a few papers out of the way in the process. Among the papers was a grainy 8 x 10 photograph of a middle-aged man who appeared to have swallowed a pufferfish. The face sparked a vague memory. A business card clipped to the photo read, "*Gerald Fitzgerald O'Reilly, Attorney at Law.*" Nigel's stomach filled his throat before dropping to his toes. "*Probate, Estate and Family*

Law," the card continued. Family law would include divorce cases. He would have thought the worm/slug/pissant combo was pretty close to the bottom, but now Nigel felt himself struggling to maintain his place among them.

Opening a desk drawer, he noticed a newly opened pouch of chocolates identical to the one he had just placed on her desk. His wife bought dark chocolates in times of stress. Nigel found a working pen and wrote on the chimp card:

My Dear Annie,

Sincerely sorry for making a complete mess of things. I absolutely promise to do better in the future. You have all my love and support.

Your Headless Chicken, Nigel

P.S. I am the chimp. Best I could do—all out of headless chicken cards.

Nigel placed the card between the vase and the chocolates, locked the office, and walked to his car feeling one step below worst possible. Now what? The waiting was the hardest part.

27

MANY OMINOUS RETURNS

New Antigua was not, as far as Nigel understood, prone to earthquakes. Yet two minutes after leaving Annie's office, while waiting for a green light at the corner of Hibbetts and 12th, Nigel felt a low rumble as if he'd parked atop a clothes dryer. Clenching the tremulous steering wheel, he looked for wobbling light posts or heaving streets. What he saw was the sunflower-yellow streak of a mobile earthquake machine. Intimidated traffic lights obviously changed to green upon its approach. Nigel revved his Fusion in pursuit.

After a few blocks, the yellow sports car whipped into the tree-shaded parking lot of the New Antigua Public Library. Nigel parked on the far side of the lot to observe Gastrick sauntering to the entrance, not to enter, but to push a book through the book-return slot. Gastrick trotted back to his car and whirled away as if not wanting to be seen at a library.

Nigel had not been in an actual library with actual books for years. He felt relieved not to be shushed by a gray-haired matron when he opened the door. Once inside, he looked to his left to see where the returned books went. He saw a wall. The room holding the returned books was accessible through a heavy wooden door affixed with an *Employees Only* sign. Nigel pressed on the door slightly. The absence of buzzers, shouts, or alarms indicated a certain openness to the public that Nigel was obliged to embrace.

Except for being crammed wall to wall with library stuff—shelves, books, desks, and the like—the room was empty. Nigel pushed his way to the outer wall where, beneath the return slot, sat a plastic bin containing a pile of books. Judging by their positions, only two books qualified as the drop-off from Gastrick. Nigel picked up the first of the two, *A Case for Love: High School Diary, Vol 14*. Not something he would have pictured Gastrick reading, but then again, who doesn't love a good high school diary. He picked up the second book, *Poisons, Potions, and Pernicious Prescriptions: A Mystery Writer's Guide to Dastardly Deeds, Book 3*. This seemed a more likely prospect for someone decades removed from high school.

Gastrick had mentioned nothing about literary ambitions. But would a butler? It's not like in the course of his duties, you'd expect him to say, "Follow me, sir. And have you read my latest novella?" That kind of crass self-promotion would be frowned upon in the butlering community. It did, however, make some sense for a butler to be a mystery author, if for no other reason than to offer a more balanced portrayal of the profession. Of course, being the butler, Gastrick could have been returning the book for any member of the household.

"Excuse me, can I help you?" came a dusky semi-feminine voice from behind.

"No, I don't think so. I think I'm finished here," said Nigel, turning around to face a quintessential example of the librarian sub-breed. She was stout and elderly, with a face like an alligator snapping turtle. Should the reader be unable to conjure a strong visual image of the alligator snapper

—*Macrochelys temminckii*—then imagine instead a stout, elderly librarian.

"What are you doing here?" she asked.

"Well, I...I had just returned this book, you see, and I...I had left my bookmark in it. I needed to get my bookmark."

"Your bookmark?"

"Yes, I used a twenty-dollar bill as a bookmark. Stupid, I know."

"Very," she said.

"Agreed, but that's just me. Some people think I'm an imbecile."

"I can see that," she said. This lady, while agreeing, somehow came off as disagreeable.

"But now that I've remedied the situation, I'll just be on my way," Nigel said, putting the conversation to an end. He handed her the book and started for the door. She looked at the book and then at Nigel.

"Are you a mystery writer?" she asked.

"Me? Oh no, not at all. More of a handyman these days."

"A handyman?"

"Yes, you know, a handyman. I take care of things. Not a pro, mind you, but I get the job done."

"Get the job done?"

You'd think a librarian would be faster on the uptake, thought Nigel. "Yes, get the job done. I'm given a list, and I eliminate —one by one—what's on the bloody list."

The librarian fixed her eyes upon Nigel. The amount of time a librarian should glower at a misplaced chap is a matter of opinion, but suffice it to say Nigel's tolerance for it grew thin from the get-go. Under the snapper's sullen stare, he thought of how nicely she'd pair with Stanley, sunning on a log in a swamp somewhere.

Finally, the librarian re-directed her eyes back to the book.

"An interesting choice of literature for a handyman," she said.

"Oh, the book, you mean? Just some research I was doing. Personal stuff, you know. Have a nice day," said Nigel, averting his gaze as he breezed past her.

Back in the car, Nigel checked his phone to find no messages. His stomach had that bottomless feel that happens when the earth gives way beneath the feet. Any conciliatory sign from the wife would patch this up in a jiffy, but until then, Nigel needed a diversion. He settled in for a long drive.

Driving down Texas country highways had often provided a tonic for his worst agitations. No matter how dragged-down he felt at the start, somewhere along the way, perspective could be found, optimism would declare itself again, and by the time he returned home, a measure of tranquility would be his. He hoped it would be so this time.

West would be the direction. It always was, especially if starting in the morning. Before aiming the Fusion westward, Nigel stopped at a gas station to resupply his tank. As soon as he got out of his car, an aggravatingly familiar growl approached from behind.

"Gassing up the chariot for some more doggie-detective action, eh, Mr. Blandwater-Cummings?"

It was Gastrick leaning against his yellow rumble machine. The dry, crusty butler had, by this time, developed a coating of slime. At least, that's how he'd evolved in Nigel's eyes, and Nigel, as a rule, steered clear of oozing butlers. Unfortunately, the Fusion's fuel door had taken this inopportune moment to refuse entry.

"Trouble fueling up?" said Gastrick. "Perhaps you might try sticking your head in."

Nigel could hear derisive laughter below the words. A clever comeback was called for. Nigel would have one ready in a few hours. He did, at least, solve his refueling issue by pulling the fuel-door release lever. "I'm quite all right. Thanks for your suggestion."

"Don't mention it. Always available to help with an important investigation. Have you managed to catch that dognapper?" he said while adjusting his driving cap. It was one of those floppy jobbers that rakish upper-class Brits wear on American television.

"I've turned over the investigation to my partner," replied Nigel. "I think you'll find some interesting developments in the case."

"Oh, really? Has someone made off with a squirrel, as well? What kind of ass-kicking would that merit?" he said with a snicker.

Nigel had once grudgingly respected the man for being a serviceable butler. But now he saw a petty man whose dignity had been imposed solely by his position. The butler suit, it seemed, was all that held in his nastier tendencies.

"You may be on to something there," said Nigel, "but I don't think squirrels are in play. My partner is one smart cookie, a former ace detective for the Houston PD. If I know her, she'll have some revelations that will turn this town on its ear." Nigel knew he was shoveling up a pile of the deep and smelly, but this guy was begging for it. If he could have, he would have buried him in it and placed a cherry on top.

"Revelations? Fascinating. I'll be most interested to hear about those revelations," said Gastrick with a sinister under-current. If the man had a handlebar mustache, he would have been twirling the tips. He abruptly finished his pump and was off in a loud, yellow flash.

Nigel, still pumping, wondered if Gastrick had stopped just for the insult. The amount of gas he pumped could scarcely have powered that yellow guzzler across town, but good riddance. Nigel had a number of questions for him. Why did he take Duffy? Did he know Oscar Griesen? Was he an author? But the least likely way to find answers, it seemed, was to ask him directly.

As aggravating as it was, this encounter was like number thirty-six on his crappy-moments-of-the-week list. The old braincase had only so much space for worry, strife, and frustration, and Nigel's was already crammed to capacity. New stuff went right out the earholes.

Within minutes, Nigel was driving past isolated ranch-style homes, meadows with cows, tin-roofed sheds, and every once in a while, a three-minute town. That is, a town that takes three minutes to drive through, inclusive of snail-friendly speed zones and two traffic lights. It was in one of these towns that Nigel, as per custom, pulled into an ancient Dairy Queen drive-through for a chocolate milkshake.

Nigel paid the girl at the window, set the cup in the cup holder, and crept away. Before reentering the highway, he grabbed the cup for a first satisfying slurp. The cup, in its holder, did not want to give itself up. Instead, it collapsed under his grip, popping off the lid and belching out a robust portion of its contents onto Nigel's hand and the car's console. With more than a little disgust, he backed the car into a parking space and reached behind his seat to grab the dirty anaconda-fighting shirt from the floorboard. As he sponged up the runaway milkshake, he felt a crumple of paper within the cloth. He retrieved a yellow sheet from the shirt pocket before finishing the cleanup.

The sheet of paper had been taken from the flooded truck of Oscar Griesen. What had seemed incidental at the time became completely forgotten a few minutes later when Nigel wrestled a snake for his last breaths. But the artifact had returned. Nigel examined the chocolate milkshake–stained document. It contained no words—just some scribbles and a few initials and numbers. Near the bottom of the note, a rectangular shape was drawn with a circle on its lower-left corner. Above this was a set of intersecting lines and numbers. Nigel recognized, in an amount of time not to be proud of, that he was looking at a crudely drawn map.

If Oscar Griesen's destination was the Sandoval estate, one might reasonably assume the rectangle represented the mansion. The circle on the lower left of the rectangle would feasibly represent the location of Abuelita's room, and an extraneous mark within the circle may have indicated an entryway—the French doors. This interpretation squared neatly with the description of Griesen's planned visit.

If the rectangle was the Sandoval mansion, then the other set of lines and numbers likely indicated directions—a map to the Sandoval place. But from where? The map contained no place names. If Nigel could determine the map's starting location, he might have the key to solving the mystery. If there had been a plot, the map's starting location might indicate the lair from which it was hatched. Nigel had only to backtrack from the Sandoval place to find the map's starting point and a possible origin for Oscar's fatal drive.

Nigel headed to the Sandoval Estate with all possible haste while not surpassing the speed limit by more than seven mph.

28

ANNIE SEES A ZEBRA

After an absurdly arduous visit to the post office, Annie returned to find her desk in a disturbed state. Its naturally disheveled and paper-strewn surface had been mildly tidied up. Sitting center stage was a small monument consisting of a vase with lovely flowers and a pouch of her favorite chocolates. Balanced between the pouch and the vase was a red envelope containing, no doubt, a letter of explanation and/or apology.

Even before opening it, she understood what it represented. Cards from a husband appeared under two situations: thoughtless appeasement—Valentine's Day, anniversary—or thoughtful desperation. Nigel, the desperate, was offering the card as a capitulation. He had recognized the error of his ways and was ready for his punishment and reformation. It represented a victory, but Annie, like a horse trainer mounting a wild mustang, felt a tinge of remorse at seeing a noble beast subjugated. Nevertheless, victory warms the heart.

Annie had reluctantly gone to the silent treatment because her preferred methods didn't work on Nigel. As an investigator, she had developed domination techniques that could drive powerful, hardened felons crouching into corners. But not Nigel. He would sit there and absorb every type of abuse, then say, "Now, how can I do better?" Nigel might appear weak-willed, but he could be unbearably, frustratingly strong. He was like those spindly palm trees that bend every which way in a hurricane, but after the storm passes, stand tall over the fallen oaks as they're chopped up and hauled away.

Annie opened the envelope and laughed at the card. It was weak by Nigel's standards, but still charming, somehow a perfect expression of minimally disguised pain. She could not continue her campaign for much longer. Once she was done with her work, she would thank him for the gifts and put the nastiness behind them—except for the all-important "laying down of the law" talk.

Annie's cell phone buzzed with a text message from Mother.

Stanley is leaving me. That pathetic husband of yours put some idea in his head. What do I do now?

Stanley, the perfect pack-mule, had busted out of the barn? Stanley? Annie never cared for him, never understood the relationship, and never comprehended the attraction. And she could not understand how Nigel had anything to do with his leaving.

Annie: *Why do you think Nigel caused it?*
Mother: *Who else? Stanley and that imbecile were talking!!! Find out what he said!*
Annie: *I'll ask, but I don't think so. I'll come by when I finish my work. Stay strong. Look for silver linings.*

Annie texted Nigel next.

Mother said Stanley walked out. She thinks you're at fault. What did you say to him?

Annie felt for her mother. It must have been a shock, but at the same time, it was hard to see it as a tragedy. Maybe her mother could explain Stanley's mysterious charms. If she couldn't, maybe it was time to move on.

Annie resumed her work searching for the long-lost Sandoval daughter, Esmerelda. She picked up a note pad to review her information. Essie, as she was called, had left the Sandoval home at age nineteen, an act of defiance toward her domineering mother after being forbidden to marry. She had scarcely been heard from since, and not at all for the past thirty-five years. Annie's computer search had revealed three husbands, three divorces, and two children. Her cities of residence had included Redding, California; Branson, Missouri; Maryville, Tennessee; Orlando, Florida; and finally, Dallas, Texas.

Most interestingly, Annie uncovered no criminal record or suspicious activities of any kind until two months ago, when Esmerelda was arrested for perpetrating an annuity scam against senior citizens. Annie found this exceedingly odd. Essie, as far as she could tell, had no education or background in financial matters. In fact, her investigation revealed an occasional hand-to-mouth existence with sporadic employment in several different fields—none dealing with sophisticated financial products. How would a minimally skilled, low-level worker become involved in such a scam?

Annie unwrapped a square of chocolate to fortify her for the work ahead. According to the court records, Essie worked with a partner who called himself Rory Rufus MacDougall. The DA asserted that Essie, in the guise of a fortune-teller, pumped her elderly clients for financial information, and upon encountering a lamb ready for fleecing, predicted an imminent financial difficulty. Of course, the clients could avoid financial ruin with the immediate intervention of a skilled financial planner. Enter the dastardly Mr. MacDougall —birthname: Gilbert Ray Stenson—in the role of financial savior offering crummy annuity packages. Financial savior, perhaps, but not for his elderly clients.

Essie was arrested based on an anonymous tip, but MacDougall skipped town. Essie maintained her innocence throughout, stating that as far as she knew, they had been helping the old folks. The judge wasn't buying it and sentenced her to six months. Annie searched to find out where Essie was being held and came across this eye-expander. Esmerelda Sandoval was listed as escaped. She had escaped two weeks ago.

This bit of news opened up a dirty brown satchel full of questions Annie had not anticipated. Where is Esmerelda now? Where is her partner-in-crime? Are they on speaking terms? Could Abuelita be correct that her long lost daughter had returned? And if so, why now? Annie, feeling her mind wobble, grabbed a fresh pencil—Ticonderoga, Number 2— and held it under her nose for a good, long sniff of cedar.

Could the misplaced documents—wills, financial records, and the like—have anything to do with this? The missing documents had reappeared as mysteriously as they had disappeared. Annie had ascribed the incident to either the liquor-induced, blacked-out bumblings of Mrs. Sandoval or the forgetful shufflings of Abuelita. Now, she wasn't so sure.

Annie learned long ago not to build a hypothesis around one captivating detail. As one of her instructors had put it, when you hear the thundering of hooves, don't go chasing zebras. Look for horses.

Annie sat back in her chair and rubbed her eyes, reminding herself that solving mysteries was fun. Feeling insufficiently invigorated by the weak aroma from her pencil, she opened the desk drawer, pulled out a box of large eight-count Crayola crayons, popped the lid, and inhaled deeply. Thus inspired, she looked down at her desk and picked up the 8x10 of the lawyer in the neighboring office. He had attracted her attention on the flimsiest of suppositions. He seemed to have no clients, and his arrival coincided with some of the strange happenings at the Sandovals'. Nothing more. Studying the face, she wondered what kind of man lurked behind those bulging eyes. She read the attached business card. Gerald Fitzgerald O'Reilly. *Sounds like an alias,* she thought. She said it out loud, "Gerald Fitzgerald O'Reilly." *Contains a certain rhythm,* she thought. "Rory Rufus MacDougall," she said to herself. She turned to her computer to see if there might be a mug shot for Gilbert Ray Stenson, aka Rory Rufus Macdougall.

There was a knock at the door.

29

ALL ROADS LEAD TO NOWHERE

Nigel sat in his car at the turn-in to the Sandoval property. He held the ragged little map before his eyes, lowering it slowly to survey the road ahead. After thumping his chin with an insistent forefinger, he rotated the paper 180 degrees and repeated the procedure. He scratched his head, spun the paper another 180 degrees, and pronounced the results "perfect." From here, he would follow the map in reverse order to find the location of where Oscar Griesen's final drive had begun.

As he prepared to pull into traffic, an image in his rearview mirror stopped him cold. A lady in a pink gown approached riding a rickety bicycle. The gown would have been flowing had it not been bunched up around her midsection, freeing her bare legs to operate the peddles. Nigel watched her turn into the Sandovals' drive.

It was the work of a moment for Nigel to connect this oddly-attired biker to the moonlit specter he'd seen earlier. Somehow, seeing the figure in broad daylight, pedaling a bicycle, flushed the gothic allusions right down the toilet. Nevertheless, having failed to make an acquaintance with the original pink-clad ghost, he was determined to get an interview this time.

He turned into the drive and drove some distance past the cycler before pulling over. Standing by his opened car door, he yelled out at the approaching cyclist, "Miss! Oh, Miss!"

Stopping appeared at odds with her travel plans. She swung wide as she approached Nigel and his car.

"Miss, do you have a second? I think we've met before," called out Nigel.

Slowed, but showing no signs of stopping, she eyed Nigel as if he were handing out free samples of the plague.

Nigel eyed her back, not with suspicion, but with confoundedness. He had, for reasons unknown, supposed ghostly specters in flowing pink gowns to be youngish and possibly lovely. Not this one. Nigel reckoned she had slogged more summers than he had, and from the looks of it, some had been pretty desiccating. Her hair resembled a derelict eagle's nest taken over by mud daubers.

"Miss," hailed Nigel. "Were you by any chance traipsing around yonder estate a couple nights ago? Say, about midnight?"

Without acknowledging the question, the sweaty ghost brought her bike to an awkward stop. She re-bunched her gown and scowled at Nigel as if he had suggested a shampoo. In that spirit, she pointed skyward with the middle finger of each hand before continuing on her way.

"Eleven, was it?" yelled Nigel as she cycled away.

In response to his supposition, she displayed a middle digit, this time with a waggle. Neither one nor eleven seemed correct to Nigel's thinking. This was his first encounter with a specter, and apart from her single-mindedness, he couldn't claim to be impressed. Perhaps he'd caught her on a bad day.

On the whole, the ghostly visitor scene was growing more tiresome by the minute. This cycling ragamuffin could be the long-lost daughter Annie was commissioned to find, or she could be the lady Abuelita had mistaken for that long-lost daughter. Or, she could be the estate's bat wrangler, for all he knew. Whatever the case, Nigel already had one mystery to solve, and he'd had quite enough of specters in pink. The ratty old ghost would go her way, and he would go his.

If Nigel interpreted the map correctly, he would follow the road north toward town for about six miles before turning left on a street labeled BW. At 6.2 miles, he came to a cross street called Bentwater Drive. The next instruction made sense as well, validating his methodology. Nigel followed the map to its logical end, which led to a highly illogical conclusion.

He had envisioned ending up at a secluded hideaway with armed thugs milling about the perimeter, or perhaps a nondescript residence guarded by a calico cat. Nigel would have accepted either destination. But where he found himself lacked both thugs and calico cats. He was at the strip shopping center where Annie's office was located—a fine bastion for trading in melons, greeting cards, and laminate flooring, but a sorry excuse for an evil lair. The shopping center, Nigel reasoned, was likely nothing more than a convenient meeting place or an agreed upon-point of reference.

Nigel's phone buzzed with a text message from Annie.

Mother said Stanley walked out. She thinks you're at fault. What did you say to him?

Nigel felt his head being acted upon by a plunging anvil. Whatever goodwill his little gifts might have spawned was now demolished. Already seething, Annie was, by now, gnashing her tusks with rage. With her office a few hundred feet away, Nigel strained to see if a mushroom cloud might be emerging from it. Cloud or no cloud, the fallout was coming his way.

With his marriage sinking and his investigation run aground, Nigel considered pointing the car west and not stopping until he was under a hundred feet of Pacific Ocean. He'd have done it if not for the inconvenient flashback of Oscar's parents burdened with the death and tarnished reputation of their son. Nigel didn't know what he could do about any of it, but he allowed his car to creep along.

He passed Wong's Chinese Restaurant, then a cellular store, then a postal/UPS depot, then Bob's Liquor, where he was tempted to stop but didn't. He kept the car crawling forward past the main tenant, a Wynn Brothers Supermarket, then Mary's Craft Shop, Todd's BarBQ, an empty space, and Sally Johnston's Plyometrics and Dance Studio. He rounded the corner occupied by New Antigua Flooring. The east side of the shopping center contained a row of smaller spaces with a Smiley's Dental, a CPA's office, an empty space, Annie's office, another empty space, and finally, O'Reilly, Attorney at Law. That was it. Nothing declared itself a haven for shady activities. It was all far too normal for Nigel's liking.

Annie's truck was parked directly in front of her office. Nigel pulled into a space directly opposite, facing out toward an empty field. He would have to face Annie sometime, but the idea of going in now made him quiver. Instead, he focused his thoughts on the Griesen case.

He envisioned a meeting taking place in this approximate location—perhaps in a shop, or perhaps in the parking lot—where someone posing as Abuelita's online lover, Fritz, furnished Oscar Griesen with the map, a bouquet of hand-cut roses, a bag of supplements, and verbal instructions for his photo assignment. The true identity of Fritz was the missing puzzle piece. Did this location, implied by the map, provide a hint?

Nigel looked around the parking lot as if a clue were just waiting to be discovered. And then he saw it…maybe.

At the far end of the lot, parked in front of the lawyer's office, was a very large, dark gray SUV. It could have been the one Nigel saw barreling down the road when he discovered Oscar Griesen's truck. But the SUV was not what had caught his eye. Nigel scooted forward in his car seat to improve his viewing angle around the hulking vehicle. There it was. On the other side of the SUV, just within his line of sight, were several inches worth of bright, sunflower-yellow rear fascia. The kind of rear fascia that belongs on a European sports car.

Nigel would not be mistaken for a powerhouse thinker, but the cogs and sprockets were whizzing now. Gastrick seemed to be everywhere. He'd been seen disposing of the family dog, he'd been at the library, and now at the lawyer's office. What reason might the butler have to visit a lawyer? In truth, there could be all kinds of reasons. But this location happened to be the starting point for Oscar Griesen's death ride. And here was Gastrick at this lawyer's office. A coincidence?

Nigel recalled two things Annie had told him about investigations. First, she didn't believe in coincidences. In an investigation, coincidences are clues. Second, she said when you hear hoofbeats, think horses, not zebras. Think of the obvious first. Nigel wished he could talk to Annie about this fascinating puzzle. Of course, if he opened his mouth about the case, she'd stuff a sock in it before running him over with the nearest available road grader. But maybe she'd helped already. Nigel recalled the photo of the pop-eyed lawyer, O'Reilly, which he'd seen in Annie's office. It was grainy like an enlargement—a surveillance photo, perhaps. She must have suspected him of something.

So, the lawyer-suspect was meeting with the butler, Gastrick—the butler who works at the Sandoval estate where Oscar Griesen was headed the night he died. Oscar Griesen who died on a photography assignment ordered by the never-seen Fritz. Suddenly, instead of a collection of random puzzle pieces, Nigel saw a picture.

Gastrick could be Mr. Inside. He knew the family secrets and had access to all sorts of useful information. O'Reilly—AKA Fritz—could be Mr. Outside, the con man, knowledgeable in the tradecraft of deception, laying out an enticing line for a vulnerable, elderly victim. If he was a lawyer, as he claimed, he'd know the legal ins and outs of acquiring property through marriage and inheritance. It was a catfishing scheme with a level of sophistication to match the stakes. Oscar Griesen may well have been an innocent pawn—a hired hand acting as an unwitting delivery boy.

Nigel's heart was beating like the hooves of a hundred zebra late for the grand opening of a new watering hole. Yes, there was probably some horsey explanation, but Nigel had trouble seeing it, what with all those stripes flashing before his eyes. Consequences be damned. He couldn't wait to share his insights with Annie. He pictured her bright eyes widening with delight as he explained the devious, twisted plot. He imagined the two of them joyfully plugging pertinent information into each other's scenarios until, together, they had constructed an unassailable account of depraved criminality they could both be proud of. Nigel sunk into his seat, weighed down with a hard-earned sense of accomplishment. All his issues would soon be resolved.

Wham!

Nigel's eyes jumped to his rearview mirror.

30

SIX LEGS OF SALVATION

In the rearview, Nigel saw Annie's office door fly open. Out came Gastrick, holding the door for the bulgy-eyed lawyer exiting, back first. From beneath his smothering hugs, Nigel saw flailing female limbs. Gastrick ran the thirty feet to the attorney's office to hold the door for the shuffling abductor and his abductee. Once inside, the door slammed behind them. The operation took seconds.

Nigel was petrified. He had just seen his wife being kidnapped. *911*, he thought. *911*. He picked up his cell phone and froze, trying to remember how to call 911.

"I'm at the shopping center," he yelled. "The Wynn Brothers shopping center. There's been a kidnapping. At the lawyer's office. It's urgent. The lawyer's office at the Wynn Brothers shopping center. Hurry!"

Nigel dropped the phone and got out of the car. What to do? Wait for the police or attempt a rescue?

Flashing back to his last conversation with Gastrick, Nigel now realized his effusive testament to Annie's detective skills may not have played to her advantage. Flashing back to the library, Gastrick's curious choice of reading material now presented terrifying possibilities. Nigel had to do something, but what?

Men facing grave circumstances often describe themselves as becoming possessed by a crystal-clear vision propelling them toward decisive action. Nigel was not one of those men. His mind resembled a demolition derby of dreadful visions, one after another trying to occupy the same space. To shake some sense from his brain, he paced, he hopped up and down; he hit his head with his fists.

If he were to crash the office, might they do something drastic? *But they've already done something drastic. Maybe something more drastic. They may already be doing something more drastic. They may have weapons,* Nigel thought. He had nothing. What chance would a flailing, has-been middle manager have against a murderous butler and an over-sized, bug-eyed attorney-at-law? Hardly any. But standing there pounding his temples didn't seem effective either.

Nigel squatted down and pounded his fist in the dirt, then his panicked left eye detected a flash of black and orange moving across the landscape—a cow-killer ant. He grabbed it with his left hand and slapped it against his right forearm. A second later, the palm of his left hand burned and pulsed with a searing pain he had, previous day excepted, never encountered before. He writhed, hopped, and emitted the kind of gurgled screams heard around industrial accidents.

The pain was far more intense than the sepia-faded version he recalled from twenty-four hours earlier. The reverberations sizzled from his hand to his arm, straight into his head, displacing the clangorous, contradictory thoughts with a simple, brain-saturating agony. On his knees, the world crackled around him as if he'd been plunked into a red-hot frying pan.

He let loose a series of grunts that grew angrier by the minute. His wife had been kidnapped, and he'd been stung by an ant. The pain of it all was congealing into a searing malevolent force. His vision became an encompassing red swirl with a butler and an attorney at the center of it. He grunted several more times and rubbed dirt in his hair, and as he struggled to raise himself, he saw another shimmer of black and orange. He reached into his pocket, pulled out a fast-food napkin, and leapt to ensnare the cow-killer ant. He lightly twisted the paper and ran toward the attorney's office.

The door was locked. Nigel pounded.

"Hello! Hello! Is anyone in there? I need a lawyer!" shouted Nigel.

No answer.

"Please. I need legal advice. It's an emergency," said Nigel. Even in his dazed state, he realized how ludicrous that statement was.

The door opened just enough for a reddened, over-sized face to be visible from inside.

"I'm sorry, but—"

In a single motion, Nigel slapped the cow-killer against the man's neck. As his hand made contact against the wobbling flesh, Nigel was seized with panic. He had not prepared the bug for its mission. Not that cow-killer ants need to be trained, mind you, but when enlisting one as a weapon to be slapped against an opponent's neck, one ought to orient the creature to produce a better than fifty-fifty chance the right person gets stung. Nigel's blood congealed in his veins while the bug dallied.

It was, therefore, a great relief to see the lawyer's eyes expand to the size of tennis balls while quivering in their sockets. The hefty man crumpled to the floor, screaming and convulsing on his way down. Nigel shoved open the door, striking against an unseen part—hopefully, a part sensitive to being struck—of the squirming body. Beyond the writhing form sat Annie, tied up in one of those cheap plastic office chairs facing a large desk. She hummed an odd, atonal tune. As Nigel approached, he saw her mouth covered by duct tape, her hands tied, and her feet bound to the legs of the chair with electrical cable.

"I'll have you out of here soon enough, dear," said Nigel, kneeling in front of the chair as he went to work unleashing her feet.

Annie expelled a series of grunts and hums with enough vigor to rock the chair, impeding Nigel's efforts to untie her.

"I know you're happy to see me," said Nigel, "but if you can just contain your enthusiasm for a minute, I'll have you out of this chair. Please, time is of the essence, but we must remain calm."

The humming and rocking continued with, if anything, increased energy. Between Annie's maniacal grunts and the downed attorney's death-beckoning gurgles, the place sounded like hell's waiting room. A frustrated Nigel looked up at Annie. Her head bobbed as if she were front-row at an AC/DC concert. Her pupils shifted back and forth within scarily intense eyes. Nigel wondered if she'd been given a drug.

Having caught Nigel's attention, Annie stopped the head banging and gazed straight into his eyes.

Nigel recoiled while the tingle of frozen spiders ran up his spine.

Her gaze, accompanied by a grunt channeled from a white rhinoceros, said to Nigel, "Listen to me now, or you have breathed your last breath."

Nigel listened. Annie re-started a slower version of her head banging routine, accompanied by a slower rendition of grunting. Perhaps sensing the declining communication value of such a gesture, she added a series of forceful chin juts.

Was she suggesting a direction or a location?

"Over there?" asked Nigel, turning to point over his

shoulder. "Grunt once for yes, or twice for no."

Annie let out a single exasperated grunt.

"Ah! Now we're getting somewhere. Over there. What's over there? Grunt once for— No, that won't work, will it?" Nigel turned to look behind him. There was a door in the vicinity. "Is it the door? Grunt once—"

Annie's eyes widened as she expelled three staccato grunts while punching her head forward.

"Three grunts? You didn't let me finish. Once for—"

Nigel heard a door fly open behind him.

"Hold on!" said Nigel, looking back over his shoulder to see a charging Gastrick. The butler, sporting a demonic grimace unusual for one in his profession, leapt onto Nigel's back. His left arm encircled Nigel's neck while the right arm extended upward beyond view.

Startled and staggered, Nigel rocked backward. His momentum slammed the two of them—the butler first—into the wall. By pure instinct, Nigel raised his hands to catch the butler's right forearm on a downward plunge. Stopped just shy of penetrating his chest was the point of a dagger. With all the force he could muster, Nigel backed into the wall again, slamming Gastrick a second time. The slam had little effect but caused a half-dozen of Annie's individually wrapped chocolate squares to come flying from the man's pockets. Nigel's personal opinion of Gastrick, already at a low ebb, hit rock bottom.

The butler's grip tightened around his neck. With his airways being constricted, time was not on his side, and he knew it. The butler's knife arm, struggling against Nigel's two-handed grip, moved upward in preparation for another stab attempt. In desperation, Nigel relaxed his arms. As the dagger began its downswing, he stepped toward the desk and dropped. The knife, plummeting toward Nigel's pounding heart, instead landed full force on top of the desk inches from where he was now crouched. The blade snapped off, a predictable outcome when your dagger is a cheap souvenir letter opener.

With the knife out of play, the choke hold posed the existential threat. Nigel lowered his chin to shield his throat, a position he could not long sustain. Anticipating a blow from the butler's free hand, he turned his head, sending the fist glancing off the cranium

In the meantime, the lawyer, still sprawled on the floor, had put aside his gurgles in favor of groans. He would soon realize death was not imminent. If he entered the fray, the battle was lost.

Having failed with the fist, the butler surrounded Nigel's neck with both arms. Nigel countered by kicking the butler's legs and putting his elbows into his ribs. He raised his right foot and brought it down hard on the butler's foot. Gastrick roared as if bludgeoned to the soul.

"You bastard!" yelled the butler. "Those are 1963 Chelsea boots! You'll die for this!"

Having found the soft spot, Nigel continued to stomp even while his trachea continued to be crushed. Out of the corner of his eye, he saw the lawyer—still groaning—raise himself to a sitting position. Straining for the slightest wisps of oxygen, he saw something else he'd not seen before. On top of a moving box, within arm's length of the groggy attorney, was a snub-nosed revolver.

While the big man wallowed on the floor like a walrus with a hangover, the revolver waited like instant death. Nigel could feel himself losing strength by the second. Sound became muffled, and a creeping darkness collapsed inward. Nigel strained to see Annie struggling to free herself from the chair. He suppressed any thought that he might be seeing her for the last time.

There was a rap at the door.

31

SHOCK(S) OF A LIFETIME

"The police!" Nigel choked out. *About time*, he thought.

The gladiators froze in place, expecting the door to spring open unleashing a bouquet of loaded weapons backed by men in blue. The attorney, aroused to a wobbly consciousness by the knock, sat up. Nigel saw him glance toward the gun.

The door opened gingerly. It was not the police. The four distressed faces looked with mouths agape as the door widened, revealing a woman with supernaturally smooth skin topped with impressively sculpted yellow hair. Her eyes darted quickly from the dazed fat man sitting on the floor, to the bluish man being choked from behind, to the butlerish man doing the choking, to the lady tied up in a chair.

"Ooooh," she said, being somewhat at a loss for words.

"Cam Logan?" gurgled the dazed attorney in a tone one might use for a long-lost loved one who'd turned up at their own memorial service—awe, surprise, and reverence all mixed together.

The visitor did not respond. Her hazel eyes, framed by lashes that could have raked leaves, darted across the scene.

A furrow would have come to her immaculately dermabrasioned forehead had the necessary muscles not been paralyzed by recent botox injections. "Sorry, I thought this was the acupuncturist," she said, slamming the door behind her.

Before this momentary interruption, the melee had been heading inexorably toward a tragic end—a *fait acompli,* one might say, had it been in France. And so it would have been had the interruption come by way of a pregnant mother struggling with morning sickness, or a postal clerk pained by persistent bursitis, or a middle-aged woman wishing to quell anxiety induced by flying tarantulas. In such cases, the donnybrook would have proceeded quite happily along its murderous way. But that is not what happened. The intrusion came by way of Cam Logan—country singer, TV star, and local celebrity—seeking treatment for a non-specific mood disorder following the receipt of divorce papers from husband number five after being accused of a dalliance—rightly, but just the once—involving ex-husband number three and his yoga instructor. The redoubtable Ms. Logan enjoyed varying degrees of fandom among the combatants, and this made all the difference.

Gastrick, the murderous butler, held a soft spot for Ms. Logan. Having grown up in New Antigua, a place devoid of glamor and tinsel, he—like most long-term residents—felt a certain local pride in Cam Logan's selection of New Antigua as a locale to have a place in. Though not a voracious fan of her music—its appeal being too broad to permit serious consideration—he nevertheless supported her ascent as a local icon. Seeing her for the first time, up close and personal, stirred within him a desire to absorb the image in a mental snapshot, to be compared at a later time to the full-length poster affixed to his closet door of a younger, hotter Cam Logan.

Nigel's association with Cam Logan had been confined to a single sighting of a cubic yard of her fiberglass-like hair at last night's football game. His interest in the visitor, therefore, was secondary to re-establishing his ongoing relationship with oxygen. The Cam Logan interlude forestalled his descent into unconsciousness and provided a much-needed respite to reconsider his strategy. This he did. A component of that new strategy was to act now while the butler was dumbstruck.

Nigel jumped up and forward, bending himself at the waist. The surprised butler, being so firmly attached, had no option but to go with the flow. The two belligerents went airborne together into a forward roll.

Below this twirling mass of humanity sat the thunder-struck attorney. Having just recovered from one shock of a lifetime, Cam Logan's appearance counted as shock of a life-time number two. Two shocks of a lifetime within a ten-minute span had, for the moment, rendered the attorney a useless nub. Cam Logan was to this evil lawyer, for lack of a better term, a kind of goddess. He had followed her career for the past two decades in a manner that would be embarrassing to admit. While making little effort to hear her music, he made every effort to catch her TV appearances, YouTube videos, and—if published with flattering pictures—gossip articles. Seeing this siren up close, even at a reconditioned fifty years of age, filled the lawyer's head with sticky love goop. So transfixed was he that shock of a lifetime number three was to arrive—as shocks of a lifetime so often do—without warning.

The whirling Nigel/butler mass, falling atop the lawyer's mid-section, laid him out like a round, puffy pancake. Lawyers of O'Reilly's dimensions are fairly packed with air, which—under normal circumstances—is excreted in small amounts under controlled conditions to the detriment of bystanders. However, in the present case of two adult males landing forcibly upon the belly, lawyer gas was expelled in a single great huff. Windows rattled and ears popped, and the lawyer emitted a sorrowful groan like something you'd hear from a sailing ship run aground. Gastrick, sandwiched between the pudgy lawyer and Nigel's plummeting mass, let loose his own groan, followed by another groan from O'Reilly, then a groan from Nigel to complete the set.

Gastrick slid off the attorney and onto the floor, still clamped to Nigel's neck. Despite Nigel's twisting and further attempts to strike with feet and elbows, Gastrick held tight, applying even more pressure. The gun remained on the box within reach of the lawyer, who—at this point—moved as purposefully as a beached whale. His arms may as well have been flippers.

Nigel, in Gastrick's ever-tightening clutches, felt himself fading. He had heard that at such moments, one sees a warm, welcoming light. What Nigel saw was something resembling the underside of a cheap office chair. At least one of its spindly legs came down forcefully onto Gastrick's torso, forcing out a rude yell. The chair raised up and came down a second time. Gastrick released Nigel to grab the legs of the tormenting furniture, heaving it—along with its occupant, Annie—onto its side. Annie had managed to free her feet, but with arms and upper body still bound to the chair, she was not able to right herself for another charge.

Nigel had to get the revolver. Gastrick, having dealt with the chair, appeared slow to understand his own peril. Nigel lunged for the gun, kicking blindly at the trailing butler.

With revolver in hand, he rolled over and pointed at the rising Gastrick. "Stop right there, or I'll shoot!" Nigel had never used a firearm, but he would under the circumstances. The gun was surprisingly light for something so deadly.

Gastrick smiled. "Let's get him," he said to a partner who wasn't getting anyone.

The lawyer was still trying to re-inflate himself.

Nigel scooted away while maintaining his aim. "Stop right there and put your hands up!"

Gastrick laughed and came toward him.

Nigel didn't want to shoot, but the murderous butler was mere feet away and coming forward. He had no choice. Nigel aimed for the chest and pulled the trigger. He missed. Over Gastrick's left shoulder sailed a powerful stream of water. "Hold on!" said Nigel.

Gastrick, smiling diabolically, leapt.

Nigel coiled himself in preparation.

At some point during this desperate tussle, the lower part of the butler's white shirt had become untucked and unfastened. To put it bluntly, Gastrick's uniform—in the vicinity of his belly button—was a shameful mess. This would not have mattered had Nigel not spotted a slab of pale skin peeking through the hurtling butler's dishevelment. Nigel knew what he was seeing—an Achilles heel in the form of a soft, white underbelly. Nigel understood soft underbellies; every reptile had one—yes, even turtles underneath their rock-hard carapaces. This snake of a butler would be no exception. Whether by plunging knife, roundhouse kick, or playful tickle, the soft underbelly was the place to be when it came to demobilizing scaly creatures. And here it was, Gastrick's soft underbelly, flying toward Nigel as if on a silver platter.

Nigel barely had time to aim and kick, but that's what he did. That flash of tummy flesh had provided the inspiration. One sharp heel in Gastrick's soft underbelly, and all would be over. But Nigel did not go for the underbelly. No, Nigel's kick did not make it that far north. When Nigel's shoe made contact, the butler's eyes bulged out of their sockets as if punched from behind by a pair of speeding marbles, or nuts.

The diving butler fell to the side, landing once again atop the lawyer. Gastrick groaned. O'Reilly groaned. Gastrick groaned again. O'Reilly groaned once more. Nigel could have listened to it all day.

The office door swung violently open.

"Hands up, errh, in the open! Everybody! Police! Drop your stuff, errh, weapons!" yelled the rubber-faced cop. He scanned the room, swinging his outstretched pistol from side to side like a weathervane in a cyclone. A couple minutes later, his partner arrived, followed thereafter by two more officers, and later bolstered by an additional four more.

Within the hour, half the New Antigua Police Department had converged on the tiny office. But as is so often the case, the early birds captured the best worms. In this case, the "worms" were selfies with a polite, if harried, Cam Logan, captured during the happy intersection of her departure and their arrival. The second officer, known to possess the coolest of heads, even coaxed a dedication: "To all the guys at the station. Love our boys in blue. Support the troops. XOXO, Cam Logan." It was later to be framed and hung in a place of honor back at headquarters, along with eight-by-tens of their hard-earned selfies.

Engulfed by a sea of uniformed officers, the four combatants each proclaimed their innocence while being handcuffed. After forty minutes of police discussions and autograph ogling, the quartet was hauled off to the hoosegow.

Sorting things out at the police station took much longer than one might suppose. This, despite Nigel's vehement and vociferous declarations as to the unassailability of his account. So confident was he, in fact, that he offered to present his case to the nearest baboon population with the hope of "speeding up the process." The process got slower from there.

A couple of issues delayed the proceedings. First off, the

lawyer and the butler were unknown quantities, whereas Nigel—in just a few short days—had established himself as the area's most reliable troublemaker. Even before the day's arrests, the rubber-faced deputy had been poring over case records to find unsolved crimes that might be attributed to Nigel. He had become—what's known in local police circles as—"a desirable apprehension" or "a perp in need of a crime."

The other problem was Annie. Despite her extensive police background, her communication skills were lackluster with a piece of tape covering her mouth. Every effort to remove the tape at the police station, even by a registered nurse, ended in failure. The fiends had utilized a brand of duct tape not approved for human lips. Annie's statement, consisting of grunts and hums, was deemed unusable.

The villains maintained a doe-eyed innocence while casting Nigel and Annie as murderous thugs with liberal tendencies. As much as the police wanted Nigel in jail, the butler's and the lawyer's stories deteriorated in ways familiar to many a politician; they couldn't keep their lies straight. Initially, the two recounted similar stories casting themselves as victims of an elaborate extortion scheme. However, it wasn't long before the two reprobates, when challenged to explain conflicting details, were pointing their crooked fingers at each other. In the end, the police had no choice but to arrest the felons and let Nigel and Annie walk.

The drive home, by Nigel's reckoning, was uncharacteristically tranquil for such an eventful day. Why shouldn't it be? A man doesn't get to play the knight in shining armor rescuing his damsel in distress every day of the week. Not even every other.

"Quite the day, eh, dear?" said Nigel.

Nigel couldn't tell if it was a growl or a purr coming from

Annie. Once he got her home and pulled the tape off, she could tell him all about it.

"How're your eggs?" asked Nigel, who'd graciously volunteered to cook breakfast.

"Horrible," said Annie, scraping tape adhesive off her cheek.

"Too much salt?"

"Too much WD40."

"Sorry about that, but it was either WD40 or the tape. I could have gone either way myself, but you seemed to think the tape needed to come off. In a week, you'll barely taste it, I'm sure."

"Tell me," said Annie. "How did you know I was being held in the lawyer's office?"

"Funny thing, really. I was out and about, and I contracted this sudden urge to see you."

"A sudden urge?"

"To see you. Sure, it happens. You get that, right? Usually, I fight it off, but not then. So, I made a beeline to your office, and there you were being carted off like a sack of potatoes by Popeye the Lawyerman and his henchman, Evil Butler. It was a lucky thing. That I was there, I mean."

"Just a lucky thing? Are you sure?"

Nigel mulled this over. He could tell her the whole story about the rediscovered map, the library book, and the encounter at the gas pump where he—quite innocently, it should be emphasized—tipped off the murderous butler, Gastrick, to her brilliant detective work. He could tell her that story. Then again, had he wished to tell that story, he would have done so when she was properly bound and taped.

"Maybe it was something more than luck: a sixth sense,

divine intervention, angels, true love's whisper across the ether. Take your pick," said Nigel.

"An angel. I'll take that."

"Really? I feel left out."

"My angel, Nigel."

"Ah! That has a ring to it."

32

NOT QUITE AN IMBECILE

Annie and Nigel made the Monday morning trip to the police station so Annie could provide her statement with a functioning mouth. After her detailed explanation of facts, the two were invited to attend a police press briefing already in progress.

The police press briefing had once been a regularly scheduled occurrence. However, several years of steeply declining circulation had resulted in the local press curtailing the free donuts. Since then, the briefings were an ad hoc affair. The local press, Agatha by name, called for a briefing on the Sandoval case because of its implications for the golf course.

The meeting took place in conference room B with free—but regrettable—coffee supplied to any participant that didn't know better. Along with Sheriff White were two members of the local press: Agatha, editor for the *New Antigua Gazette*; and her upstart rival, Edgaretta, publisher of the *New Antigua Roundup* website. Annie and Nigel were ushered into the room as questions were being answered.

"There's no murder here. I came all this way for no murder? What possible interest is this to my readers?" asked news veteran, Agatha. Agatha was a newshound, the last of a breed, who wore a visor and smelled of ink. Her paper hadn't turned a profit in eight years, but there was no way she was shutting down. She was addicted to the smell of newsprint, literally.

"Well, there was a death, if that helps," said the defensive sheriff.

"People die every day, especially in this town," interjected Edgaretta. Edgaretta, across the table from Agatha, was thirty-ish, with a nose ring, an assortment of tattoos, and dark-brown hair dyed like vanilla ice cream with a green swirl. "That doesn't make much of a story. Besides, you said he died innocent. This Oscar Griesen was merely an unknowing pawn in the scheme. I'm not sure that counts as feature material."

"You wouldn't know feature material if it peed on your laptop," said Agatha.

"Laptop? Where'd you learn a word like that?" snapped Edgaretta. "Next thing you know, you'll be talking about podcasts."

"Ladies, ladies, I warned you once already. Let's have some decorum," said the sheriff, looking like a grandfather babysitting the kids with no Wi-Fi. "We don't make the crimes; we just solve them. If this crime ain't good enough for you, then I suggest you go out and make your own."

Agatha shattered a pencil point on her legal pad. Edgaretta typed extra loudly into her laptop. Nostrils flared all around.

"Tell me, Sheriff," said Agatha, "this evil lawyer was from out of town. Dallas, wasn't it? How did he know about Abuelita Sandoval and her money?

"He had some kind of business dealings with her daughter, Esmerelda Sandoval. He must have learned about the old lady from her. He had her pegged as an easy mark."

"I don't know any Esmerelda Sandoval," said Agatha. "Have you questioned her?"

"No, ma'am. She was arrested a couple weeks ago for conspiracy to commit fraud. That business she was running with the evil lawyer was some kind of racket. She was arrested but escaped before her trial and is presently at large. No one knows where she is."

"Excuse me, Sheriff," said Nigel. "I believe she may be in the area."

"Who are you?" said Agatha, eyeing him like a stray anchovy on her pepperoni pizza.

"I'm a detective hired by the Sandovals."

"A detective?" said Edgaretta with a strong whiff of skepticism.

"Dog detective."

"Ah," she said, dispensing with the skepticism. "Why did they need a dog detective?"

"To find their dog, Duffy."

"Duffy?" said Edgaretta. "Was that a hideous-looking mutt?"

"An apt description, yes."

"I remember," said Edgaretta. "I did a story on him once: 'The County's Ugliest Dog.'"

"That's just the kind of story you'd find on an internet news site," said Agatha.

"Yeah? The kind of story you'd find in a mirror," replied Edgaretta.

"Ladies, ladies," said the sheriff, shaking his head. "I can end this thing right here and now. I'll do it if you two can't keep your claws to yourselves."

"So, what was going on with this dog?" said Agatha, seizing the initiative.

"The butler was taking the dog away," said Nigel.

"The Evil Butler? The one under arrest?"

"Yes. The same."

"He was taking him away as part of the crime?"

"I believe so," said Nigel, "but I'm not positive. Getting rid of the dog certainly would help facilitate the crime. On the other hand, he didn't much like taking the dog's temperature—"

"Taking the dog's temperature?" said Agatha.

"You know," said Nigel, thrusting forward a straightened index finger.

"With his finger?" said Agatha.

"A thermometer," said Nigel. "But he still didn't like it. He was taking the dog to his property out in No Way—"

"Cam Logan has a place out there," said Agatha.

Edgaretta rolled her eyes while mouthing Agatha's words. The sheriff shot her a stern look and raised a finger.

"Apparently, so did the butler. A mobile home he rented out to Oscar Griesen. But the dog kept escaping from that place and ending up at my place. It may have been the butler's undoing."

"How is that?" said the sheriff.

"Yes, how is that?" repeated Annie.

"If not for the dog, I wouldn't have been involved in the case. If I hadn't been involved, who knows how this would've turned out?"

"Really?" said the sheriff.

"Really?" repeated Annie.

"Who knows?" said Nigel, pleading his cause. Nigel wasn't about to say it, but didn't his tip-off to the butler bring the whole matter to a head?

"Okay," said the sheriff, shaking his head. "What about this Esmerelda? You know something?"

"Do you have a picture of her?" asked Nigel.

"Here you go," said the sheriff, pulling it from a file.

The picture was disturbingly nothing like the woman he'd

seen. This girl was young, attractive, and into vintage fashions.

"This a recent picture?" asked Nigel.

"1968."

"Okay. I'm guessing she looks different today. Probably the woman I saw. I believe you can find Esmerelda haunting the Sandoval estate, or thereabouts. Try walking around the place at night. She's kind of shy."

"I'll have a look," said the sheriff.

"But Sheriff," interjected Agatha, "you said the evil lawyer planned to kill old lady Sandoval for her money and property. If he'd never met her, how'd he ever hope to get her property?

"That's a whole 'nother aspect to this crime, and one we're still sorting out. The lawyer had assumed the identity of Fritz, Abuelita's online lover. He'd nurtured this relationship with the intent of becoming the primary beneficiary to Abuelita's property."

"So, he assumed a fake identity to finagle himself into her inheritance?" asked Edgaretta.

"Yep," said the sheriff.

"The identity is not fake, exactly," said Annie. "This lawyer's racket was bilking old people. Having dealt with these fraud cases before, I'd guess that Fritz is an actual person, and this lawyer has some form of caregiver—or power of attorney—status. If that's the case, the attorney can make just about anything look legal on paper. When old Fritz dies, this lawyer gets the whole shebang, including the Sandoval estate, if he's wormed his way in. Of course, Fritz is probably in some nursing home with no idea about any of this."

Classic Annie, thought Nigel. *Hard to put anything over on her.*

"Who are you, if I may ask?" said Agatha.

"My name is Annie Novak. I was hired as a detective by the Sandoval estate."

"You're also a detective?"

"A people detective, formerly with the Houston PD."

"I see," said Agatha. "A person with true credentials. As one professional to another, maybe I should interview you while Edgaretta deals with that dog detective."

"Agatha," interjected the sheriff, "behave, please."

"But even if this lawyer knew about old lady Sandoval's situation, how did he wangle his way into her good graces?" asked Edgaretta before Agatha had a chance.

"The butler," stated the sheriff, Annie, and Nigel simultaneously.

"If I may," said the sheriff. "The lawyer had fingered the butler as a source of documents, email addresses, and inside information to help gain the confidence of old lady Sandoval. The butler entered the scheme after he was contacted by the lawyer posing as an interested party in reopening the golf course. The butler had been a former manager at the course. He was the perfect inside man after being promised a general manager's position when the course reopened."

"What was the supposed murder weapon for old lady Sandoval?" asked Agatha. "Was it the snake?"

"The snake?" howled Edgaretta. "How absurd! Of course it wasn't the snake. What kind of nitwit would think a big snake would make a suitable murder weapon? I mean—"

"No, not the snake, the pills," said the sheriff. "The pills were not as labeled. They're currently being analyzed to determine their exact ingredients, but we suspect some form of poison that would have led to her death over time. The butler, of course, might have been the one to administer it."

"I vote yes," said Nigel.

"What do you mean, vote yes?" said the sheriff.

"I vote yes that the butler was an accessory to the murder

plot. He knew the deliverer of the poison, Oscar Griesen. In fact, Oscar was living on his property. The butler would have known about Oscar's services as a photographer and as a big snake provider. And I maintain that the butler was involved in preparing the poison. If you consult a book in the series called *A Mystery Writer's Guide to Dastardly Deeds, Volume 3,* you will likely find your poison among the listings."

"Is this poison commonly used to put down dogs?" quipped Agatha.

"Book three, you said?" asked Edgaretta, typing into her laptop.

"What do you think you're doing?" asked Agatha.

"I'm reading the book."

"Reading the book? On the computer? You must be daft!" said Agatha.

"Speaking of daft, I'm afraid the butler may be preparing himself to enter an insanity plea," said the sheriff."

"Why would you say that?" asked Agatha.

"In his statement, he rambled on and on about some galoshes like they was made of gold. Then when he was issued his jail garb, he refused to hand over his shoes. Didn't want anyone to touch them. Started yelling something about sixty-three Chelsea. Crazy as a wet hen, I think."

"Don't get caught with your back turned," said Nigel.

"I'll be careful. This is a wrap, everyone. I've got to head over to Mrs. Stoppelschuk's house for the vigil."

"The vigil? Has she taken a turn for the worse?" asked Agatha.

"Ha!" said Edgaretta. "And you call yourself a journalist."

"No," said the sheriff, "they administered some extra-powerful medicine for that bowel blockage of hers, and they're expecting some movement this afternoon. There'll be a crowd on her lawn waiting for news. Should there be a breakthrough, I'll be there to keep things contained. Y'all take care, now."

"I'll be there, too," said Edgaretta, preparing herself to leave.

"You know," said Annie, leaning toward Nigel as if drawn by a gravitational force, "some people think you're an imbecile."

"And you?"

After a moment's thought, she whispered, "Not quite."

Nigel leaned in to kiss Annie on the lips.

"Geeez, get a room!" shouted Agatha.

Edgaretta snapped a picture and began typing her caption, "Private Eyes—Not So Private Lips."

EPILOGUE

In Texas, a crisp autumn day is a special thing. Special not for its attributes—crystalline air, invigorating temperatures, and radiant sun—but for its rarity: roughly three per year. One of those days had fortuitously fallen on the second Saturday in October, a date reserved for the volunteer bake sale to raise money for Mrs. Stoppelschuk's medical bills following her latest bowel blockage, which—in one of life's tragic ironies— had been accompanied by the onset of an overactive bladder.

For the event, the FLONA—Fine Ladies of New Antigua —had erected, outside Wynn Brother's grocery store, a long table covered in white butcher's paper and adorned with festive bunting left over from the Fourth of July bake sale. The Fine Ladies were now in the process of receiving the many donated baked goods from the town's kind-hearted individuals, along with others who had been cajoled into contributing. Bake sales and arm-twisting were specialties of the Fine Ladies of New Antigua. The Wynn Brothers could testify to this, but they never, ever would. Nigel had been generously volunteered by his wife to supply a pastry.

"Ooh, what do we have here?" cooed an enthusiastic elderly woman in her finest liniment-infused woolly sweater.

"A pie," said Nigel, holding out his handiwork. "Cherry."

"Fantastic!" said the lady. "We already have a couple, but you can never have too many cherry pies."

"Certainly not," said Nigel.

A quick glance at the table turned up two cherry pies priced at ten dollars each.

"I'll just have a look, if you don't mind," said the lady as she rolled her gaze across the crusty brown landscape. "Okay, I see. Let's try for six on this one."

"Excuse me. I noticed the other two are priced at ten."

"Well, you know, too much supply drives down the price. Supply and demand, as they say."

"This one, if you didn't notice, was baked totally from scratch."

"You baked it?" she said, looking across the tops of her glasses. "Yourself?"

"Yes. From scratch."

"Let's have another look then." Balancing the pie in her left hand while holding her glasses at a just-so angle with her right, she slowly rotated the pastry in front of her face. Her eyes, shifting back and forth as if watching a tennis match, assessed the bumpy surface of the slowly spinning dessert. Lowering the pie to waist level, she cocked her head to one side, affording her appraising left eye a more holistic view. She repeated the maneuver for the sake of her right eye. She then gently raised and lowered the pie several times in a manner familiar to prison guards accustomed to finding implements. "Mmmmm," she said. "I'll tell you what, let's go with five."

"Five dollars? I might as well take it myself—"

"That would be fantastic! Better for everyone."

"What do you mean, better for everyone?" said Nigel.

"We get the donation, you get this delicious pie, and our standards are maintained. See. Better all around."

Nigel slapped down a fiver and snatched up the pie. Turning toward his car, he saw Stanley approaching with a large pie carrier.

"Nigel, old man, how are you?" called Stanley. "Haven't seen you in what? A month?"

"At least," replied Nigel. "You're donating a dessert? Is that from Kayda? I didn't know you two were back together."

"No, no, no. Back together with that hellhound? Not on your life. I'm with someone else now, and she insisted I bake something for the sale, so I whipped up a cherry pie."

"A cherry pie, eh? Seems a popular dish. They already have a couple," advised Nigel.

"I don't mind the competition. Do you?"

"Absolutely not. Brings out the best. Do you mind if I have a look?"

"Not at all, old man."

Stanley pried off the cover of the carrier to expose something more along the lines of a 3D wall-hanging than a pie. The dessert was covered in a crusty lattice interspersed here and there with intricate crusty vines that sprouted perfectly formed crusty roses. The center of the pie exposed the cherry filling through a perfectly formed heart-shaped opening. All was not well with the cherry heart, however, as it had been penetrated by a crusty arrow shot from the crusty bow in the hand of a crusty cherub floating about near the edge. Had Nigel not been told it was a pie, he would have thought it an *objet d'art* absconded from some baroque palace, or perhaps a garden decoration from The Home & Garden Tchotchke Palace. Either way, it was one impressive looking edible.

"You didn't make this, did you?" said Nigel, holding his own pie behind his back.

"Of course, I did."

"I mean all those crusty doodads. Surely, you didn't sculpt those yourself."

"You bet I did. I try to give my pies a little class. Of course, that's not really the hard part."

"It isn't?"

"No," said Stanley, "the hard part is the treatment of the filling to obtain the perfect balance of sweetness and tartness. I analyzed each of the cherries, all 938 of them."

"There are 938 cherries in this pie?"

"Oh, no. Don't be silly. Only 142 made the cut. The rest we used to make dog food."

"All this time I've known you, Stanley, I never knew you were a baker."

"Pipefitter," said Stanley.

"Pipefitter?"

"That was my profession. I just started baking after leaving that terrible woman. Exploring my creative side."

Just then, the appraiser stepped up and bellowed forth like an explorer who'd just laid eyes on a new continent. "Magnificent! This is a pie!" she declared, looking at Stanley's creation. "What price can we possibly put on a work of such brilliance? Perhaps we can auction it off to the highest bidder. Let me clear a place of honor," she said, tossing aside various low-rent desserts.

"I really have to be going," said Stanley. "My girl is waiting."

He pointed a thumb over his shoulder to a stretch limousine parked in the fire lane. The windows were severely blackened, but even so, Nigel could see a familiar mass of blond, fiberglass hair.

"She wants me to open a pie shop," said Stanley. "Maybe someday, we can have you guys over for dinner. She has a place out there. Gotta go." Stanley skipped to the limo and dove in headfirst through the opened door. Nigel had no sooner turned to walk to his car when Annie appeared.

"Where are you going with that?" she said.

"I was just going to put it in the car. I bought it."

"Good. What is it?"

"Cherry pie."

"I thought *you* baked a cherry pie?"

"I did. Seems to have stoked my appetite for cherry pie," said Nigel.

Annie leaned toward the pie for a closer inspection.

"Just had to have one."

"That's the one you got?" she said. "They must have some better ones on the table. What happened to yours?"

"Mine? Sold already. I wangled this one for just five bucks."

"Mmmmm, should have held out for four."

"With that strategy, you could end up with nothing," said Nigel. He made his way toward the car, but not before running into Stefanie Sandoval and her annoying mate bearing a prominent bandage on his forehead.

"Hello, Stefanie. How are you getting along?" said Nigel.

"We're doing fine, mostly," said Stef, "though Rob took quite a hit to the head yesterday."

"I can see that," said Nigel, attempting not to sound happy. The bulky bandage covered half his forehead but did not hide a left eye ringed in blue and purple. "Stefanie appears unscathed. But you, old chap," he said to Rob, "might need to improve your defense."

"Don't think that would have helped," he replied. "Strangest thing. I saw something in the bushes up at the house. When I went to investigate, falling out of the sky was a galosh, straight onto my head."

"Gosh. A galosh, did you say? Out of the clear blue? Wasn't even raining? You need to be more careful."

"I imagine it was left on the house by a roofer," he said. "Probably been up there a long time. The thing looked like it had been exposed to lots of sun."

"And saltwater," said Nigel.

"Listen," interjected Stefanie. "Before you get away, I'd like to tell you how much we appreciate what you've done. I know you were treated kind of rough—"

"Just a little, but I probably deserved it."

"No doubt, but still, you were doing your best, I suppose. What's that you're carrying? You've bought something already?"

"Cherry pie," said Nigel. "Just five bucks."

"If you'd waited to the end of the day," said Rob, eyeing the pie with a grimace, "you could have gotten it for two. They always drop the price to get rid of the rejects."

Nigel deposited the pie in his car and turned back toward the table, which had begun to draw a sizable crowd. His wife was conversing with a stout, elderly lady in librarian attire with snapping turtle-ish features. The lady had the unnerving habit of speaking to Annie while staring at Nigel. He found this so discomforting that he adopted a zigzag approach on his return to determine if her gaze was random, or if she were tracking his movements. She was tracking.

Nigel, tucking limbs close to body, hovered safely out of snapping range until the scaly librarian had paddled off.

"You know that old tortoise?" said Nigel.

"Don't make fun. I think she's senile," said Annie.

"What makes you think?"

"She said she was worried about the baked goods, and I asked why. She said 'poison,' and I asked why. She nodded toward you. I said, 'He's not worth poisoning,' and she said, 'He's a poisoner.' I told her that I had eaten some of your baked goods and they weren't that bad, and she says, 'Does he write?' I said, 'I wouldn't think.' She said, 'As I feared.

He's a bad one, all right. The FBI should be notified,' and off she went."

"You suppose the FBI would take her seriously?" said Nigel.

"I don't think so. They're trained to recognize someone that snaps."

"Good. They'll know to guard their fingers."

"Well, if it isn't the detectives," said a familiar voice from behind. It was Mrs. Sandoval. She seemed taller than Nigel had remembered because she was standing.

"Hello there, Mrs. Sandoval. You're looking good. The sun flatters you," said Nigel.

"It's probably because I've quit drinking," she said, pulling Nigel near.

"Really?" said a skeptical Nigel. "That's splendid. So, did you just wake up one day and decide enough is enough? Cold turkey, as they say?"

"Cold turkey. That's right, no alcohol from midnight to noon each day. It's a rule now. I seldom break it," she said proudly.

"How is Abuelita doing?" asked Annie.

"Well, she turned pretty mean after her Fritz was exposed to be, you know."

"Jailbird?" said Nigel, taking an elbow from Annie.

"Not so much that, but an unsuitable lover. But since Esmerelda came back, she's been like a new woman."

"I understand," said Annie. "Having her daughter around must be very comforting."

"It is for sure. And," said Mrs. Sandoval, "Esmerelda grows her own mushrooms. We had no idea how much Abuelita missed her. They're both very grateful to you, Ms. Annie, for helping to reunite them."

"Really, it was nothing. I just did the detective work that got her off the hook. It was the Evil Attorney that drove her back into her mother's arms."

"She understands that, but for whatever reason, she prefers to heap praise on you instead of her would-be assassin," said Mrs. Sandoval.

"Tell dear Abuelita that she has our best wishes," said Nigel, "and that a nice mention in the will is all the appreciation we could ever hope for."

"I'll let her know. And that reminds me, Mr. Nigel, we still need to discuss your starting date."

Nigel felt a sizzle on the back of his neck, which moved across to the front of his face as Annie repositioned herself.

"Perhaps we can discuss that at a different time," said Nigel.

"I think now would be a fine time," said Annie.

"Oh? Do you have some thoughts on the matter?" asked Nigel.

"Well," stammered Annie, surprised at being allowed into the conversation, "since we work at the same firm, we need to coordinate our assignments. It's best if we get these things out in the open."

"I could not agree more—" began Nigel.

"Good," said Annie. "Discuss."

"I could not agree more, *if*, as you say, we were working at the same firm. However, if I take this position, I regret that I must tender my resignation."

"Tender your resignation?" said Annie.

"Yes. I would not be allowed to continue in my role as dog detective."

"Why not?" asked Annie.

"The Sandovals would not allow it, and neither would I. It would not be proper for me to go about chasing down pets while ignoring my regular job at the Sandovals'."

"A regular job at the Sandovals?" said Annie, throwing a wicked side-eye. "Doing what exactly?"

"Buttling. The Sandovals are in need of a butler. I am up for the position."

Annie stepped back, then pulled her head back still further. From this stilted vantage point, she looked Nigel over from top to bottom, and back again as if not making sense of the thing. Nigel felt like a piece of abstract art strung up on a museum wall, or worse, a photo of Duffy.

Feeling over-scrutinized, Nigel crept backward until he encountered the edge of the dessert table, whereupon he crossed his feet and leaned against it. He held this position for what felt like an eternity waiting for a pronouncement from Annie.

"Eeeeeeeeh," she yelled when a loud snap preceded Nigel dropping to the ground beneath an onslaught of bouncing, sliding, and tumbling desserts. The crowd, having jumped away from the initial calamity, re-formed in a semi-circle around the recumbent Nigel emerging from beneath a cloud of powdered sugar.

"I feel I've started already," said Nigel. "Biscuit, Milady?" he said, holding up a broken oatmeal cookie. "Tea to go with that? Milk? White Russian?"

The End

How do you think Nigel will do as a butler? A skeptic, eh? Pick up *The Butler Defective* to find out.

GET A FREEBIE!

Hey reader, D. R. here. If you'd like a little more D. R, then sign up for my newsletter and download this free novelette.

If *The Dating Defective*, a joyful one-hour read, were to appear on the retail market, it would command a price of $1999.99. That's why I'm giving it away for free. Who needs that kind of money? In addition to this epic, you'll receive infrequent emails keeping you abreast of my novelistic mishaps. To sign up, just go to www.drlowreyauthor.com.

By the way, congratulations on finding me. Not many have. Why not poke those D. R. Lowrey-illiterates by entering an Amazon rating or review for *Defective for Hire*. (On the Amazon book page, look to the left in the review section) D. R. would sure appreciate it.

ABOUT THE AUTHOR

D. R. Lowrey, the non-award-winning, critically-untainted author of comedic fiction, writes from the hothouse of Houston, Texas, often while not wearing a shirt.

It wasn't always like this. For years, D. R. clung tenaciously to a shirt-wearing job that paid real money in exchange for his soul. When that job went kaput, he investigated the possibilities of a career in the hardware retail business, or, alternatively, writing fine literature. Fine literature, as it turns out, is hard to write. Harder even than selling door hinges. Having acquired such wisdom, D. R. took to writing stuff more aligned with his true personality—uncultured, absurd, insubstantial. He now foists these works upon the reading public.

Some refer to his books as a "beach read." D. R. disagrees. He feels that if you require a beach to read a book, your time is better spent wading amongst the sharks and stingrays. He suggests reading in the comfort of your own living room, preferably on furniture suitable for napping, while siphoning a favorite beverage. Experience shows that after extensive siphonings, his books do indeed start to resemble fine literature...what with the words, punctuation, and all.

D. R. enjoys thoughtful, non-violent interaction with his readers. He views such discourse as an ongoing referendum on whether to write or sell latex paint.

Check out www.drlowreyauthor.com if you're desperate for something to do.

The Bumbling Brit Abroad Mysteries 1 - 4
Read the entire Nigel saga!

Book 1: Defective for Hire

Nigel escapes the rat race by settling in smalltown Texas. Tranquility he wants, but the town has other ideas. Animal attacks, interminable to-do lists, and an unwanted murder soon have him yearning for simpler days among the rats.

Book 2: The Butler Defective

For most butlers, cleaning up after a murder would be the absolute worst. Not for Nigel. When his arrival as the new English butler coincides with the discovery of a dead body, conclusions are easily drawn, but not easily dismissed. There'll be a lot more cleaning up to do if he's to avoid hard time in the Big House.

Book 3: The Demented Defective

Every person in New Antigua, Texas seems to have just stepped off the crazy train. So why is Nigel the only one hiding from the whitecoats with the butterfly nets? Could it be they're out to silence the one person who knows the town is the epicenter of a global telepathic struggle?

Book 4: The Dancing Defective

Have things finally settled down at the Sandoval estate? Yes, but only because the Sandovals have all vanished. If Nigel is to find them, he'll first have to solve the big mystery behind all the extreme nuttiness. And even that is not enough. He'll also have to dance!

Made in the USA
Columbia, SC
08 April 2022